The Fire Hills

Oliver Eade

Best wishes
Oliver Eade

www.olivereadebooks.org

Type set in Georgia
UK spelling observed

ISBN: 978-1-912513-54-3

Silver Quill Publishing

Dedicated to Donald and Ishbel Gordon
'Mr & Mrs Trimontium'

In Memory of James Curle (1862 -1944)

Laid to rest in Melrose Abbey.
Lawyer and archaeologist who had
the foresight to recognize the major
significance of findings from 1905 to 1910
at the site of an old Roman fort at
Newstead, Melrose.

'Once we accept our limits, we go beyond them.'
Albert Einstein 1879-1955

Acknowledgements

As always, I must thank my wife, Yvonne, for her endless tolerance and encouragement; also, Iona McGregor for her helpful proofreading suggestions, plus others in Silver Quill Publishing for their support. I am indebted to Donald Gordon for correcting my schoolboy Latin, and to the Trimontium Trust for bringing back to life an important chapter in the history of the Scottish Borders that might otherwise have been lost forever.

Reviews of the author's previous publications:

Moon Rabbit

'...Ideal introduction into Chinese culture, written in a way that is perfect to be read aloud and enjoyed by children of all ages...'

Sunday Express, 2009

'...A Magical Experience...beautifully written and illustrated children's story...'

P.A. News, 2010

Northwards

'...A witty and heartwarming novel packed with adventure...'

Sunday Express, 2010

A Single Petal

'...Carefully researched, well plotted and more full-blooded than you might expect, A Single Petal's spiritual dimension is solidly grounded in traditional narrative rules...'

Alastair Mabbott, The Herald, 2013

'...There's an abundance of beauty in this book...: it is a sensitive, poetic account of the faith, fears and irresistible forces within a community...'

Raymond Hume, The Writer, 2020

The Terminus

'...Once you pick up this chilling book, be prepared to climb onto an emotional roller-coaster...'

Wendy Leighton-Porter, award winning author of the 'Shadows of the Past series', 2013

Parth Path

'...A momentous novel... the reader is drawn into a post-apocalyptic nightmare... In the face of overwhelming evil, good prevails...'

Iona Carroll, author of the 'Oisin Kelly series', 2018

The Kelpie's Eyes

'...An extraordinarily good fantasy novel... so well-handled that it grips throughout...'

Frost Magazine, 2018

In the Blink of an Eye
'...Powerful stories following key developments in medicine... clearly written and hugely informative...'

Ray Cartwright, Emeritus Professor of Medicine, 2021

After the god of fire and the goddess of the land came together in an embrace that no elements could disengage, three towering hills were all that remained of their passion. Life appeared... first plants, then animals. Amongst these was the deer whose powerful god, Corunna, was worshipped by those who lived on the northernmost of those bleak hills forged in that love-nest of the gods... ***The Fire Hills****, also known to the Celts as Aill Dun, 'Old Rock' and, two millennia later, as the Eildons.*

But a gentler deer deity, Flidais, held sway on a lush, verdant isle to the west of Britannia, now called Ireland. In a fleeting glow of orange against green, she appeared to women in need, and to their daughters and the daughters' daughters, until...

PARS PRIMA

I

Angela Leckie, Professor of the Department of Forensic Pathology, Edinburgh University, stared in disbelief at the report on her desk.

"Well?" queried Ranjit Desai. "Is it possible? Or was there contamination? All this terrible business happening. Half your staff missing. Remember the other case? They got that very wrong indeed!"

The young Indian doctor grinned. His gleaming white teeth were perfect. Like those in the skull unearthed, near the River Tweed beyond Melrose, whilst the MOD dug foundations for yet another military camp. Angela's esteemed academic colleague, Andrew McIver, head of the Department of Archaeology, had turned purple with rage on learning what they were up to on and around the site of the old Roman Fort of Trimontium, and the professor could hardly wait to tell him this latest news.

Angela, who treated her lovable post-grad student like the son she never had, shook her head. Her keen, grey eyes fixed on the sentence at the bottom of the page. She pointed to the signature beneath this, then tapped it meaningfully.

"Charlie does not make mistakes!" She looked up at the face of the eager young academic medic sharing the impossible with her. "First thing you must learn in this business, Ranjit, is whom to trust. So, with this radiocarbon testing result, our skull belongs to a male over the age of thirty of Mediterranean origin. Roughly eighteen hundred years old. Nothing surprising in that. Not down in the Borders where the Romans were all over the place. But..."

The professor searched for another report somewhere amongst the patchwork of papers littering her desk.

"Here it is!" She waved a sheet at Ranjit's broadening smile. "Ballistics never get it wrong either. A bullet fired from a contemporary UK police-issue weapon lodged in his skull."

"That is not possible." Ranjit's head did that expressive little wobble that made her want to hug him, though she never did. After all, she was almost twice his age. "Unless we are having some crazy guy who uses ancient skulls for target practice."

"Ranjit, it is not our job to guess what is or is not possible. Remember, you are not a detective. You're a scientist. Anyway, he was clearly alive when he got shot. So, what we have to do is to make sense of what we see and know to be true. And if you can make sense of this then..."

The professor winked at her student.

"Then I can use it in my thesis?"

"This, Ranjit, will *be* your thesis. Who knows? It might become your whole career. Your life. A Nobel Prize! But first, that spiral CT scan we looked at yesterday. Bring it up on your computer. There was something I saw that could be a missing piece of our jigsaw puzzle."

"Madam Professor, my little daughter is very much liking jigsaw puzzles!"

Angela laughed. They loved to tease each other, with Ranjit calling his boss 'Madam Professor' and Angela responding with 'Doctor Postgrad'.

"One thing, Doctor Postgrad," she added. "Do not—and I mean *not*—tell anyone else."

"Ranjit Desai is more secure than the Bank of England!" reassured Ranjit.

"Not good enough!"

"Bank of Scotland?"

"Just as bad!"

"I have it! As secure as the box in your drawer in which you keep the departmental slush fund!"

"That's more like it, Ranjit. Now... let's look again at that scan. At where the bullet was lodged in the cranium. You see, having got that far, it should have shot clean through our victim."

"Like I said, an execution. Linked to the disappearances in the Borders, perhaps? Your first suspicion, Professor, if I remember correctly."

"Till I saw this," replied Angela patting the radiocarbon test report. "This young man must have disappeared an awful long time ago. Or maybe he didn't disappear at all. Maybe it's the executioner who disappeared."

Ranjit looked puzzled.

"I don't follow you," he said.

"First, look again at that image and tell me what you observe about the exit hole. At least we know the bullet was pointing outwards, away from the skull."

*****

"Go!" she screamed. "Anywhere but here. Across the river!"

Breth froze. The two Germanian thugs who held Adienna, one by each arm, chuckled. Neither understood a word of Brythonic, and not much Latin either. Larger and coarser featured than their elegant Roman commander, Octavius, who had sent a small troop of auxiliaries to get the girl on the pretext that her family was short on tax payments, the Germanians would have easily disposed of the boy with a single thrust of a *spatha*[1]. Adienna knew her loved-one's temper only too well. Her parents put it down to his red hair, but she had always reckoned there was more to it. The boy cared about things. Deeply. And he had been particularly grieved about the way the new commander treated their tribe.

The previous commander in charge of the auxiliaries in the Roman fort by the river was a lovely man. Domitius Fluvius respected the *'homunculi collis'*, or little hill people, as he affectionately called the peaceful Selgovan community living on the northernmost Fire Hill. Tongue in cheek of

---

[1] Roman sword, widely used instead of the shorter *gladius* during the second century AD.

course, as most of the Celtic tribesmen towered above the Italians.

The Romans had named their cavalry fort 'Trimontium' after the three ancient hills, conveniently establishing it beside the *Flumen Certinassa*, known to the Celts as the 'Duabs' and to us in the twenty-first century, the River Tweed. This provided access to the sea, and Domitius had allowed Breth's people unrestricted access to fishing. He had learned some of their language too, encouraged trade with their tribespeople further afield, and would sometimes scale the northernmost hill to talk with Breth's father and the tribal leaders and elders around a village fire. The men conversed mostly in Latin, and Domitius would tell his Celtic friends how he yearned for the sunny warmth of Italia, the smell of the vine and the girlish giggles of his little nieces chasing the crows away from the vegetables that grew behind the family home near *Roma*. He often spoke of the great wisdom of their Emperor, Marcus Aurelius Antoninus Augustus.

As a boy, Breth, who wished he had a name as long and important as that of the emperor, if only to impress wee Adienna, had learned from Domitius not only to speak but also to write in Latin. Often, his father would take his only child to the summit, and, looking down at the activity going on in the Roman fort, would tell the boy that, like Domitius, he could make something of himself if he were to become an auxiliary in the Roman Army. Breth even carved a *spatha* for himself from a branch of firewood and loved to pretend he was fighting the enemies of Rome in hand-to-hand combat until Adienna told him how stupid he looked waving a bit of wood in the air. Even when young, he would do nothing that displeased his pretty little fair-haired, freckle-faced friend.

Domitius was getting on in years, and Breth was none too surprised when his father informed him that the old soldier had been replaced by a younger leader. A smooth-skinned, dark-haired snake of a man who strutted amongst his auxiliaries like a cockerel in a henhouse, using his vine-stick across the back of anyone whose mere appearance displeased him.

One fateful day the reptile noticed Adienna. A month before they came for her, Adienna was walking hand in hand with Breth beside the river. All knew they were soon to be married, for the girl was now of full figure and ready for childbearing. The two had been sweethearts for as long as anyone could remember, and that day the boy had brought his lifelong friend to see a carving he had painstakingly gouged into the trunk of a riverside tree. Known for his wood skills with a knife, he had created, on the tree, the image of a young deer. He lovingly called Adienna his 'little deer', the girl being agile and fast of foot, plus her mother's ancestors came from that island to the west where, she had told him, the deer goddess, Flidais, looked after her womenfolk. His carving, he told her, would be stirred into the cauldron of Aine, the goddess of love, also from that island of Adienna's ancestors, to bring wisdom to their children. His way of proposing to her. On her sixteenth birthday.

Where the path split into two, the lower winding down to the river's edge towards the tree in question that stretched its old brown arms over the fast-flowing water, stood the new commander with two ruffian auxiliaries. Breth halted.

"You children have permission to come here?" Octavius questioned in Latin.

Children?

Breth was both taller and stronger than the Roman who addressed him.

"Our families pay their taxes," he answered staring at the ground. "And Domitius said—"

"Domitius! Pfff! Look at me, *puer parvule!*"

Breth clenched his fists to control his anger. Something he often did when annoyed. Adienna noticed.

"Don't!" she whispered in Brythonic.

Breth looked into the commander's cold, dark eyes

before the man approached his loved one. He hoped Aine had been listening when he dedicated that carving to the girl he would soon marry. Perhaps he should have addressed Alator, a warrior god whom the Romans call Mars? For the first time in his life, Breth realized that he and Adienna were not only different from the Romans, but also their inferiors. Inferiors have two choices: rise up and fight to become equal or stay low, like discarded animal bones.

Octavius showed no interest in the boy. Gazing into Adienna's fearful blue eyes, he raised his hand and, with the backs of his slender, milk-white fingers, caressed her freckled cheeks.

"Not an answer," he said without looking at Breth. "But Flavia here, she will soon know what I mean. I can see she yearns for a real man, not a *puer parvulus*."

"My name's Adienna," the girl protested. Her hand brushed against Breth's. He felt her tremble.

"Adienna non est! Flavia est!" barked the commander, before gripping Adienna's chin.

Then, smiling like a fox about to leap on a chicken, he ran his fingers through the girl's long blond hair which Breth had told her was now the colour of ripened corn because she was ready to bear him children.

"Flavia! Fair one. Never, in my blessed Italia, have I seen a girl so beautiful, so exquisite and..." He glanced scornfully at the red-haired Selgovan boy standing beside her. His hand dropped to his *spatha*. Breth watched those spider-leg fingers play with the black knob at the end of the hilt. With a single punch to the man's cleanly-shaven jaw, Breth could have sent him tumbling into the river below, but one against three armed men? From their uncouth appearance, the other two looked like devils from Germania. Trimontium was full of them. Breth had heard from his father how even the women of that land are known to tear their living enemies apart.

Octavius stepped back. Still fixed on Adienna, his fox

eyes narrowed.

"Exquisite and as ripe as the fruit waiting for me in a bowl back at Trimontium. I bet you can't wait to replace that fruit, huh... *carissima mea?*"

His smile gone, he turned to Breth:

"Back up the hill. Quick. And as for those unpaid taxes..." He looked again at Adienna. No words were needed to say what he was in mind.

Breth clutched the girl's hand. Together, they turned and retraced the path home to *Bryniau Tân*—the Fire Hills.

Rising from the broad plain carved over millennia by a river now called the Tweed, they could be seen for miles. Those hills were the reason why the legion of Gnaeus Julius Agricola chose to establish a cavalry fort so close to the river. A blessed place, most surely, but for the Selgovae it was the hills themselves that were linked to the gods. Ancient hills where the God of Fire, Bel, found passion with Liban, a beautiful Goddess of Earthly Pleasure and, together, they left their mark on the land as Breth had left his on that tree. A mark that connected him and his beloved with Flidais, the deer goddess of her mother's ancestors.

Neither of the young lovers said a word, although Adienna sensed her friend's fury. Halfway up the hill, Breth stopped.

"I'll kill him," he said.

Adienna's loving arm encircled his waist. The girl grinned.

"You'll do nothing of the sort. Just forget the bastard. I'd no more let him touch me than lie with one of their horses!"

Breth laughed. His little friend always did have a way of cooling his anger. They walked on towards a hollow halfway up the hill. A special location where, as children, they would often go to avoid the annoying demands of their parents and of the tribal elders. Breth called it their magical 'cave' after that memorable day when, older, he had fashioned a secret hideout with broken-off branches and torn bracken fronds.

Their love nest where they fondly lay undisturbed, cuddling and kissing. He dedicated the hollow to Aine and maintained it as a private haven of passion.

Standing beside this, they embraced and kissed again, and Breth declared that nothing and no one, not even the new emperor, would prevent him from marrying her.

New emperor?

Word quickly spread throughout the empire. The noble Marcus Aurelius was dead. His son Commodus, who played games with the lives of others, stepped out of the shadows to fulfil the role of full emperor, creating a shock wave of horror that spread out, like foul sewage, from *Roma*, even reaching the distant shores of Britannia.

A week after that encounter by the river, those same Germanian fiends showed up, with a gang of armed auxiliaries, in the hilltop Celtic fort at the break of day. They went straight to the wattle and daub roundhouse of Adienna's family. One of the evil pair had drawn his *spatha*, ready to run through anyone who dared to challenge him. Breth, sitting outside his family roundhouse, carving in the soft dawn light yet another deer for his beloved, stood up and watched in horror.

Adienna's father, Alun, filled the entrance to his humble home. Blond, like his daughter, tall and of slender build, he was a gentle man and no match against those devils from Germania. He took down a skinned hare that was hanging outside his hut and offered this to the auxiliaries.

"Not enough!" one of them snapped in a harsh Latin that matched his stone-hard features.

The soldier spat on the ground, pushed the Selgovan aside and disappeared into the roundhouse. The muffled scream that emerged from the tiny abode pierced Breth's soul with the precision of a Roman crossbow bolt. Moments later, the Germanian emerged gripping a struggling, kicking Adienna.

"I found the unpaid tax," laughed the brute. When the

girl lashed out with her fist, his companion grabbed the offending arm whilst the girl's father stood by, helpless.

"I'll give you more," he pleaded. "Everything I have is yours. Just free my daughter."

The men looked at each other, their filthy faces distorted by lecherous grins. Breth, carving knife in his hand, shouted,

"Leave her alone! We're to be married. Our gods will destroy you if you don't let her free."

He ran forwards. The soldier, grinning, prodded the point of his drawn *spatha* up against Adienna's slender neck. Breth halted.

"Go!" the girl screamed at Breth. "Anywhere. Across the river!"

The auxiliaries laughed. The one holding his *spatha* to Adienna's throat let go of his prey. The other immediately grabbed her freed arm whilst his accomplice slowly approached Breth, stopping just two paces from the boy.

"You dare to challenge the authority of our new emperor?" he asked. "And threaten his soldiers with your little gods of mud and straw?" Adienna, in tears, shook her head when Breth glanced at her. He looked at the small knife in his hand, then at the glinting, hard steel of his opponent's *spatha*. Dead, he could do nothing for Adienna. "No, you will not marry the girl my master calls Flavia. Instead, after she has become his, she can look at your miserable face every day. Stuck on a pole outside the fort entrance. As a reminder of how lucky she is to have a real man like Octavius."

With his childhood years spent chasing his 'little deer' over the hills, Breth, fast-footed, knew the terrain well; knew every hollow and gully, each dip and hillock. And he knew where to hide. In a flash he was gone. The heavy-footed Germanian ran after him but soon tired.

"We'll come back for you later!" he called out from the edge of the hilltop settlement to the darting figure zigzagging down the steep slope. If he'd had a crossbow, he could easily have shot the lad. He would often shoot rabbits brought by the Romans, now running wild in the land around Trimontium. “As a warning for Flavia to behave!” he added.

The boy did not stop running until he reached Aine’s ‘cave’ where a deer suddenly appeared from nowhere; a deer that shone orange like the setting sun. He stopped and glanced back up the hill, relieved to see that the auxiliary had not pursued him. After turning around, facing the ‘cave’, he watched, dumbfounded, as the deer shrank down and vanished into it, causing the surrounding ground to glow. On hands and knees, Breth crawled into the lovers’ secret place. Nothing! He rolled over onto his back, staring up at the patchwork blue sky fragmented by angled branches and bracken. He promised all the gods he could think of to make offerings for the rest of his life if they would only help him to get Adienna back. These included Corunna, their own deer god, although he knew that other-worldly vision of a deer could not have been Corunna. She appeared gentle, like Adienna, not warlike like the antlered god of battle. Being a Selgovan Celt, Breth knew little about Flidais, the goddess of Adienna’s grandmother who came from that island of mist and rain far beyond the setting sun. Brought back to the Fire Hills after a trading mission by his love’s grandfather, the woman’s beauty and kindness had become legendary in the hilltop fort.

Closing his eyes, Breth prayed again to Aine...

*****

“For God’s sake dinnae go on at her, Dad!” begged Craig. “It’s the glandular fever.”

Craig Stevens and his dad were sitting having breakfast. They could hear his sister crying in her bedroom upstairs. This angered Craig. Mrs Stevens stood up, ran her fingers through her hair then shook her head.

“But that was six months ago,” Mr Stevens pointed out.

“It’s called the post-viral fatigue syndrome, Dad. Or ME. Affects twenty-two percent of people with infectious mononucleosis. That’s glandular fever. And they’ve no idea why some go on to get ME. Bit like long COVID."

Whenever he felt annoyed, Craig would bamboozle his parents with facts gleaned from the internet. But he so loved his little sister, and truly hated the way their dad went on at her. Okay... so he, Craig, was bright and had always worked hard, if only to prove to his teachers and others at school, when younger, that having an unpronounceable surname like Szczepański was no bar to getting on in Scotland. But after classmates in S2 began to tease wee Hannah, calling her S-Z-C-Z, and making squeaky R2D2 noises at her and running around like robots, Craig said enough was enough. For his sister's sake, he demanded they change their surname to Stevens. He even told them how to do it. For £36 each, a total of £144, they could become the 'Stevens' family. "Dad doesn't drink," he explained, "so he saves at least that amount each month by not going to the Ship Inn every night. Surely you two can do this for Hannah! Anyway, there was a Hannah Stevens who landed in Virginia in 1714."

Mrs Soon-to-become-Stevens giggled. Her son, who never quite understood his mum's humour, always got his way sooner or later. But now, with Hannah just turned sixteen, and Craig in his final year at Earlston High School, she really did not know what to think.

"I ken what it's called," grumped Craig's Dad. "*And* what the doc said. But he did suggest she at least try to get on with her life."

"The Mayo Clinic says cognitive behavioural therapy can help. Why don't you and Mum—?"

"Listen, Craig," interrupted his mother, "Dad has a lot on his plate. With all this political nonsense he's got himself into." Mr Stevens frowned. "We simply can't go around dishing out money—"

"Hannah needs help, Mum! That's all I'm saying. Anyway, must get going for school. Don't wanna miss the bus again. Just let Hannah stay at home today. I'll have a talk with her when I get back. Okay?"

Mrs Stevens shrugged her shoulders. It seemed all she could do these days, what with her daughter's illness and her husband's hot-headedness by getting involved with the local SFS... **S**cotland **F**or the **S**cots.

She smiled at Craig, thankful for a son with his head screwed on and a caring nature. None of that 'me, me, me!' of most teenagers, including Hannah before the glandular fever kicked in. But she also feared for her son. Because of his father. No one quite knew which side the police were on these days, let alone what the dreaded newly formed Scottish Security Service, or 'SSS', might get up to. The disappearances—which had increased of late—were, in whispered asides, secretive texts and covert e-mails, put down to the 'SS', as Jamie preferred to call them.

And that was another thing... e-mails.

SFS had been using a code to disperse information. 'Have a good day!' meant 'Saturday' and 'what a bummer, ay?' was Sunday. Craig suggested they use Latin backwards. "Give SFS some finesse!" he said, but Jamie told his son there was little time left to teach everyone Latin.

"Besides," he added, "they'll have a computer program that would suss that out in one hundredth of a second!"

"Not if you factored in pi," suggested Craig.

"What?"

"3.14159265," replied Craig. "Etcetera... to the eighteenth figure. Plus, the day of the month. Like today it's June 4th. That's 0406. So, add the date as eight figures to the beginning of pi. Twenty-six letters in the alphabet, see. The code'll change every day. Represented by the first twenty-six numbers of your reconstructed pi. Add zeros for numbers that repeat. And use Latin, of course. Easy-peasy!"

"Hmm! For their new quantum computers too. Look, Craig, we're not all bright like you. And I dinnae want you to get mixed up in any of this. If I, too, disappear because of my SFS allegiance, just look after Mum and Hannah. That's all I ask of you."

Craig shrugged his shoulders. Like his Mum, the boy had a habit of doing this, but in other respects he was very different from both parents. And his sister. No one would have dared tease one of the best local junior rugby forwards about his name, although the girls who had goaded Hannah had little interest in the sport other than cheering for Melrose on a Saturday whilst jumping up and down in micro skirts fit for barbie dolls. It must have been one of these thirteen-year-olds, plastered to the eyeballs in make-up, and blowing kisses to Craig after he scored try after try, who texted his freckled sister:

Wot u call a droid with dots? S-Z-S-C!

At first, Hannah did not want to tell him the reason when he found her in tears, back home, after he and the lads had 'lived it up' following the match, but as he put his arms around her, and she began to sob on his shoulder, it all came out.

"Do you know who sent the text message, Sis?" he asked.

"No!" she lied.

"That does it! As from today we're changing our name!"

That was nearly three years back. Craig could not understand why his dad, or his granddad, had not done this before. It was one thing to feel proud of a great grandfather training with the Polish resistance, in Scotland, during World War II, but to expect Borders Scots to wrap their tongues around a name like 'Szczepański' was taking things too far. After all, less than thirteen percent of his and Hannah's DNA was of Polish origin. When Craig pointed this out to Jamie, his dad, the man nodded, then said,

"Yes, but it's the most important part of your DNA, son."

"No, the mutations that make me who I am are. Same for Hannah. That bitch who texted her is jealous of her freckles, ken!"

"What?"

"Didn't she tell you?"

"Nope!"

Craig could guess why Hannah had kept her dad in the dark about that text. If he had found out—and she did know who sent it—he would have thumped the shit out of the stupid child's dad. Working at the council recycling centre, Jamie had the frame of a champion wrestler.

"Never mind, Dad. You know, all the lads love Hannah for the way she is."

"Everyone does!"

"No, I mean her freckles. Dylan says she's the prettiest girl in Earlston High School. Blond hair, blue eyes and freckles. Hits the spot, he says."

Jamie, soon-to-become-Stevens because of his son, frowned.

"Hits the spot? What are you talking about?"

"Just an expression, Dad. Your daughter is beautiful. Never mind what those other girls say."

"Hmm! All the more reason for you to watch out for her and Mum if ever—"

"It'll not happen, Dad! Remember your Polish genes. How many in the SFS can boast a real resistance fighter perched on their family tree?"

Almost three years later, they were having a similar conversation, this time triggered by Hannah's illness.

"Look Craig, I'm really proud of you. How many tries you gonna score on Saturday, ay?"

Craig shrugged his shoulders.

"Whatever we need to win, Dad. Look, just think about CBT for Hannah. That's Cognitive behavioural therapy. Remember? I spoke to you and Mum about it. Got it off the internet. Maybe the doc could arrange something for her?"

"With the NHS falling apart?" Jamie paused. "Which, by the way, is one thing that's helping us get more recruits of late."

"Take care, Dad!"

"Didn't I just tell *you* to do that?"

Father and son laughed. Jamie got up and patted Craig

on the back.

"Must get to work. See you later, son!" They hi-fived before the boy picked up his school bag. "And Hannah stays at home. But only today!"

"Thanks, Dad!"

Jamie left for work whilst Craig went upstairs to speak with his sister before catching the school bus. She was still in tears.

"It's not really the ME, is it?" he asked. She shook her head. Craig sat on her bed, opened his arms wide then hugged his sister. "More of those texts, huh?" The girl nodded. "I wish you'd tell me who—"

"It'll only make things worse," Hannah interrupted.

"I honestly think CBT would help you cope with this business as well as the ME."

"Mum says it's out of the question. Paying for some trick cyclist to—"

"Don't call them that! Psychiatrists. Sort of term that bitch at the other end of your phone would use."

"Dad's word. Apparently. Oh, I just wish I was somewhere else!"

"Nope! Big brother would be seriously upset if that ever happened. Tell you what. How about you joining me and the lads in the Ship Inn tonight, huh? Dylan's turning eighteen today and wants to celebrate. Just hope he doesn't get pissed. Your presence might just stop that from happening."

Pissed? Rhymes with kissed, thought Hannah.

"Dad wouldn't—" she began.

"Dad'll never know! He's got an SFS meeting. So... it's a 'yes', then?"

"I'll see how I feel."

"Dylan's always asking after you, ken."

Hannah, her chin still resting on her brother's broad rugby player's shoulder, smiled to herself.

Seriously? she thought.

Only Craig knew about the novel she was writing. Her

other excuse for being off school that day. The heroine, same age as her, also had freckles, and the hero looked just like Dylan.

"Thanks!" Hannah said softly as Craig left her room. She pulled out her laptop from under her bed and thought about how best to escape back into the world of her novel...

Dylan once said I look like Daenerys. The Mother of Dragons. So, this has to be her story. That other Daenerys. Not the one who turns bad in the end. This one has to put up with a gang of girls who double their weight every time they put on make-up. He doesn't like make-up. Craig told me. At least, not so it changes your face. Craig says I'm not old enough to—you know—do what those girls say I do in private with a frigging teddy bear. They're animals, the lot of them.

Yeah, so this Daenerys knows about the firebox. But so do they. Only it's not real fire in that box. Just looks that way. To others. To ignorant people. It's a strange orange colour, and my Daenerys can see into the fire. And through it. It'll enable her with a power that would make those cows at school tremble like Fatso Jennie Mackay's backside on a treadmill. Problem is that the box got stolen and they've hidden it somewhere in the city.

The city? Kind of futuristic. Streamlined. And colourful. Awesome colours! But no shops or nothing. Everything's for free. Hold your hand up, and AI sensors read whether you've enough credits left for what you need. Only the gang have hacked into the system and taken whatever they want. Worse than this, they threaten to block my—I mean Daenerys's—code. Orphaned, she'll starve. She has a vision of the gang encircling her emaciated body, cackling like pantomime witches, poking her with fingers the nails of which are decorated every colour of the rainbow. Cackling on and on till she draws her last breath.

No! Can't let it happen. Not in my novel. Dylan will

rescue me. I mean her. And I mustn't call him Dylan. Hey... there's that new guy in the orphan compound the spitting image of Dylan. Keeps looking at me. I mean her. The other Daenerys. I, or rather, she smiles at him. He comes over and sits next to her.

"The box!" he whispers.

Smiling contentedly, Hannah started to type...

*****

Things had changed. Something was happening. The branches and bracken trembled. *Everything* seemed to vibrate. An orange glow, that had forced him to cover his eyes, faded. Breth knew it had to be Aine responding to his prayers, wishing to intervene now that Adienna was in danger. His hands, gripping the heather, also shook. And yet the patchwork sky above remained unchanged.

Breth heard a deep-throated sound unlike anything he had heard before. Surely that of a beast from those legends brought to life by the elders around a fire. It diminished, then vanished, only to be followed by another sound. The shrill call of a child. In a language that was neither Brythonic nor Latin.

The language of the gods?

Now confident that Aine would protect him, Breth summoned the courage to face whatever was out there. Having crawled headfirst into the 'cave', he backed out, eyes closed. One foot came up against something that was most definitely not there before. He looked round. Uncertain whether to panic at what he beheld, or feel over-joyed, he scrambled to his feet.

His foot had touched what looked like a Roman *pilum* stuck in the ground, yet it sported a dangling yellow pennant. Curiously, it emerged from a perfectly round hole. But it was the ground itself that puzzled the boy. No heather nor bracken. Only a dewy sheen of short green grass, as if one of the gods had cut every blade to a certain length. Nothing but grass. And, further away, other *pila* with yellow pennants also stuck out at right angles from similar holes. Did these holes connect, like their 'cave', with Aine? Maybe not, but the most disturbing thing, when he turned around, was the 'cave'. Rather, the lack of it.

Gone! Only a slight grass-covered depression. He looked up at the three hills. The roundhouses, the posts and the woodstore, normally visible from miles away, had also disappeared. Had Aine tricked him? Done a deal with one of those Roman gods?

Then he saw something not of this world high above the Fire Hills. A giant, bird-like creature, silvered by the morning sun, breathing a plume of smoke, not from its mouth, but from its tail, and making a noise the like of which he had never heard before. A deep, unearthly grumble. He decided to run for the safety of the woods beside the river and away from Trimontium.

On reaching the top of the slope, Breth halted. His jaw dropped. He knew, now, that he was doomed, for the Romans had not only obliterated his village on the Fire Hills but had also created buildings of their own within a javelin's reach of where he stood. Strangely alien buildings. He took off again in a blind panic. Where the grassy slope ended was a wide grey, smoothly surfaced *via* clearly built for horses, wagons and other Roman hardware. Beyond this were houses the likes of which he could never have imagined. The monster in the sky had grown louder, trailing its white breath cloud, whilst another monster, without wings, suddenly flashed past along the chariot *via*. Red and shiny and, like a chariot, bearing thick, dark wheels, albeit small, it roared as it sped off towards Trimontium. Breth stepped back, looking on in both wonder and horror. A child, carrying a sort of bag, came into view, stopped and stared at him.

"Why's that man dressed funny?" it asked, but Breth only heard words that were neither Latin nor Brythonic. A woman without a tunic appeared. She was all legs, and her dark hair was unlike that of any Roman woman he had seen. It was wild, not dissimilar to Adienna's long, wavy locks.

"Never you mind," the woman answered. Her tone was unthreatening and Breth merely gaped at her and the little boy, presumably her son. "Hurry now. Don't wanna be late for school again, do you?" she added, frowning at Breth before pulling the child along towards Trimontium.

Split-second decision making. Same in battle, as his father once told him. Not wanting to be pierced by one of those flagged *pila*, and repeatedly looking back over his shoulder, Breth sprinted towards the grey chariot *via*, hoping to reach the safety of the woods beyond the brow of the hill to his left. Woods where he and Adienna used to play so happily, and far enough away from Trimontium to connect with...

*****

Craig slowed down to text Dylan:

H says yes. C U later. CS.

No sooner had he sent the text than... BANG! His phone clattered to the ground.

"What the hell!" he exclaimed. A filthy arm reached down and picked up the phone. The arm belonged to a bearded, long-red-haired lad who, like Craig, was not looking where he was going and had crashed into him. About the same age as Craig, he wore...

Uh? What on earth is he wearing? Bloody freaky!

Craig studied the curious unshaven figure holding his mobile at arm's length and gawping at him. A walk-on extra for a movie about the Borders Reivers, perhaps?

"Cool dress you're wearing Jimmy, but... may I have my phone back? Please? Don't wanna miss the school bus."

The lad, possibly an actor, stared blankly. Clearly, he had not understood a word, but Craig also saw terror in those greenish-blue eyes. A terror far greater than would be expected of a crap-movie extra with only a run-on part.

“Polish?” he asked. “My great granddad was with the Free Poles, you know. In the last war. Me... erm... Craig Szczepański. Was. Originally, like. Dinnae understand a word of the lingo, though. So now it’s ‘Stevens’. After my little sister got bullied because of our surname.”

“Bull... *ied*?”

Craig looked down at the lad’s footwear. Just flaps of leather tied on with thin strips.

“Cool trainers, dude! Now... my phone, please!” He held out his hand, palm up. The other boy slapped it, then grinned. Craig laughed, though could not work out exactly why he found this funny. The boy also laughed. The nearby old mental hospital had been closed for years, otherwise he could have been an escapee.

Breth spoke for the first time:

“Num Romanus es?” he queried.

Of course! Craig reckoned the lad was probably part of a live television event at the Trimontium Museum in Melrose, getting a feel for his costume. Despite the post-Brexit, post-pandemic, economic crash, and subsequent political turmoil, during which the far right seized power in Westminster overnight, banning all hitherto legitimate political parties, including the SNP, it was the focus for all sorts of historically educational events.

“I get it. You’re involved with Trimontium. Right?”

The response this caused could not have been more spectacular. Not even if he had poked the boy with a cattle prod. Breth took off, with the phone, up the hill towards Bowden village. Craig, the ace rugby forward, soon caught up with him and tackled the lad to the ground. He helped Breth up, retrieved his phone, said, “Sorry!” then got to thinking...

Across Scotland, the military had created ‘special forces camps’ or SFCs, allegedly to ‘maintain order’, but obviously with control of the fast-growing SFS in mind. Jamie Stevens said it was the last straw when he got wind of such a camp being set up in a field that had been the location of the ancient Roman military fort of Trimontium. Seemed like 'giving the finger' to all who revered that local archaeological site of world-class importance. Whether this boy was connected in some way with SFS, whether he was a Polish immigrant who had escaped deportation, or whether he was merely bonkers, did not seem to matter. Craig felt sorry for the lad as he felt sorry for his sister. His inescapably caring nature never remained hidden for long.

What the heck if I do miss the first two lessons, he thought. *Maths and chemistry? I bloody know it all, anyway*. (Which was true.) *Might cheer Hannah up to get to the bottom of this freak! Well not actually his bottom, maybe, but what he's about.*

Craig beckoned to the youth to follow him back up the hill. When he held out his hand, palm up, for another slap, whatever that meant, Breth's eyes lit up. It was obvious Craig meant no harm. Breth slapped the outstretched hand, chuckled again, then followed its owner, a twenty-first century stranger, towards the housing development on Dingleton Hill. Together, they turned into another chariot *via*, then another and another, the boy's eyes almost popping out of their sockets in disbelief at everything he saw, until they reached a certain building, two storeys high, identical to the others they had passed by. Breth felt relieved that there were no more of those shiny, covered, horseless chariots on the move like the one that had roared past on the *via* towards Trimontium, although some stood stationary outside other buildings.

"How can they move without horses?" Breth asked the other boy in Latin. "*Dei Romani?*"

Craig understood only the last two words.

"Roman gods? What are you on about, dude?" He shrugged his shoulders, took out his key, opened the front door and called out:

"We've a visitor, Hannah!"

"What?" his sister shouted with irritation from her

bedroom upstairs. She felt truly annoyed to be interrupted whilst working out how to best describe her heroine's first kiss with a Dylan lookalike. "Why aren't you on the school bus?"

"Because..." Craig stepped inside and beckoned to Breth to follow him, but the red-haired boy remained in the doorway as if superglued to the ground. Craig reached forward, grabbed the lad's arm, pulled him into the house then slammed the door. If he did have something to do with the 'resistance', as he called the SFS, he did not want neighbours blabbing to the local police even if some in the force turned a blind eye to SFS goings on. Whom to trust had become a problem of late.

What Craig did not know was the cause for Breth's sudden confusion. His sister's voice. And when Hannah appeared at the foot of the stairs, dressed in tight-fitting shorts, blouse and flip-flops, her brother really did think he had made a stupid decision, for Breth went berserk. Hannah cupped a hand to her mouth as she watched a wild-looking youth wearing a shabby 'dress' grip her brother by his shirt, lift him up and push him up against the wall.

"Stop it!" she cried out, rushing forward to pull at the Selgovan boy's arms, trying to yank him away. Finally, the lad, taken by surprise, let go. Craig remained up against the wall whilst the strange boy, his eyes filled with tears, just stared at Hannah. She frowned, went up to her brother, then demanded,

"Explain, big brother!"

II

"We'll pick him up later," said the larger of the two auxiliaries, giving up the chase. "Just now, Octavius will be wanting his tax, huh?"

"Might need taming first," the other said. "The little cow tried to bite me."

"'Unharmed,' our master said! Mind you, can't imagine what he sees in her."

"Can't you?" queried his companion. He gave Adienna a lustful glance. "Must be blind, *amice!*"

Adalfarus, breathless after failing to catch up with Breth, turned to face the silent crowd of Celts held back by other auxiliaries.

"And you lot can piss off before I skewer you all!" With *spathae* drawn, and pulling the reluctant girl along by both arms, the auxiliaries left the Selgovan hilltop fort, taking the shorter though steeper of the paths down towards Trimontium.

"What's that?" Adalfarus called out as they approached a covered hollow on the lower slopes. "Those branches and bracken. They've been put there. Over a bloody great hole someone's dug out."

Adienna's heart sank. She knew only too well about the secret 'cave' where the two young lovers would often lie, fondling and saying sweet things to each other. Certain that Breth was hiding there, she bit her lower lip as Adalfarus went to examine it, kicking aside the bracken.

"Nothing!" exclaimed.

Not there. Thank the gods!

The brute stooped to pick up something. Adienna recognized her friend's wood-carving knife, but no Breth. Why had he left it?

"That stupid little boy was here all right," observed Adalfarus, examining the knife. He showed it to Adienna.

She tried to look away, but the other auxiliary, even uglier, gripped her chin and forced her to look at the knife. "*You* can use this to skin his body alive when we find him. I'll make you a purse out of his hide." He gazed with pleasure at the pain in her face, then erupted into laughter and slapped his thigh. "Joking!" he added. "Let's forget the little fool. He'll be of no consequence to you after you become the pleasured property of Octavius."

"Never!" Adienna muttered in Brythonic. The auxiliary's eyes narrowed.

"What's that?" he asked.

"Says she can't wait," the other suggested.

They both laughed and pulled Adienna on towards Trimontium where she was proudly paraded before cheering comrades.

"Unpaid tax for Octavius!" Adalfarus explained.

"Octavius? But he only just left. With twenty or so men," someone said. "Trouble out west. The messenger trembled like an earthquake when he told our commander."

"Hmm! Flavia will have to wait, then. And none of you lot touches her. Hear me? He'll have plans for this one. In Italia, perhaps. But trouble out west again? They have their own bloody forts!"

"*Big* trouble!"

"Selgovae?"

"Selgovae! Like her! Don't you think we should just... you know... whatever Octavius said she was good for. He'll never know. We'll dispose of her afterwards and say she wasn't there. Ran off with that irritating little village boy. Is that his toy knife?"

The other soldier indicated Breth's knife. Adalfarus approached the man, pushed him backwards then held Breth's 'toy' knife to his throat.

"In the absence of Octavius, you will respect my authority. Until he returns, no one touches Flavia here. Do I make myself clear?"

No match against the brawn of Adalfarus, the minion nodded. Also, in Trimontium, levels of authority were to be respected at all costs, and Adalfarus and his chum were expected to keep other auxiliaries in order whilst he was away. Insubordination was treated severely. Often, this involved death of the perpetrator.

Adienna-turned-Flavia was taken to the *praetorium*[2], beyond the main barracks, where Octavius resided, and handed over to the commander's woman-servant.

"Treat her well, Donia," Adalfarus ordered. He grinned. "But only because the little bitch is of value for our commander."

The woman, from the Votadini tribe, spoke Brythonic. As soon as Adalfarus had left to celebrate his personal triumph in the company of his friend, she sat, with her arm across Adienna's shoulders, softly chanting an old Celtic song, repeatedly running her boney fingers through the girl's long blond hair and stroking her freckled cheeks. Adienna thought she would never, ever, stop crying.

"Hungry?" Donia asked.

Adienna shook her head.

"Some water, then?"

The girl nodded. The woman fetched water in a glass. Adienna had never seen anything made from glass. Holding it up, she gazed at the light streaming from the open doorway through that miracle of transparency, patterned with colours like those of a rainbow. "That's right, my girl," she said in Brythonic. "We must see through them. Even the Romans have their weaknesses. Do not give up, whatever you may think or whatever happens."

Wiping away tears, Adienna looked at her quizzically.

"What do you mean, 'See through them'?"

"For a start, he'll not bed you himself."

"How do you know this?"

---

[2] Commander's quarters in a Roman fort

"I see right through that man." She leaned over and whispered something in the girl's ear. Adienna appeared shocked.

"How d'you know?"

Donia pointed to her eyes and her ears.

"Are you sure?"

"As sure as you are the most beautiful girl to have ever set foot in this place."

"Hmm! With these?" The girl pointed to her freckled cheeks. Donia smiled.

"Those are special. Like a gift from a goddess," she replied, then paused, squinting at the seated girl. "He has other plans for you. I know it. Plans that ensure you must remain a virgin. For now. And perhaps for someone of our own kind."

Adienna's eyes lit up.

"Breth?"

Donia frowned and shook her head.

"Breth is my childhood sweetheart," the girl continued. "We're to be married. I couldn't stand for anyone else to touch me. Not like that!"

Donia patted Adienna's cheek.

"They won't!" she assured. "Not yet. Because of this business out west. But we must get thinking. Together. My master will need to strike a bargain. Your people are strong in the west. But... well, you see, for their chieftain, freckles like yours will be truly special. And—"

"I don't believe you! I'm one of them."

"Just so, my dear child. Just so!"

*****

"Was halfway down the hill to the bus stop. Had just texted Dylan about meeting up tonight to celebrate his eighteenth. With you. To cheer you up. Then this dude here just crashes into me from bloody nowhere. Knocked my phone to the ground. Starts speaking in Polish or something."

"How d'you know it's Polish?" Hannah asked.

"'Cos I can't bloody understand him."

Hannah tried hard, but failed, to look away from the terrified boy who would not take his eyes off her.

"So... you know all the languages in the world?" she asked her brother whilst still staring at Breth.

"Na! I just wondered whether he has something to with Dad's... you know..."

The girl turned to face her brother.

"SFS?"

"An immigrant, maybe?" continued Craig. "Threatened with deportation by the Westminster government? Joined the SFS hoping he can stay in a free Scotland?"

"And who doesn't speak a word of English?" Hannah was sceptical. Breth tapped her shoulder. She turned and frowned. He pointed at her shorts and shook his head.

"I think he disapproves, Sis," suggested Craig.

"Look, Craig, thanks for your support with Dad and all that, but bringing home a goof like this! What the hell got into you?"

"He needs help," replied Craig.

Hannah buried her fingers in her hair and clenched her fists. Something she did when annoyed. Like her mother.

"Ugh!" she exclaimed. But neither she nor Craig were prepared for what happened next. The boy reached up and, very gently, took hold of the girl's wrists and lowered her arms to her side. Again, he pointed to her shorts and shook his head.

"Look, go change into jeans. Then we'll try and figure this out. I'll get my iPad. Use Google translate." Whilst fiddling with his iPad, Craig added, "Can take a later Earlston bus to school. Make up some semi-plausible excuse for being late."

Hannah disappeared upstairs then re-appeared wearing tight jeans. Again, Breth pointed to these and shook his head.

"God, he's so-o-o bloody fussy!"

“I think he’s telling us something,” said Craig. “To do with modesty, perhaps?”

“What’s he bleeding want me to wear?”

“Try a dress, only not too short.”

When the girl showed up in a knee-length dress that she would not normally be seen dead in, the boy seemed happier. Craig busily scanned ‘Google Translate’ whilst Breth stared at the iPad as if witnessing something only the gods might comprehend.

*****

Breth had run from the hilltop Selgovan fort because he knew he was fast, plus those over-confident Roman bullies were without crossbows or slings. After hiding in that secret place, and seeking comfort and wisdom from Celtic gods, he now found himself transported to a land of gods so strange that even the wisest of village elders would have been rendered speechless. Worst of all, Adienna, who had first appeared almost naked, no longer seemed to recognize him. Nor did she understand their language. Not even Latin. That’s how he came to realize that the gods responsible for this could not have been Roman. Like the young man standing beside him who only understood a word or two of Latin. Although he appeared to be familiar with Adienna, Breth could tell there was no desire between the two. This puzzled him, for he could not imagine any male not feeling fire in his loins in the girl’s presence.

Unless he prefers boys?

That gesture earlier on, holding his hand out? Should Breth feel worried? No! The fellow really did have friendship written across his face. He bore not a *spatha* but a warmth of spirit, and, as he stood touching and flicking at the shining tablet held in his left hand, causing pictures and letters to appear, only to vanish moments later, a voice inside Breth’s head, perhaps that of one of his own gods, told the Selgovan that this boy might be trying to help both himself and Adienna. After all, better that the girl was here in a land of strange gods rather than imprisoned in Trimontium to await the unwanted attentions of the new commander, even if she could no longer speak Brythonic.

The boy showed him the tablet on which had appeared, in large Latin letters:

C... R... A... I... G

Breth was thankful he had learned not only how to speak Latin, but to also how to read the words of the Romans. When the boy pointed to those letters, then to himself and said, "C... R... A... I... G, Craig," Breth understood. He repeated "Craig", pointing to the other boy, then, pointing to himself, said, "Breth."

"Getting somewhere now," observed Craig. He pointed to Hannah, typed H... A... N... N... A... H, saying, "Hannah."

Breth frowned and shook his head.

"Adienna!" he insisted, pointing to Craig's sister.

Craig also shook his head.

"Hannah," he repeated.

Breth became upset. Adienna looked at him. There was no mistaking those sky-blue eyes and the freckles. He knew each and every one of these by heart. He gazed at her as she stared back at him. "Adienna?" he said softly. Then, in Brythonic: "Why won't you recognize me?" Tears filled his eyes. The girl looked away, biting her lower lip. Adienna always did this when something was wrong, and all of this was very wrong.

The tablet was again shown to him, this time bearing the letters P... O... L... I... S... H? Breth shook his head. S... E... R... B... I... A... N? Another shake of the head. L... A... T... V... I... A... N? Breth gazed at the letters for a while, then pointed to five of these one by one. The L, the A, the T, the I and N. He missed out the 'V' and the second 'A'. The boy called Craig tapped at the tablet.

'NONNE LINGUAM LATINAM INTELLEGIS?' appeared.

Breth nodded.

"De montibus ignis venio[3]," he replied in Latin, clearly the language of choice in this mysterious land of gods who resided in tablets that could be held in the hand.

"Hannah... we have a problem!" said Craig in mock-American, mimicking the famous Apollo 13 announcement, from space, *'Houston... we have a problem!'*

---

[3] I come from the Fire Hills

III

Domitius Fluvius bowed to his younger superior who wore a toga fastened by a silver cross-bow *fibula*[4]. He glanced over his shoulder to ensure the servant had left before declaring his reason for intruding on the busy general's time.

The Roman army had become top-heavy. It was difficult for Domitius to know exactly whom to approach, and how. What he did know was that things would soon become impossible for the men in Trimontium to keep control over the surrounding land because of the cruel treatment being meted out to a people he had grown not only to respect, but to love inasmuch as a soldier can ever love those he is paid to suppress.

The missive that Domitius had received, whilst hurrying home through Gallia, came from his second-in-command, Marcus, renamed by Domitius in honour of their recently deceased great emperor Marcus Aurelius. Demoted by Octavius, the man could take no more of the beheadings and crucifixions and the burning of native roundhouses. He fled to take refuge in the forest after sending a trusted messenger on the fastest horse he could find to catch up with Domitius. What the coded words revealed brought tears to the old soldier's eyes. There could only be one outcome: rebellion. And not just around Trimontium, at the limit of the Roman Empire and of the territory of the Selgovae and the Votadini. Further west, tribespeople would be less forgiving. As soon as they got wind of what Octavius was up to, they would strike back. And harder than the new commander could ever imagine. Domitius had seen this happen whilst fighting in Germania where even the women proved to be ruthless in the extreme. Witnesses there said it was worse than seeing someone getting mauled by an angry bear or being eaten

[4] Roman brooch-clasp for fastening a toga

alive by lions in the arena.

"Forgive me, Publius Petronius, noblest of generals," began Domitius, "but the matter I wish to bring to your attention is, I believe, something that would benefit from your wisdom and insight. I—"

The general laughed, took Domitius by the hand and gave him a couple of hearty slaps on the back. Anyone unaware of the general's ways would have thought the military lion of a man was trying to kill his former underling, but Domitius knew the younger man too well to suspect him of anything other than friendship.

"Come... somewhere quiet away from our new emperor's spies," warned Publius. "Never know whom to trust these days."

With a wink and a smile, the younger man ushered his old comrade-in-arms inside the *Tabularium* at the sunset end of the *Forum Romanum* where, by bribing a military official with a *denarius*, Domitius had tracked down his former commander. Now, whilst hopefully on a fast track to higher station, Publius knew that uttering just one word that displeased Emperor Commodus could end his life. He also knew that his old comrade was the only man who might help him prevent Octavius and his Germanian thugs from pitching not only Trimontium, but the whole of Britannia into chaos.

Marcus Aurelius's son could not have been more different from the beloved father. Glorious decimation of the Celts north of the Wall of Hadrianus would, in the demonic mind of Commodus, be seen by the gods as a sign of personal imperial strength. But no one knew the strengths of those Caledonian tribespeople, the Selgovae and the Votadini, better than Publius's old chum Domitius. The brutality of the smooth-talking new commander, and his auxiliaries, in tune with the ways of the new emperor, might succeed in gaining riches, even land, for the fort, but only at the expense of a backlash that could be even more terrible than what the old friends had witnessed in Germania under Marcus Aurelius during the campaign against the Marcomanni. And the fact that this brutality was being inflicted by Octavius, as an antidote to his predecessor's generosity towards the locals, truly piqued Publius.

The general agreed that Rome could not afford to ignore the warnings hidden in the covertly worded missive Domitius received from the messenger, coded with references to the *epistulae*[5] of Gaius Plinius Caecilius Secundus whose writing Domitius and Marcus often discussed at Trimontium following the establishment of peace. Now those years of relative peace under Marcus Aurelius had come to an end.

Coding had been a game for the two men since there was little to do in the cavalry fort under *Pax Romana* apart from overseeing the collection of taxes and intervening in minor disputes. For the sake of caution, they decided that when communicating about Trimontium, in the future, should the need arise, this would be done using a code that related to the younger Plinius's depiction of the Vesuvius eruption which killed Domitius's great grandfather at Pompeii. Both men knew that the Selgovae called the three hills overlooking Trimontium the 'Fire Hills' in their own language. Why, they had no idea, but the Vesuvius reference seemed relevant when dealing with Trimonium-related matters. A separate code based on Plinius's writings about the Christians was used for all other issues, partly because the bravery of their martyrs had always impressed Domitius. He had even wondered whether Marcus Aurelius, a stoic philosopher, might have been influenced by the wisdom of their deified Jewish leader so cruelly crucified for his belief in one God, his 'true Father'.

Decoded, the missive informed the retired soldier that the monster who had taken over at Trimontium was

---

[5] letters

extending his territory, claiming that forts in Northern Britannia had grown weak under the likes of Domitius, and that the Selgovae should be taught a lesson they would never forget. He also planned to drive wedges between the tribespeople, playing one community against the other. 'Selling' the beautiful daughter of a respected elder from one village, to be used and abused by the chieftain of a neighbouring community, would, in his reckoning, make life so much easier for the Romans. But the Selgovae were far from stupid. Their gods were cunning, too. The path chosen by Octavius could only lead to the beginning of the end of Rome's mighty influence in this far-flung province.

"So, what do you want me to do about this? It's a bit like playing *ludus latrunculorum*[6] in the dark, blindfolded and with your hands tied behind your back." Publius guffawed at his own humour. "Much the same as trying to make sense of what's going on in the *Senatus Populusque Romanus* with that animal Commodus on the imperial throne, right?" Another mischievous wink from the general was enough to inform Domitius that the other man was on board with any plan to stop Octavius in his tracks.

"Three men and a donkey," replied Domitius.

The general laughed so much he had to hold on to the older man for support.

"I love it, my friend," he said, after recovering his composure. "I take it you mean yourself and not a real donkey?"

Domitius, grinning like an ass, nodded. "With four horses," he added.

"Hmm! And the men? Auxiliaries or—?"

"The best you've got."

"Legionaries, then. But if you're planning to murder Octavius, we're not having this conversation."

"We go unarmed. Apart from *spathae*. Disguised as

---

[6]Roman two-player board game of military tactics, resembling chess.

Christians. Wearing their little crucifixes. Have you not read the *epistulae* of Gaius Plinius the younger?"

"No time for all that nonsense. But what you say makes sense. I've already heard from another source that the man you talk of is a *diabolus*." Publius chuckled. "*Diabolus pulchellus puer* (pretty devil boy) is how he was described to me. Face of an angel, mind and heart of a devil. He and our emperor were once partners in evil, you know. When Commodus was but a child. Tortured animals together. It's why you were replaced by one so young. So, you, my old donkey, must take care. If Commodus ever finds out about our plan, he'll think up ways of disposing of you in the arena, in front of his cheering crowds, that would make *hades infernum*[7] seem like paradise. But you might just be lucky. Because he leaves the running of the empire to a man called Perennis, the poor blighter. He'd simply have you strangled. Far less painful. More respectful and—"

"One thing Octavius doesn't have, my source tells me, is respect from his underlings," interrupted Domitius. "Apart from a small circle of Germanian auxiliary thugs."

"Hmm! And we know what the Germanians did to some of our best in the wars against the Marcomanni."

"But remember how we overcame all of that? In the end? Under our great emperor Marcus Aurelius? Making friends, not enemies? The enemies that Octavius is now creating are our friends."

"Were, Domitius. *Were!* Take care and be back here at dawn tomorrow." He chuckled again. "Before the emperor's goons get wind of this. The monster himself will be in his harem, of course. And that's another thing. The men of *Roma*—or Commodiana, as he'd have us call our beloved city—get their women to uglify themselves. Any woman considered beautiful is dragged away to join his whores, married or not."

---

[7] Hell

IV

"You're mad!" scoffed Hannah. She glanced at the youth standing beside her brother. The boy could not seem to keep his eyes off her. "And as for this lump of—" She looked up at the ceiling as though she might see, written across it, a word that could describe the gangly, red-haired creep her brother had brought into the house. "Ugh!" she exclaimed with fists clenched like those of a champion boxer.

Craig chuckled. He loved it when his little sister expressed her exasperation with such physical body language.

"Hannah, let's all three of us go into the living room and work this out."

"With that Neanderthal?"

"He is *not* a Neanderthal! Just needs a bit of a shave. And he's called Breth. Apparently. Breath of fresh air in this crap awful place, ay?" Hannah didn't even smile at her brother's feeble attempt to humour her. "Look, before you blow a fuse—and it's good to see you worked up, Sis, rather than have you moping—"

"I never mope!"

"Whatever! There's something going on and you're gonna help me get to the bottom of it. Whether you like it or not."

Hannah glanced again at Breth. The strange boy smiled. *Maybe if he shaves, and wears something decent, he could pass for human,* she reckoned.

Craig took Breth to the sofa. Both sat. Hannah remained standing. A clear message that, were she to sit down, she would be displaying approval for the creature her brother had brought in. With the iPad on his lap, and Breth's startled eyes darting between this and Hannah, as if trying to work out which was the more puzzling, Craig spoke in a mix of schoolboy and internet Latin, with Breth responding in

Brythonic-modified Latin...

"Where... do... you... live?"

"*Bryniau Tân. Erm... colles ignis.*" To explain this, the Selgovan boy pointed upwards, facing the window. Craig understood.

"Alone?"

Breth laughed at the suggestion.

"I wish!"

"Wish what?" asked Craig in Latin.

"I wish I lived alone with you, Adienna," he replied in Brythonic, looking at Hannah. "Marry?" he suggested in Latin, pointing to her. Hannah looked away.

"Others?" queried Craig, in Latin, via his iPad. "On the *colles ignis?*" pointing to the window.

Breth appeared puzzled, then, patting his chest with pride, came out with...

"*Multi, multi sunt!*[8] *Selgovae sumus. Animosi*[9]*!*"

It was common knowledge that the iron age fort perched near the summit of the northernmost Eildon Hill, its ancient contours obvious when carpeted with snow, had been peopled not by the Votadini tribe of the East, as once taught, but by the Selgovae. Unaware of any post-Brexit, post-pandemic hippy community residing up there, Craig could only assume the guy was an out-of-work, Latin-taught, foreign actor posing as an ancient Selgovan. But he could not have been more than eighteen years old, if that. With such an amazing grasp of Latin, this made no sense. He should either still be at school or starting uni.

"*Houses there?*" Craig asked in Latin.

Breth nodded.

"Round houses. Not Roman!" he answered. The fire in the boy's eyes troubled Craig. "Adienna (the lad pointed to Hannah again) not Roman! *Non Flavia est!*"

---

[8]There are many

[9] Proud

"What's he saying?" questioned Hannah. Breth frowned at her.

"All this..." Breth spread his arms to take in the living room. "From our cave?" He pointed to Hannah then himself. "Aine's cave!"

"Hannah, go and make him a cup of tea. Think I need one too. Bring some biscuits."

Hannah, torn between a wish to escape the piercing green eyes of the freak seated beside her brother, and a curiosity to stay and discover who he really was, left the room. Instead of going directly to the kitchen, she hovered in the hallway, adjusted her hair in the mirror and listened...

"Where is this cave?" Craig typed into Google Translate.

"*Pila* and holes," was Breth's reply in Latin. "Aine angry with the Romans. Octavius bad. His men from Germania took Adienna for him. *Tributum!*"

Craig Googled *'tributum'*.

"Tax?" he queried, puzzled.

"Adienna."

"What year is it?" Craig asked in Google Latin.

Breth laughed so much he had to hold on to the sofa. "What year?" he repeated, pointing to Craig. He laughed again. "Why do you ask? The year of Bruttius and Condianus!"

For several moments Craig remained silent as he trawled the internet to work out what this meant. Meanwhile, in the hallway, Hannah bit her lower lip then hurried on into the kitchen where, in her head, the Dylan, with whom she was in love, had been challenged to a dual by a young man she called a Neanderthal.

"Oh man!" Craig exclaimed on learning from his iPad the significance of the year of Bruttius and Condianus. "That's AD bloody 180!"

*****

"But... how can Octavius prefer boys to girls?" asked Adienna. "Surely he's a man?"

Donia smiled.

“Some men have no desire for women,” she informed the girl.

“So, he’ll use me like money? To barter with our people out west? Because they’re fierce and annoying? But surely they would just return me to my father.”

“Where a beautiful woman is concerned, all men turn evil.”

“I don’t believe it. Breth could never be bad. Not in that way. He’s honourable. He was going to show me something special beside the river when we met Octavius and his bullies. His way of showing his love.”

Donia stroked Adienna’s flushed freckled cheeks before gently wiping away the tears.

“You must both be strong for what has to be. You know, my grandfather told me that before the Romans came, our men were forever fighting each other. At least the Romans put a stop to that. Brought us together in our combined hatred of them.”

“No! Domitius was a lovely man. You know, there was a time when Breth wanted to become an auxiliary in the Roman army. Because of Domitius.”

“Hmm! Auxiliary but never a legionary. However clever. All a pretence, don’t you see? To appease their gods. They say mercy is rewarded. And that’ll be part of my master’s plan. Show them mercy if they accept a beautiful gift for their chieftain.”

“I don’t understand. I only want to be back with Breth. Then we’ll escape to the land of the free in the North.”

“Up there? And put yourselves at the mercy of those monsters the Romans call the *Picti*?”

“How d’you know they’re monsters? Could be more of that Roman pretence you talk about.”

“Stories from the old times. Before the likes of Octavius contaminated our blessed land. Tales of creatures too terrible to even imagine. Monsters like the boobries. Giant black birds that can swallow cows whole. No, you'll not be wanting to go up there, with or without Breth. But my own people in the east—"

"Votadini?"

"Of course! I know them well. Why do you think my father agreed to me coming here when my husband and sons got killed?" A mischievous grin appeared on the woman's face. Adienna, too, smiled.

"To be a spy? Truly?"

Donia heard voices outside and put a forefinger to her lips.

"Now, my girl. Let us get Flavia looking even more beautiful for her new master, eh?" she said more loudly, with a wink and another smile. But there was something about the smile. The curve of her lips, perhaps. Like that of Roman crossbow.

*****

A three-day ride across country for Octavius and a small troop of cavalry and legionaries. They had no fear. The roads were straight, their scout, a local man whose only allegiance was to the god of greed, could be trusted, and all were well-armed with crossbows and slings. When they reached the brow of a hill overlooking the Roman fort to the west, built by Agricola, the commander reined back his horse. Smoke plumed from within the fort, the outhouses appeared deserted and decapitated bodies of Roman auxiliaries lay strewn in front of the unguarded fort entrance.

"Now you see why our new young emperor chose *me* to lead you in this godforsaken land. That, my friends, is what would happen to you if I'd played along with the weakness shown by my predecessor." A glance from Octavius at his favourite legionary (and bedmate) was all that was needed. The man spat on his hands, took his crossbow, chose a bolt from the quiver at his side and waited. "Let us hope all has gone according to plan back at Trimontium, huh? With that unpaid tax," remarked the commander.

*****

The fathers of Breth and Adienna shared their grief on the summit of the middle Fire Hill which, for them, now, was a place of prayer driven by anger. An anger soon replaced by fury. Fury matched only by that of the God of Fire.

"I would rather die trying to get Adienna back for your son than allow that fiend to defile her purity! I swear I'll tear him apart limb by limb."

Never had Breth's father heard his friend-since-childhood talk this way. Like his daughter, Alun was the gentlest of souls.

"Brave words, but I'm afraid there's little we can do against the might of Rome."

"Do you remember that story Domitius once told us? From an auxiliary who came from that land the people he calls Christians regard as sacred?"

"About the peasant boy who slayed a cruel giant with a slingshot?"

Breth's father, Gorsedd, nodded. He smiled.

"I do remember. If only we could have Domitius back, huh? You'll have heard from the elders, no doubt. About what's happening in the west."

"No. Tell me. I wasn't listening to the gossip. Too upset."

"A runner arrived late last night. From the west. They're planning to destroy the Roman fort there."

"D'you think this tax nonsense could be linked? Is this Rome showing us her muscles and her weakness at the same time?"

"Possibly. But..." Gorsedd paused. "Remember Domitius telling us rumours about the emperor being ill? And about his fear of the man's son who was supposed to be assisting him?"

"Mad and dangerous, he called the boy."

"Perhaps the beloved emperor, Marcus Aurelius, has died. His son might have sent Octavius, and others like him, to do his dirty work here in Britannia."

"We could get reinforcements. From our friends the Votadini."

Gorsedd frowned.

"Votadini? Friends? I'd rather sleep with a wild boar than keep company with that lot!"

"But not with Octavius, you wouldn't!"

"What are you getting at?"

"It's been my one comfort since they took Adienna away. The only time the new commander came to our village himself. Remember? Two full moons ago. With ten of his men, all armed. Unlike Domitius would have been. Did you not notice the way he looked at your son?"

"At Breth?"

"Yes, at Breth. Not Adienna. Like I said, it may not be the commander we should fear, but those devils out west if he hands Adienna over to them to buy their allegiance. It's why we might be better off with the Votadini."

"What do you mean, devils out west? Aren't they our own?"

"The chief there. He's taken to beheadings like the tribes down south. Believes it'll make him more powerful, some say. By owning their souls."

"Who tells you these things?"

Adienna's father, Alun, looked down at the fort of Trimontium below where, on the parade ground, auxiliaries practised the art of killing whilst decent folk toiled the land beyond its strong walls and protective ditches.

"The birds," he replied. "The birds that open their wee souls to the world when the sun goddess shows herself each morning. The birds that fly free and sing about freedom. These birds are trying to tell us things. About what we should do to be like them."

Gorsedd had always known his friend as a cautious man, but the Romans taking his daughter had forced to the surface someone quite different.

"I agree, we must free ourselves from the Roman

scourge!" he declared. But he feared for his headstrong son.

*****

Breth watched as Craig typed away on his iPad. He listened carefully to the other boy's curious Latin. It was even worse than that of those uncouth Germanian auxiliaries.

"You live on those hills with your family?" asked Craig.

"Ita vero[10]!"

"In AD 180?" The Selgovan boy looked puzzled. "Erm... the year of Bruttius and Condianus?" Breth nodded. "Under the Romans?" Another nod and a scowl.

"This cave where there are 'holes and *pila* in the ground'... is that near where we..." Craig smacked his hands together to imitate their earlier collision at the bottom of the golf course.

"Ita vero!"

"Not spears. Or *pila*," Craig informed Breth. "Markers for 'golf-holes'." Google, unable to provide a sensible Latin translation, merely regurgitated 'golf-holes'. The Selgovan boy shrugged his shoulders. "Hmm! My sister's always doing that too. So, who... is... Adienna?"

Breth pointed to the door leading to the kitchen from where sounds of Hannah making tea filtered into the living room.

"No, I'm afraid not, dude," Craig replied in English. "That's my little sister, Hannah!" he added, after translating this into Latin with his iPad.

Breth smiled. The word *'soror'* was a relief, but also a puzzle. Adienna's big brother had died when they were children. Killed by a wild boar, it was said, although Adienna always doubted this. But this boy looked nothing like her brother, Aydhan.

"Hannah!" Craig insisted.

"Hannah?" echoed Breth. *"Gemina Adiennae?"*

Craig typed on his iPad. As he had thought, in Latin

---

[10] Yes!

gemina was the female for 'twin'. So, this boy, whom he still struggled to believe had suddenly arrived from ancient Britain, presumed Hannah had, in a past parallel world, an identical twin called Adienna? Perhaps, he reckoned, this might be a good starting point. He gave Breth a thumbs-up, nodded and agreed. After a Google translate search...

"*Ita vero! Hannah Adiennaque geminae sunt!*"

Craig tried to say this using an accent similar to that of the Italian waiter in the restaurant in Melrose where his parents had been fond of eating out before things turned politically nasty. He held up his right hand, palm forwards and Breth slapped this then chuckled. Hannah entered with a tray bearing three mugs of tea and a plate of biscuits she had made at the weekend.

Made these for Dylan's birthday, damn it! she thought, trying, unsuccessfully, to avoid Breth's eyes.

"Hannah, please sit down," Craig said after his sister placed the tray on the coffee table. "You're just gonna have to believe this."

Glancing uneasily at the Selgovan boy, she sat on the armchair opposite, pulling down the hem of her skirt.

"Breth here is no actor, Hannah. Not crazy, either. And he seems to accept you're the twin of a girl called Adienna."

"Not that again! I really will call the police if you don't..."

"The police? With Dad being in the SFS? Listen, Hannah. I'm telling the truth when I say Breth would never harm you. Worship you, maybe, but harm, no way. You see—now don't freak out, sis—he really is an ancient Briton."

"What do you mean? Not much older than me, by the look of it. And I'm only just sixteen. Worst luck. Otherwise, me and Dylan might have already—"

"Not his age! When he's from."

Hannah's jaw dropped.

"Tell me I'm not dreaming," she said.

"And he believes you're the twin of a girl he knows. Someone called Adienna. Seemingly she's kind of special for him."

Special? Hannah's heart missed a beat, then took off at a gallop.

"Poor girl!" she said. "But you're joking, huh?"

"When did I last tell a joke?"

Hannah grinned.

"Before I was born, I guess. But what makes you think this... this *freak* is what you call an ancient Briton."

"Hannah! Have some respect! He's no freak. Just look at him. He's totally bloody lost. And terrified! It's the things he says, too. And I dinnae ken anyone at Earlston High who understands Latin like him. Or speaks it like—I dunno—like he's used to doing. Comes natural to him. Not that Latin has been his normal—"

"Normal? Bloody hell, there's nothing normal about that—"

"Hannah, he's human! Like you and me. We've just gotta work things out. Together. Only..."

"Only what?"

"Can't miss English before lunch. So..."

"Hang on, Craig. Surely you're not gonna—?"

"Like I said, I promise you'll be safe with him. Okay, he needs a shave. And a change into my jeans and one of my tops. Looks like we're pretty much the same size and shape. Then—"

"Then I'll call the police."

"Shut up! You bloody won't!" Craig rarely lost his temper with Hannah, but she was beginning to get on his nerves. She looked hurt, but neither brother nor sister was prepared for what happened next. Breth sprang from the sofa and pulled Craig up by his shirt.

"Paenitet dicere ei!"

Craig broke free...

"Cool it, dude." He retrieved his iPad. "Better look that up," he added. Moments later, "Erm... wants me to apologize to you, Sis." He went over to Hannah, hugged her, looked back at Breth then said, "Okay now?" Breth got up and did the same, but in a rather more affectionate way. The girl, uncertain whether she should resist his embrace, felt confused. She blushed.

"He smells," she said quietly. "Take him up to the bathroom and sort him out. Shave him and put proper clothes on him, then we'll talk before you leave me alone with... with an ancient bloody Briton. And I'm going back to the kitchen to get a knife. Just in case."

Twenty minutes later, Craig and Breth re-appeared. Hannah felt even more confused, for the young man standing beside her brother was fiendishly handsome. His straggled red hair had been cut short by her brother.

"It's called a Caesar cut. Got it off the internet. Like it?" Craig asked on seeing how his sister gaped at their guest. When Breth smiled at her she feared her insides would melt.

I love Dylan, I love Dylan... she kept repeating inside her head as a Hollywood hero lookalike sat down opposite her. He pointed to the knife she held and shook his head. She agreed. She no longer had a need for it and placed it on the coffee table.

"I'll get you a pen and paper," Craig said to Hannah. "Plus, you can use my iPad. When I get back this afternoon, I'll expect you to have taught him basic English, at least. He seems pretty bright, ken."

"But what about Mum and Dad?" Hannah queried, wondering how on earth they were going to explain the presence of a spruced up ancient Briton in the living room.

"Leave that to me. He could prove useful for Dad. Who knows?"

"Who knows? God, I feel I know bloody nothing!"

"Language, Hannah! And use the table. For a proper lesson in English."

Hannah, now even more afraid of the Selgovan boy, but for a different reason, beckoned to Breth to join her at the table. After Craig had left to catch the bus to Earlston, she wrote on a blank sheet of paper: 'ENGLISH'.

"English," she said, pointing to the letters. "I teach you," she continued with appropriate 'I' and 'you' hand gestures. "Okay?"

"English," repeated Breth. "Okay!"

His smile created havoc with the girl's insides. Pointing to a chair at the table, and blushing crimson again, she said, "There. We sit. You. Me."

Please don't smile again, please don't. Not like that. I love Dylan, I love...

Breth smiled again. Hannah smiled back and they sat together at the table. At first in silence, then...

"Right! English. So..."

V

Adienna, at Donia's suggestion, lay down on a low wooden bed in the far corner of the room whilst the Votadini woman-servant left to get on with her daily chores. If only the girl had known more about this seemingly gentle-hearted soul, or about the tribal conflict between the Votadini and the Selgovae that had smouldered since long before the Romans moved north of the great wall built by their Emperor Hadrianus.

Later, Donia met up with Octavius's new second-in-command, a powerfully built man and older than his superior. His name was Lucius, meaning 'light'. Ironic when he must have been as heavy as a bull, although Latin, less confusing than English, has only one meaning for *'lux'*. Unlike the commander, his amorous attentions favoured the female sex. If, in Octavius's absence, she could make a deal with her own people in the east, the girl handed to her by those Germanian auxiliaries might be used to pay of both Lucius and, albeit by then 'used', her tribal chief, Ninian.

The woman was fed up with the way Octavius treated her. Fed up with his contempt and with the floggings. She knew many of the legionaries who had remained behind after his departure, and the auxiliaries, hated him. If Ninian's men could help Lucius dispose of the Germanians, and establish control before the return of Octavius, her life would be significantly easier. And the stupid young girl whom Octavius insisted should be called 'Flavia' would be none the worse off, ending up as a Votadini chieftain's whore rather than that of a chief of the child's own tribe.

*****

Jamie Stevens and his friends from SFS met up, as planned, by the river, away from security cameras. Like rabbits during the Roman times, these had spread across Scotland, and, by using face-recognition technology, 'they' knew where anyone was at a given time, and with whom. Not even the streets of Melrose were safe, nor, indeed, the fields around the new military camp at Trimontium.

"Arms," whispered Alex Laidlaw, a police sergeant in his public life. A man to be trusted, he had always been on their side. "Only went into the force to maintain the order we'll need to take back our country," he had once said at an early secret SFS meeting. He reckoned more than half the police were with them, but no one knew who. The same with Scottish army regiments.

"Shooters? But—?" began Jamie.

"Indeed," agreed Jonny Aveyard. "But only to be used if really needed. If they realize what they're taking on, they might just go away!"

Jonny, jokingly nicknamed 'Jonny English' because of his Yorkshire accent, was, ironically, the most hardened of the local SFS supporters. He felt a far greater allegiance with Celtic descendants north of Bradford than Norman descendants 'running' (or 'ruining'?) the country from Westminster in the south. He had met his wife, Morag, at a bus stop in Glasgow when he went there, partly out of curiosity, to look for work. Never before had he been in a city where complete strangers treated him like a friend.

"You wish! And where to?" he asked.

"Ah, well..." Alex hesitated. "As for the shooters, we thought *your* place, Jamie. You could dispose of them quickly if it came to that. In the council tip."

Jamie shook his head.

"You wish! But when? And how many?"

"Crate arriving tonight. Dozen or so guns."

It was wee Jonny who had insisted they should be armed on the day in question, though Jamie was all for Gandhi-style passive resistance. Craig's suggestion, he explained. But the others were less forgiving. Particularly after the disappearances started. Gandhi, according to Craig, succeeded in peacefully freeing India from British oppression, Jamie informed them. But the recycling centre worker had to admit that none of the police special team identified to 'investigate' the local disappearances were known to Alex. A cover up? Maybe Jonny was right. Action, not passive resistance.

Jamie was hugely proud of his brilliant son. His own failure to achieve any sort of academic distinction could be put down to disagreements with his quarter-Polish father. The man, bullied as a child, had encouraged his brainy son to do better than anyone else at school, but the young Jamie rebelled. He sank from top to bottom of the class, had no interest in going on to university, and did various manual jobs before ending up as a recycling centre worker. But he always kept himself fit, training three times a week in the gym. Craig rebelled in the opposite direction, wanting only to be top in everything. Including rugby, the one passion that he shared with his dad.

"You said they might just go away. How?" Freddie the butcher asked, unable to believe troops, sent by Westminster to suppress them, would ever 'just go away' if asked to. Like Jonny, he hated what millionaire politicians down south had done to the country.

"Best no one present kens," replied Alex. He grinned. "Perhaps us lot aren't the only ones who can conveniently disappear. But..." He beckoned for the others to come close, as if the fish in the nearby river might be listening. "Firearms training. In the Moffat hills. Assuming the consignment arrives tonight. Only a few sheep up there. No security cameras. This coming weekend. Okay, lads? And no questions asked where the shooters come from."

When Jamie arrived home, later, his plan was to take his son aside and explain everything. No way could he allow the boy to get mixed up in any of this, but for the sakes of his son's and daughter's futures, he could not give up on the SFS. He would never forgive himself if he missed the opportunity to secure for them a country where they would be treated as equals rather than as second-class citizens in a Disunited Kingdom.

But when he walked into the living room back home to find his family had a guest, a red-haired young man dressed in his son's clothes, he just stood and stared, fearing the worst...

*****

As soon as one of the Selgovan brigands appeared from a smoking building, the legionary released the bolt from his crossbow. The man dropped like a felled deer. There were shouts and more figures emerged. A ghastly chorus of sling-shot whistles must have terrified these men, for they scattered in all directions. Moments later, none remained standing. The horses' hooves scuffed the ground before the commander and his troop descended cautiously down the slope towards the stricken fort, *spathae* drawn. Once within the walls, they dismounted and conducted a building-by-building search, kicking over corpses of Roman auxiliaries and Selgovan warriors mingled in death like flotsam on a beach. Some stank, suggesting that most of the killing had been done a day or two before. Maybe the men they had just seen off were looters.

One of Octavius's legionaries called out. A tribesman was still alive. The sling shot had only grazed and stunned him. Octavius strode over and pulled the man up. It was comical to see the Selgovan tower over the small Italian, but there was no humour in what the commander did next. With the point of his *spatha,* he chose to play with the iron torc encircling the man's thick neck before slitting his throat. Two pairs of evil eyes became locked in mental combat. Octavius paused. The eyes' owners understood each other. Octavius could make use of this Celtic giant. His *spatha* travelled up the other man's neck before coming to rest on his cheek where he abruptly slashed a large 'T'. Blood oozed, but the Selgovan's cold gaze remained unchanged. Octavius grinned.

"That's so you and your miserable people remember. 'T' for Trimontium. You show us respect and we ensure your safety. Rise up against Trimontium and Rome, and you will be beaten down till none are left alive. Women and children go first. Which reminds me. I have a proposition for your little chieftain." Almost funny coming from a man as diminutive as Octavius, but no one laughed. "You can lead the way, barbarian."

With his wrists bound in front of him, the captured man, pulled along by a rope held by Octavius on horseback, led his troop away from the Roman fort, along a valley, then up a steep slope, towards a tribal fort perched on a hilltop. On seeing one of their fiercest thus tamed, with his face bloodied, the villagers, drunk from Roman wine after celebrating their recent triumph over the might of their overlords, stood and stared whilst Octavius was escorted to the largest roundhouse. The injured Selgovan called out. A small, older, stocky man appeared at the entrance, naked from the waist up, as was the young girl hovering in the shadows behind him. Octavius laughed.

"Good! I see you like your women to be young, old friend," he said in Latin. His smile vanished, his elegant features turned as hard and sharp as the glistening blade of his drawn *spatha*. "Now bring them all out here. All your women. Including the little bitch you've been playing with. Celebrating in bed with someone's unfortunate daughter, huh? Yes, bring the children too. Line them all up together with your women. In front of my friends here."

He turned to address his legionaries, still mounted.

"And don't waste your shot, boys. Every whistle must finish with a dead child or woman, unless..." Octavius turned to face the aging Selgovan chieftain. "Unless, of course, you agree to my demands."

No one moved. Not a word was spoken. Octavius's fox eyes had already taken in every detail of the pitiful defences. His bound captive, a monster of a man, would decide their fate. After leaping from his horse, the Trimontium commander approached the chieftain and held the point of his *spatha* up against the old man's throat.

"I'll let your women and children live on condition this hunk of Celtic muscle (with a nod, he indicated the Selgovan giant) and all of your thugs who are fit to fight, become auxiliaries. Working for me. Under my command. My men from Germania will have them well-trained in a day or two back at Trimontium. And you, their chieftain will get a little reward. One of your own kind and far more pleasing to look at than that little wench who was warming your bed. Now... have all your women and children out here where I can see each and every one of them whilst you turn things over inside that thick skull of yours."

One of the younger men of the village stepped forwards and translated Octavius's proposition for his chieftain. The old man grunted then nodded without taking his eyes off Octavius. Soon, in twos and threes, women and children emerged from roundhouses to stand in a wide crescent in front of the legionaries still mounted and with slings dangling. Nothing engendered so much fear amongst the Celts as a Roman sling. The children, struggling to hold back tears that might have made them the first targets, trembled whilst the women only stared, speechless.

The chieftain spoke to the younger man who disappeared off into the village. Moments later, a sizeable force of men, strong from toil on the land, had amassed in front of the Romans. Octavius lowered his *spatha,* but his legionaries remained poised to wipe out all the women and children in response to a single word from their commander.

"Good!" exclaimed Octavius. "Leave your weapons here. They're mere toys compared with what my auxiliaries will have you using back at Trimontium. If you fight well and stay alive, some of you may even get to see your women and children again."

Two of the legionaries marshalled the men into a

cowering line.

"She has blond hair and eyes the colour of sky, my friend," Octavius said to the chieftain as he remounted his horse. "Pity she doesn't have a brother, huh?" He laughed, then, herded like sheep, the Selgovan men were led away from their hilltop fort.

*****

On seeing his dad gawp at Breth, Craig jumped up from the sofa.

"It's okay, Dad. Hannah's been teaching him English. He's a refugee, like. An immigrant. Fleeing from what's happening south of the border. He might be of help to SFS."

Craig glanced at Hannah. He knew that lying wasn't her thing and could tell from her eyes she was far from happy. But their dad merely grinned and held out his hand for Breth to shake, though recoiled when the Selgovan boy slapped it.

"Don't worry, Dad. It's a foreign thing. Like high-fiving, I guess. Could be Polish, ay?"

"Not something my granddad ever mentioned."

"Modern Polish."

"What's your name?" Jamie asked in Polish.

Craig laughed at the way Breth looked at his father.

"Your accent's hopeless, Dad. He's called Breth."

"Breth? Doesn't sound very Polish to me."

"Changed it, maybe. Like Stevens for Szczepański. Perhaps his parents have disappeared. And maybe he'd heard about the resistance north of the border. And—"

"Shut up, Craig!" blurted Hanna. "It's nothing like that, Dad. He's an ancient Briton."

"A what?"

"Breth. He bumped into Craig running off the golf course— and—well, he did look weird at first, but he's cleaned up pretty good and—"

"Wait a minute, Hannah. You're telling me this lad who was sitting next to you is some sort of an actor? From an event at Trimontium?"

“Ugh!” The girl gripped her hair and tugged at her flaxen locks out of sheer frustration. As before, the Selgovan boy reached up and gently pulled her hands down.

“Adienna always does this,” he said to Hannah in Brythonic. “But can twins really be so alike?” He pointed to her cheeks. “The freckles too. Each one exactly the same as Adienna’s? I’ve stroked them all a thousand times over!”

“Cannae understand a word,” interrupted Jamie. “Sounds a bit like Gaelic. You sure he’s nae frae Harris?”

“Dad...” began Hannah, struggling to break free from the gaze of those green eyes. “I’ve been with him all day. I know you won’t believe me, but he really does live on top of the Eildons. Rather, did. Something to do with a cave on the golf course and a deer goddess. As far as I can make out.”

“Wait a minute. You’ve been alone with this... this—”

“I’m so sorry I called you a Neanderthal,” Hannah said softly to the boy beside her.

“Ancient Selgovan, Dad!” explained Craig.

“An ancient Selgovan?” Jamie glowered at his daughter. “Without your brother? Doing... doing...?”

“Teaching him English, Dad. And other stuff. Like life in the twenty-first century. In Scotland,” added Hannah.

“He thinks she’s the twin of a girl called Adienna. Someone from his own world,” remarked Craig. “That explains what he did just now. Reaching up to Hannah like. He’d never harm her, ken. I can vouch for it. Or I’d not have left them alone together.”

“I need a cup of tea,” sighed Jamie Stevens. “Then when your Mum gets back, we all sit together and get to the bottom of this... this *bloody* nonsense!” He turned and headed for the kitchen, muttering, “Nonsense, nonsense, nonsense!”

“He understands you!” Hannah called out as her father reached the door. Jamie stopped and, without turning around, listened to what his daughter had to say: “I mean what you’re going through with your SFS thing. The Romans were as bad as the English. Disappearances and stuff. Worse, maybe. They've got this girl he thinks is my twin. Called Adienna."

"Adienna," agreed Breth. Not for one moment had he taken his eyes off Hannah.

"Dad, can't you see Hannah's a different person now?" said Craig. "Whoever he is, her ME seems to have gone. Like she's got her cheeky old self back!"

"Cheeky?" queried Hannah.

"You know what I mean, Sis!"

"Like I said," interrupted their father, "we'll have this out when Mum's back. She'll be none too pleased, Hannah."

He left. Breth was frowning. He pointed to the girl beside him.

"You trouble?" he asked. He pointed to himself and raised his eyebrows.

"Na!" answered Craig. "Dinnae worry. I usually get round Mum. And she *always* gets round Dad." He looked thoughtful. "Well, sometimes always! So... we'll ease the pressure by taking Breth with us to the Ship Inn after tea, Hannah. Get him to meet Dylan and the clan, right?"

A mistake he had to live with.

VI

All day, Donia came and went, hovering like a mother eagle guarding her chick. From time to time, Adienna would hear shouts and swearing and the noise of fighting. The Romans' behaviour fell far short of what she had been led to believe during those childhood years when, as a fledgling 'auxiliary', Breth played with his wooden '*spatha*' to 'protect the glory of Rome'. Rome and, of course, his little blonde friend. She now prayed to Aine that, with help from the goddess, her sweetheart would be able to outwit Octavius's brutes, and, by some divine miracle, rescue her from a fate worse than death. She feared she could no more trust the commander's woman-servant than the dogs she had seen scavenging in the courtyard outside the *praetorium*.

That first night, the girl barely slept a wink. Every voice, every horse whinny, indeed every sound within the fort seemed magnified to a point where she was sure all its occupants were talking about her all the time. Muttering about what would soon happen to her. When Donia found her the following morning, cowering in a corner, her face wet with tears, the woman helped her up, took her to the bench and brought her bread and milk.

"Don't trouble yourself so, Flavia. I have contacts in Trimontium," she said. "We'll get you out of here. To *my* people."

"Who hate us Selgovae. Stop pretending. We share nothing. And if you call me Flavia again, I'll... I'll..." But her mind offered no sensible suggestion as to what she would do.

"Yes, my dear. No doubt you will. Meanwhile, stop this stupid behaviour and listen to me. In a few days, my contact will have a force of Votadini warriors ready to take on Octavius's auxiliaries. Plus, he has enough loyal legionaries in Trimontium to bring Octavius to heel. We hand you into the safe hands of my people. Octavius and his bullies get the same treatment he's been handing out to anyone he dislikes. Their heads on spikes, huh?" Adienna stared blankly as the woman-servant mimed the spiking of Roman heads then patted the girl's cheek. "And we restore *Pax Romana* in the land of our gods. These wishes we must surely share."

Adienna thought for a while. Maybe she had misjudged Donia because of those silly tribal disputes of their forbears. She agreed to eat and drink and keep up her strength, if only to be fit to confront whatever might be in store for her when this 'contact' returned with a band of Votadini ruffians. And, when alone, she would pray to Aine that Breth might somehow show up and take her away—*far* away—from the fort, from the Romans, from their slim, smooth-faced commander who preferred boys to girls, from tribal conflict and from the Fire Hills.

But what about her parents? Why hadn't her father done more to stop those brutes taking her from her home on a hill that was sacred for ancient Selgovan gods?

For days on end, Adienna ate, drank, agonized, ate, prayed, swore, drank, prayed and prayed and slept until, early one morning, an unfamiliar noise awoke her from a fretful dream...

*****

"What makes you think the Votadini tribespeople will be remotely interested in helping us get Adienna back?" asked Gorsedd. "Or my son, for that matter!"

"Because they'll be next. Look, we lived in peace together because of Domitius and his emperor. But now those Italian bastards are only here for what they can get from us, Selgovae and Votadini alike."

"So, you want twenty or so of our strongest to join forces with whatever our brethren in the east can offer, go down to Trimontium and get ourselves slaughtered? Just to prove that the Romans are a bunch of murdering bastards?"

"No. We pick them off. One by one. Where they can't see us hidden in the forest. Hit 'em when they go fishing. Destroy their boats. Intercept their messengers."

"And Adienna? She'll be the first to feel the wrath of their revenge."

Alun, the girl's father, paused, then nodded.

"Listen, I've an idea..." he began.

*****

Tea was no problem. Breth, a quick learner, had been taught by Hannah how to hold a cup, a knife and a fork. She had shown him the fridge, the food inside it, the butter and cheese. She laughed to see his face when she poured milk from a carton into a glass. She laughed a lot that day. Possibly more than any since her family name was changed to Stevens. Breth, too, was happy.

When Ellen, the girl's mum, arrived home to discover her husband in a state of shock after learning his daughter had spent most of the day alone with an ancient Celt whose home was the long-gone settlement on the northernmost Eildon Hill, Hannah jumped up from the sofa, ran to hug her mother, then took the puzzled woman by the hand to introduce her to Breth.

"He's really very polite," she said. She wanted to say so much more about her feelings concerning the Selgovan boy, but all that came out was 'polite'.

"Oh!" exclaimed Ellen Stevens.

"Your daughter's been alone in the house all day with an ancient bloody Celt and all you can say is, 'Oh!'" her husband remarked.

"Blame me, Dad," intervened Craig. "He bumped into me coming off the golf course. You cannot believe how he looked then."

"It's true, Mum. And I said to get rid of him. Like he was some kinda freak, but..." Hannah paused and stared admiringly at Breth as if trying to decide what she should now say about him.

"Cleaned up very nicely like you said he would, Sis," observed Craig. "Don't you agree, Mum?" His mother responded by raising her eyebrows. "Dad, he honestly might help you. Hannah's found out from him what a load of bastards the Romans were."

"Bastards!" echoed Breth.

They all stared at him. Then, quite suddenly, Ellen Stevens burst into laughter. She held on to Hannah for support. Never had her children seen her laugh quite like that. Hannah frowned.

"It's true, Mum! And it's not funny," she protested. Her mother took in a few deep breaths but kept bursting into giggles.

"No, Hannah. You're right," she finally agreed. "An ancient Celt joins us for tea. Not funny at all! Dead serious." Then she began to giggle again.

"Ugh!" exclaimed Hannah. She tugged at her hair. Much to her father's annoyance, Breth stood up and gently lowered his daughter's hands. "I'm so sorry, Breth," she said. "I just wish my parents would take me seriously sometimes."

"Sometimes?" echoed Breth.

"Like I told you, Dad, he'd never harm Hannah," insisted Craig. "Worship her, yes. Harm, no! The point is, he's incredibly bright. Awesome, in fact. And he might be able to help you SFS guys. I know it."

"Let's all have tea!" Ellen Stevens suggested. Then she giggled again.

Whilst his mother was in the kitchen, still giggling, Craig unveiled his plan to his father. One concocted in his head during a boring current affairs class that day, and that his sister was none too happy about. Muffled bursts of laughter from their mother kept interrupting his train of thought, but the plan was no laughing matter. After tea, when Hannah, her mother and the red-haired boy from the past were together, washing up, talking and, intermittently, Ellen laughing, Jamie Stevens thought seriously about his son's plan. Later, when Hannah, Craig and Breth had left for the Ship Inn, it was he who suggested they put the Selgovan boy up for the night before deciding on a more permanent solution.

"Breth might yet prove useful, as Craig suggested," he reckoned. Whatever disagreements father and son might have, both knew that Craig's brain would always win the day. Besides, Jamie Stevens' mind was still struggling with that special 'consignment' about which he dared not tell his wife, but perhaps Craig was right. By being open about the origin of the strange boy in their house, international attention might focus on what was happening at the old Trimontium site from where, in the distant past, Romans, not English troops, held sway over the locals. As a consequence, perhaps no need for guns.

*****

Of late, Dylan had thought almost exclusively about the sister of his lifelong best friend. Over the previous four years, he had watched her transform from a cute little freckle-faced child with long blond hair into a young woman of captivating beauty. And when Craig told him about the recent cyber-bullying that she had to put up with from catty, jealous classmates, he decided to take the plunge. He would become her boyfriend and protector. But did she really fancy him, as Craig had implied?

Of course she does! Or must!?

So, she would be at the Ship Inn that evening. He would get drunk, kiss her for real in front of all the lads, declare his love and swear vengeance on those girls who had been making her life a total nightmare.

He was already pissed as a newt when Craig and Hannah entered. With Breth.

Oh my God, she's lovelier than ever. But who the heck is that red-haired creep?

VII

Domitius set off on horseback, at first light, with his three legionary companions. Their mission had the full blessing of Publius, a general whose reputation had spread throughout the Empire, but whose future had become uncertain because of Commodus. Disguised as Christians, armed only with *spathae* hidden under humble cloaks as befitted members of that curious sect that had attracted so much attention, they travelled fast up though Italia, taking only three full moons to cross Gallia before reaching the northern coast from where a *Classis Britannica* boat hastened them across the narrow sea. Rebellion in the south of Britannia had been well and truly crushed, and, with *Pax Romana* having been restored by the legions of Marcus Aurelius, Domitius had no difficulty in recruiting auxiliaries from Roman forts and camps on their way north. Continuing along *Via Domitiana* (now Dere Street) beyond the wall built by that other great emperor, Hadrianus, and reaching a long, straight road that curled up and down over the hills marking the southernmost boundary of Trimontium territory, Domitius experienced a curious elation. Back home in Italia, his little nieces had become young women and no longer wished to play games with him. His sister, a one-time beauty, had lost her softness. It had been displaced by an irritability that, at times, rivalled Mount Vesuvius. Her older sons had left home and had families of their own. The one-time commander of Trimontium was now little more than a grey-haired ex-soldier. A sort of living decoration for her small family villa with its sunbaked olive groves and vineyards, and perhaps a reminder of what once made Rome great. But here, in the wilderness of the far reaches of Britannia, where he had put into practice what he had learned in Germania—that by making good friends he could weaken his enemies—*here* he felt strangely happy. Almost as if he were returning to his true home. But he feared that Octavius might have already undone all the good he had spent years in the making.

Arriving at the summit of the last of those hills, Domitius reined in his horse. The others followed suit. The ageing ex-commander dismounted. Nearby was a small stone hut he knew so well. After clambering up on top of this, he looked out across the wide plain towards those three hills balanced on the horizon above the green forest. The Selgovan settlement was on the northernmost hill. Were they too late, he wondered? He looked back at his small army of men from all over the empire. Men who truly believed in *Pax Romana* and were therefore determined to make sure that Octavius and his Germanian bullies did not destroy everything that the legions of Marcus Aurelius had so carefully built up. He told the legionaries to pitch camp and rest in preparation for what might prove to be the most important battle of his distinguished military career.

*****

"Craig, my old pal. Have a drink with me. And what'll Hannah be having, ay? G & T?" As an audible aside to his mates, he added, "And not too much of the 'T', right? Can't have her denying me what we both yearn for, guys." He winked at his pals. "Ken what I mean?"

Craig had never seen Dylan drunk. The gangly youth stank like a brewery, his eyes had become little windows of ugly lust, and, for the first time in their twelve-year friendship, the younger lad felt he really did not know the newly turned eighteen-year-old.

"Don't be stupid," Craig said. "I only brought my sister along to cheer her up. How many times have I told you? No one in my family touches alcohol! Because of our granddad." Then for the barman's benefit, he added, "Anyway, Hannah's only just sixteen."

Jamie Stevens had never stopped going on about his granddad exsanguinating from his gullet because of alcohol. "Bloody awful way to go," he had said at least a hundred times. "Literally!" Like Hannah, Grandpa SZSC took the teasing and xenophobic innuendos to heart. "And those bastards drove him to it!" Craig's father, bright but vehemently non-academic, rebelled not only against the drink, but the whole damn system. In the gym, he grew muscles that ensured no one got on the wrong side of him as well as catching the eye of a certain young Ellen Murray.

"Oh, damn your shitty grandpa! Give Hannah a break." Dylan turned again to face his mates propping up the bar, all as pissed as he was. "Guys, there's only one reason why Hannah Stevens has come here tonight!" He staggered over to Hannah who remained in the doorway beside Breth. Her brother was held back by the others. "She's dying for it! I ken she is!"

The lads restraining Craig laughed as Dylan roughly pulled the girl forwards, then held her face firmly with both hands. He was about to force a kiss on her tightly closed lips when a fist slammed up on his jaw. He fell back against the counter. Before he could recover his composure, Breth, grabbed him by his clothes and threw him to the ground.

"Say sorry!" he demanded. The first words he had uttered since leaving the house. In English.

"Enough of this, boys," warned the barman.

"Who the hell is this red-haired git?" slurred Dylan from the floor.

"He's my friend," answered Craig. "Hannah's too."

"Little whore! Smash his head in, lads."

"Leave! Now! All of you. Or I'll call the police." The barman yelled as he and another customer pulled Dylan to his feet.

"Police, huh? Sounds good to me," said Dylan, rubbing his jaw. "Might get an informer's fee if I tip them off about your dad, Craig. We all know what he's been up to, the bleeding Polish bastard."

Craig broke free from those holding him back, punched his friend in the belly, then on the nose, took Hannah by the arm and beckoned to Breth to follow them out of the pub. But the Selgovan boy wasn't quick enough. Outside, five drunken youths set on him, punching and kicking, even when he was down on the ground.

"Stop it!" screamed Hannah. "I hate you, Dylan!"

A few well-aimed blows from Craig scattered those who were laying into Breth. They all fled save Dylan who seemed to come to his senses as Hannah, weeping, knelt and fondled Breth.

"Hannah... I'm so sorry," Dylan said shakily, standing right behind her. "I was pissed. I *am* pissed. It's my eighteenth, ken. I so wanted to kiss you and say how much I—"

"Shut up, filthy coward!" shouted Hannah.

"But—?" Dylan got no further with his explanation, for Hannah, after helping Breth up, turned around and slapped him hard across his bruised face.

"I *hate* cowards!" she shouted. "Just clear off!"

As Dylan staggered away, muttering and swearing vengeance on the whole Stevens family and 'that red-haired creep', Hannah took a hankie from her bag and tenderly wiped the blood from Breth's face.

"I'll kill him," she said.

"No need, Sis. He's no longer my friend," reassured Craig.

"I'll still kill him!"

"It's called jealousy. Shakespeare wrote about it in Othello."

"Damn Shakespeare. And Othello. It was five against one. You saw them!"

"Well, Breth did give Dylan a bit of walloping in the pub."

"He was defending my honour!"

"Honour!" repeated Breth.

Craig, like his mum, had a habit of suddenly bursting into giggles if he found something funny. For some reason, he found Breth's repetition of 'honour' hilarious. Or maybe it was relief that all the tension of the previous few minutes had dissipated. Hannah too laughed, before hugging Breth and stroking his grazed cheek. She so wanted Breth to do with her what Dylan had tried to do, but she knew that in front of her brother and in the street was not the time and place.

"A walk by the river, Craig?" she suggested. Her brother agreed. They took Breth over the old swing bridge, then down to the water's edge where, the river being shallow, Hannah bathed the Selgovan boy's wounds. Three abreast, they followed the riverside path in the direction of the towering Victorian viaduct across which, in happier times now gone forever, trains thundered over the River Tweed to join the main line connecting Edinburgh with the south. As they walked, Hannah continued with the lesson in English she began that morning. She was now even more determined for Breth to learn and speak a language that could not have been more foreign to the boy, but one thing had become apparent to her and to Craig: Breth was super bright.

They halted on reaching a stone bearing a plaque in memory of someone who had died a few years ago. From there on, the path shrank, lost in trees clinging precariously to the steep-wooded bank.

"Dangerous," said Craig. "Erm... *periculosum?*"

"Periculosum?" Breth echoed, staring at the plaque.

"That? No, it's just a plaque. In memory of a man affectionately known as 'Tubby'," Craig informed him. '*In Memoriam*. A farmer. Owned land here. A good man, we're told. And into rugby. Like me."

"Rug... by? *Periculosum?* Dangerous? Man die?"

Both Craig and Hannah laughed.

"Not normally," replied Craig. "Fabulous game. Teamwork. Working together. But that's where it's all falling apart, Dad says. We're no longer together in this bloody country. Just them and us. Like you guys and the Romans.

Not like rugby. No teamwork."

"*Romani?* Here?"

Craig chuckled again.

"Not now. But were. Further on. Across the river. That's where the Romans were. And it's why Dad's all fired up about the military takeover at the Trimontium site."

Breth flinched.

"Trimontium," he muttered. "*Scelesti sunt!* Romani bad. Dylan bad. *Nunc* Adienna *et* Breth... *res bona est.* Is good thing."

"By the way, Breth. Thanks for curing my sister," said Craig.

"Curing?" queried Breth.

"Hey! You make me sound like bacon!" objected Hannah.

"Bacon?" Breth, frowning, pointed to Hannah.

"Hardly, mate. You've cured her ME. Worked a miracle. No need for any more doctors."

"...Any more doctors?" echoed Breth.

"Yeah!" yelled Hannah. She shouted across the river. "No more doctors! Never again!"

Breth took hold of her arm. She turned.

"Adienna," he whispered.

She so wanted him to kiss her, there and then, that... that she kissed him. Quickly, whilst Craig had stooped to pick up a piece of driftwood to throw into the river.

Although his lips responded to the all-too-brief touch of hers, for the first time in her life Hannah felt the sharp pang of jealousy. Who was this accursed Adienna whom Breth reckoned must be her twin? She now knew what Dylan must have suffered on seeing her enter the pub with the Selgovan boy.

VIII

The two Selgovan men left the Fire Hills fort before dawn. Alone, and staying clear of dwellings and roads, they cut through woods, away from the river, then scaled hill after hill on towards the territory of the Votadini, foes in the distant past. But now? Because of what was happening, not only in Trimontium but also out west and further north, the Votadini were their only hope of ever seeing Adienna and Breth again. Knowledge that the snake in charge of Trimontium preferred to focus his desires on boys rather than girls was of no comfort. His evil intentions might be foisted upon Breth, if captured, whilst the boy's intended wife would be sold off like livestock to someone equally loathsome.

The threat that this would be the maverick, womanizing Selgovan chieftain in the west strengthened the determination of the two life-long friends to get Adienna back. But the man was also the reason why they had told no one other than their wives. Their own chieftain was a weakling who would have eagerly offered Adienna to the man as a sop to stop him from further antagonizing the Romans. Although Gorsedd and Alun had no idea how they might persuade the Votadini to supply men enough to take on the forces of Octavius, and demand Adienna's release, events had transformed the girl's father from gentle lamb to lion-hearted beast, whilst in the chest of Gorsedd, like that of his son, the flame of the Fire God never went out.

Thankfully, friendly tribesmen they met on the way seemed only too keen to join the two fathers. Close to the Votadini stronghold, a force of over fifty Celts set up camp whilst Gorsedd and Alun, alone, approached the fortified settlement. Unarmed, they were perceived as no threat. Also, past skirmishes and battles over land, women and livestock had been long forgotten, and the men were well received.

They were fed and given undiluted Roman wine from one of several *amphorae* gifted by Domitius whilst sharing resentment against the invaders from Italia. And it all came out: the terror inflicted on the Selgovae by the monster who had replaced the kind, gentle Domitius, plus Adienna's abduction and Breth's disappearance.

Ninian, their chieftain, laughed when told of Breth's escape.

"He just ran away from them? Like a deer?" Gorsedd hung his head in shame. He knew that his son had always referred to Adienna as his 'little deer' and loved her to bits. How come he had not found the courage to challenge those auxiliaries? Ninian sensed the Selgovan's shame. "I was laughing at their expense, not your son's. Alive, he might yet save her. So... they have their weaknesses, those Romans! Without their slings and crossbows, they're little more than sheep. Hand to hand fighting, and we'd turn them into piles of pig food."

Alun smiled. Then he thought of Domitius, both kind and honorable.

"They're not all bad," he said. "And from what's been told to us by the elders, it seems we Selgovae and you Votadini are closer now than we've ever been. Because of Romans like Domitius."

"We're brothers in the eyes of our gods, my friends."

"Then, brother, will you help us?"

"Now there we might have a problem."

"How come?" Gorsedd and Alun exchanged glances.

"They're here."

"Who?"

"The Romans. Arrived on horseback two days ago."

Alun froze. After journeying all that way, had they walked into a trap?

*****

Thankfully, the 'consignment' arrived before Hannah and Craig returned home with their ancient Celtic friend.

Ellen Stevens was busy in the kitchen. The doorbell rang, but she knew nothing about the nailed-down crate left on the doorstep.

"Just a circular," Jamie called out to his wife. He never was good at lying.

Circular? No way! Ellen frowned as she continued to iron whilst listening to the radio. She just wished it would all end. Before the recent political turmoil, life had been so easy. No hatred, no enemies. Just doing her best for Jamie and the kids. Now everything seemed of secondary importance to merely staying alive, and not becoming another 'disappeared'.

Jamie stood in the open doorway scratching his head. No sign of either a delivery man or a van. Only a crate. His wife's suspicion that something more than a circular had been delivered was confirmed when she heard the trapdoor to the loft being opened. She sighed then smiled on hearing her husband's hopeless attempt to tread the steps quietly, muttering curses as he struggled with something heavy, but she was no longer smiling when Jamie appeared in the kitchen and asked whether she wanted to watch the telly.

"Na! I want you to tell me the truth, Jamie Stevens. What's happening?"

"Better you dinnae ken, love."

"Show me the circular!"

"Like I said, you dinnae want to ken." Ellen put down the iron and turned to face her husband. Before she could open her mouth, he wrapped his arms around her. "Now, how about a hug and some telly? Kids might be late."

"What *do* you make of Breth?" Ellen asked.

"What *can* I make of him? Seems a nice enough lad. But all that ancient Celt crap? Look..." He kissed her, then stroked her cheek. "If you want to go to bed, I'll stay up. Find out more when they get back. But—?"

"No! *I* will find out more. From you. About that delivery. I'm not stupid."

"Course you're not. After all, where does Craig get his clever genes from?"

"Hmm! D'you think Breth really is super bright like the kids say?"

Her husband shrugged his shoulders.

"Asking the wrong person, love. But the way he looks at..." Jamie paused.

"At Hannah?"

"Mmm!"

"You have to realize she's growing up, Jamie. And Craig believes part of the bullying by those girls is because the boys at school have noticed how beautiful she is."

"Why doesn't Craig have a girlfriend?"

"You really don't see it, do you?"

"See what?"

"Ugh!" She broke away from her husband then, turning to face him, gripped her hair with both hands just like her daughter. "He's always too busy trying to prove himself. For you! I do wish you'd get to know your son better rather than play dangerous games with your mates in SFS."

She emphasised the word 'dangerous' by stabbing two fingers, gun-like, at her temple. Jamie frowned.

"They're not games!" he announced quietly before leaving the kitchen. At the same time the front door opened.

"Mum!" Craig called out.

Ellen joined Jamie in the hallway. Hannah, in tears, was being hugged by her father. Ellen was horrified to see the state of Breth. No words were needed to understand what had happened.

"Who did that to him?" she asked.

"Dylan and his mates. I tried to stop them, Mum, but..." began Craig.

"They're a bunch of bloody cowards," added Hannah. "Breth was only defending my honour when he hit Dylan."

"Oh! So *he* started it, then?"

"No! Not exactly! Look, have you got a plaster for that

cut on his cheek? And something for his bruises? Arni... whatever you call the stuff."

"Arnica. Aye! Your dad's a living lump of bruises. Gets through shiploads of the stuff. But Craig, this sounds serious. Dylan's always been your best mate."

Craig glanced at Hannah.

"Othello," he replied.

"Quit the riddles. Tell me what really happened."

So, after Hannah took Breth, by the hand, upstairs to tend to his cuts and bruises, Craig filled his parents in on the events in the pub.

"Well, as your dad would say, 'I told you so'. 'The scourge of humanity', he calls it. Alcohol. Right, Jamie? Poor Dylan, though. He'll never forget his eighteenth."

"Poor Dylan? He threatened to grass on Dad. Tell the police."

Jamie appeared alarmed.

"What the heck!" he exclaimed. "What's he bloody ken? What've you told him?"

"Nothing, Dad. Honest."

"His Mum?" suggested Ellen. "She's a right sponge. Picks up on all the gossip. And word gets around, Jamie. Small town talk, ken. It's what I've been trying to tell you."

"Oh, my God!"

"This just gets worse and worse. Can't you see what happens if you get yourself mixed up in all this stupid SFS business, Jamie?" bemoaned Ellen.

Jamie grunted and stomped off, leaving Ellen and Craig in the hallway.

"It isn't stupid, Mum. It's all about identity. About who he is. Dad's a proud man. You know that. And pure Scottish now that we're the Stevens family."

"No. It's about power. Between 'them' and 'us'. And it's doing my head in. He's putting his family at risk. Hannah included. As if she hasn't had enough to put up with, with all that business at school. Then the ME."

"It's better."

"What is?"

"Her ME. Tons better. Because of Breth. I'm sure of it. Plus, he saved her from that cowardly creep I thought of as a friend."

"Saved her?"

Craig grinned.

"You should've seen Dylan's face after Breth socked him one. For trying to force a kiss on Hannah. And wanting to get her pissed, too. It bloody served him right. He has no damn respect for my little sister!"

"But he's keen on her. Always has been."

"Aye... well that's the Othello bit, see. Blind jealousy as soon as Breth entered."

"He's a good-looking lad, I'll give you that."

"Dylan?"

"No Breth. But this plan of yours. Your Dad refuses to tell me anything."

"Well, if he refuses, I can't tell you either. Not that I ken all his secrets. Where's Breth sleeping tonight, by the way?"

"As far from Hannah as possible!" Mrs Stevens chuckled. "Or Dad might finish the job that Dylan started!"

"On the sofa?"

"Na! The shed in the garden. Just big enough for the spare mattress."

"Hope he's not arachnophobic."

"If he really is an ancient Celt—and that's had me chuckling all evening—it'll be like a 5-star hotel for him. Come to think of it, I'd better go upstairs and see what they're up to. It's gone awful quiet!"

Hannah had taken Breth into her bedroom where she sat him down on her bed before kneeling before him and cleaning his wounds after rolling up his trousers. She gently rubbed the fresh, swollen, purple bruises on his shins where he had been kicked, lingering over the Breth's fine red hairs. She spent as much time as she could applying the arnica. The boy, not wishing to show any response to pain, remained impassive, but when tears started to trickle down Hannah's freckled cheeks, he reached out and wiped them with the back of his hand.

"My fault!" she whispered. "All of this!"

"Fault?"

His soft voice seemed to touch something inside the girl. A buried memory, perhaps? Waiting, like an archaeological treasure, to be unearthed? She patted her chest, then said,

"Me! Bad!"

Breth shook his head.

"Hannah good! Adienna good. *Puella bona est.*"

Hannah laughed.

"Must remember that! I'm a *'puella bona'* whatever it means. Look, can I show you some pictures?"

"Pictures?"

"Of me and Craig. From when we were little."

She left him seated in deep thought, a Rodin statue with rolled-up trouser legs, whilst she went to retrieve her photo albums from a drawer. After sitting down beside him, with their hips touching, she inwardly smiled at her so far successful attempt to displace the annoying Adienna from her pedestal inside the boy's head. She opened the album at the first page. Herself, on a beach, as a five-year-old. She was totally unprepared for what happened next. The Selgovan boy reached out with a finger and touched the image of the child in the photo. He was frowning and his eyes filled with tears. He repeatedly poked at the page, as if trying to make the young Hannah, captured in the photo, come to life. Hannah hadn't even thought about the possibility of Breth never having seen perfect human likeness trapped on a piece of paper. Indeed, it was unlikely he had even seen any of the realistic Roman portrait paintings discovered in archaeological ruins.

Hannah took hold of his hand which was getting increasingly agitated because the little child Hannah in the photo failed to respond to his searching finger. No longer could he hold back.

"Adienna!" he cried out, clutching the photo to his chest.

"It's okay, Breth. I'm here." She put her arms around the boy. "That's me."

"You?" he queried. "Adienna *es tu*?"

For a few seconds Hannah remained silent, not knowing what to say, but somehow, she no longer felt jealous of her ancient Celtic rival.

"I think so," she whispered, not knowing why. Her mother entered and Hannah sprang back.

"Think what?" Mrs Stevens asked.

"Nothing! I was showing Breth old photos. That's all." But her mother never missed a thing. She saw the moistening of the boy's eyes.

"You can help Craig set up the mattress for Breth in the garden shed. His sleeping quarters!"

"Oh Mum! What about those ginormous spiders?"

"They don't bite."

"Look like they might. Oh, why can't he sleep on the sofa downstairs? You're being so cruel! He's really, really badly injured!"

"Garden shed! End of discussion. Plus, young lady, you and I must have a little talk."

"Ugh!" Hannah ran her hands through her hair then gripped and tugged at it. "It's so unfair! Everyone's being so mean to Breth. He did get beaten up, ken!"

"Downstairs!"

At the doorway, Hannah turned. "Keep my photo album, Breth." She returned to put the book in his hands and closed his fingers over it, then pointed to the book and to Breth. He nodded his understanding, stood up and followed Hannah out of the bedroom. Downstairs, Craig was already lugging the spare mattress through the back door.

"So bloody unfair!" his sister muttered. "Forcing him to sleep outside. Particularly when he's mortally injured."

Craig laughed.

"Hell's bells! Only this morning you were calling him a Neanderthal," he reminded his sister.

"That was before."

"Before what?"

"Before he got cleaned up. He's different now."

Breth appeared at the top of the stairs. Craig looked from Hannah to Breth and back to Hannah.

"And you, my little sister, are different too."

Is it true? Am I really Adienna? Could I be that lucky?

"Adienna is me," replied Hannah looking at Breth. "I know it now." She turned to face her brother. "And we're to be married!"

"Oh my God!" Craig dropped the mattress.

"God?" echoed Breth. *"Deus?"*

IX

What Donia did not know was that Lucius, the man Octavius had left in charge, and to whom she had promised a night with the Selgovan virgin of exceptional beauty, was not the person she thought he was. Secretly, he had a wife and daughter, a girl not much younger than 'Flavia', back in Italia. He was no fiend, like his superior, and had remained in communication with the deposed second-in-command, Marcus. To use Votadini brawn to remove Octavius appealed to both men. So, much to the woman-servant's annoyance, he had already left without ravaging the girl and taking her as damaged, though still valuable, goods to her own tribespeople in the east.

He set off alone. There were enough able legionaries left behind in Trimontium to keep the auxiliaries from Germania under control. Lucius had given orders to supply the brutes with sufficient wine to pickle them until he could return with a sizeable Celtic army and, if the messenger whom he sent had caught up with Domitius, a Roman force as well. His hope was that, on seeing their superior strength, Octavius would concede without battle and return to his family's vineyards with a recommendation from his predecessor that he should be retired with full military glory.

Lucius found the Votadini welcoming. They knew that he was no threat. And he found out more about Octavius's woman-servant. Described by her own father as a 'viper lurking behind the mask of kindness', it transpired there was no truth in the rumour that her husband and son had been killed. She had left them for the embraces of a Germanian auxiliary who took her back to Trimontium then used her to pay off his gambling debts. Domitius, who always tried to see the best in people, took her under his wing and employed her as his woman-servant. But she remained bitter not only against the Romans, whom she tried, unsuccessfully, to play for her own benefit, but also her own people. They did not want her back. Perhaps the offering of a beautiful Selgovan girl might have softened the Votadini chieftain, Ninius, but, thinking of his own daughter back in Italia, Lucius was having none of it. The girl would remain in Trimontium, guarded by trusted legionaries, until the old order could be restored. Then she would be returned to her family in the Selgovan settlement on the three hills that gave their fort its name.

It came as a surprise when he was summoned from his tent to meet the two Selgovan men. Even more so when he learned of the Celtic force camped on a nearby hill. On learning that one of the men was the father of the girl whom Octavius called 'Flavia', and whose real name was Adienna, he became even more determined to rid Trimontium of the elegant commander who preferred boys to girls.

At first, Breth's father was wracked with suspicion. Why had Octavius replaced Domitius's chosen second-in-command? What went on between this man of muscle and that reptile who had gone west to 'subdue rebellious Selgovae', as Lucius had informed them? The Roman's answer was simple: the less he spoke, the better. Because of the man's silence and physique, Octavius had assumed him to be a dumb bull who would do as he was told. Lucius reassured the Selgovans that this was far from the truth.

*****

On his return, Octavius's anger, on hearing from his woman-servant that Lucius had been gone seven days, erupted like Mount Vesuvius. Why he vented this by flogging her, even he had no idea. Just seemed a good excuse to practice with his whip. He'd have preferred to unleash his frustration on the 'little Selgovan bitch', but he didn't want to offer up a gift of damaged goods. Of course, if she had been a boy, he would not have been so forgiving.

Donia, in turn, took it out on Adienna who now saw another side to the Votadini woman. After flinging a jug of water over the sleeping girl, she yanked her up off the couch and told her to "Get on with your bloody work!"

"What work?" Adienna asked, blinking.

"What work?" mimicked Donia in a squeaky little voice. "Everything!" bellowed Donia. "See that brush over there? Sweep! I've just had to suffer the master's wrath because of the mess you've made. Got lashed instead of you 'cos your skin's too bloody precious." She rubbed her sides where the commander's whip had curled and bitten her like a serpent from hell. She spat at Adienna's feet. "Work, damn you!"

No one could tell Octavius exactly where or why his second-in-command had gone. That the remaining auxiliaries had not run amok on his return was a miracle. In fact, this worried him. Why, during his and Lucius's absence, had peace reigned instead of chaos? There was a curious calm within the fort that unnerved the Italian. On his command they all gathered in the central compound, together with his new Celtic auxiliaries from out west. Just to annoy his 'old faithfuls', he appointed, as his personal bodyguard, the hulk who bore a healing 'T' cut onto his broad face. Also, the brute was to be awarded special privileges, including extra wine rations.

"This man is favoured both by the gods and by me. He survived a slingshot delivered by one of my best legionaries. That's more than any of you miserable lot can lay claim to. You will look up to him!"

The stony features of the Celt gave nothing away other than the sheer lunacy of attempting to come into conflict with the monster. But he was an unlikely bedfellow of their silken-featured commander. The weight of the man would have crushed the life out of the Italian lover of boys.

"His name shall be Bikkus. After their word for small." Octavius was the only one who laughed at his weak humour. "So..." He drew his *spatha* and approached the ranks of legionaries and auxiliaries. "Is there anyone present who does not know where Lucius is?"

His soldiers were only too aware of their leader's obtuse ways of getting to the truth. No one stepped forwards, although all fitted the description. None had any idea of the whereabouts of the second-in-command.

Octavius grabbed the nearest auxiliary, the only man of slender build like himself.

"I'm so glad you honour our blessed new emperor by knowing everything that goes on in Trimontium, *amicus meus!*" The man looked to his companions for support. None was forthcoming. "Tell me, why is Lucius not here?"

Even before the man's trembling lips could vocalise any meaningful words, with an upwards thrust of his weapon Octavius dispatched the auxiliary to the afterlife. He held the limp body dangling on his *spatha* before pulling it back and sneering as the man slumped, lifeless, to the ground.

"I will not tolerate untruthfulness in my fort. I ask again. Where is Lucius?"

"Gone to seek help from the Votadini," someone shouted. Before Octavius could fix on the legionary who had dared voice these words, others shouted out in unison, "Went to the Votadini. Yes, the Votadini!"

Octavius re-sheathed his *spatha*.

"Now that's more like it! To win support against the rebellious Selgovae, no doubt?"

Silence.

"Pfff!" The commander spat on the ground. "Well, thank the gods he didn't take the girl!"

*****

The following morning, Craig found Hannah alone in the kitchen.

"Dad and Mum left for work already?" he asked.

"No. Mum's taking a day off. Phoned the office." She smiled. "You know Mum. She told them the truth about Breth, put the phone down, then had a good laugh."

"You mean she told her boss we have an ancient Celt in the house?"

"Kind of awkward, the truth, aye?" She looked at her brother. "Was so hoping to give Breth another lesson this morning, but she says I'm better and have to go to school."

"She's right, Sis. Work's the only thing that can help get you and me out of this shit hole."

"Melrose is not a shit hole. Not with..." She went quiet.

"I'll check on him. He obviously didn't want to let on in front of you, but—"

"What are you on about?"

"I wasnae born yesterday, Sis. I saw the way you two look at each other. He won't want you thinking him a weakling. It's a male thing. But he got kicked in the head. Might be bleeding inside his skull or something."

Hannah's eyes doubled in size. She sprang from her chair and ran to the garden door. Craig chuckled. Moments later she re-appeared with a very fit looking Breth. Both grinned from ear to ear.

"Mum's gonna *have* to buy him some clothes," she said.

"But he's the same size as me."

"No, his *own* clothes. I'll go and tell her. And do give him some breakfast, Craig. He must be starving. Bet they get up early on top of the Eildons. I mean *did*. The Fire Hills or whatever. Oh, must I really go to school today? Can't I pretend I'm—?"

"Pretend? Be like Mum. Stick to the truth for once."

"For once? Ugh!" She gripped her hair. Breth reached up and gently lowered her arms. Their fingers, intertwined, lingered together for a few moments. Hannah glanced at Craig then picked up her school bag.

"See you on the bus," her brother called out to her just before she left. "And *I'll* have a word with Mum. She understands." Hannah halted at the front door.

"Really?" she called back.

"Really! Much more than you think."

Hannah smiled all way to the bus stop.

*****

"He's called Lucius," said Domitius.

The old soldier plus the legionaries chosen by Publius—three of the best—were seated away from their army of able auxiliaries, now swelled by a motley of fierce-looking Celts who were only too pleased to take on the new Trimontium commander, knowledge of whose cruelty had even spread northwards to the tribes scattered across the hills and forests of Caledonia. But for the famed benevolence of his much-loved predecessor, now leader of a curious mix of Roman and Celtic fighters, the Celts might have attacked rather than joined them. Domitius's kindness, which belied a keen military sense, had become as legendary as Octavius's evil.

"He might be old," Publius had told the three legionaries, "but he's the sharpest soldier I've known in my many campaigns. Listen to him carefully. Be his eyes and ears."

The legionaries made sure every one of their fighters was well fed and watered. Gifts were promised if they succeeded in ridding the province of the reptile in charge of the Trimontium cavalry fort.

"Can this Lucius be trusted?" asked one of the legionaries, between mouthfuls of meat he gnawed off a mutton joint.

"I know him only as a bear without a voice," joked Domitius.

The others laughed.

"Not your typical Italian, then!"

"His forbears were from the East. He came here to teach the Celts how to behave."

"One of those monsters from the East, ay?"

"Monster? Not Lucius! The rain and the mists of Britannia changed him, perhaps. I could always tell from his unspeaking eyes that he was different from his wild forbears. A huge bear, yes, but a tamed one. Mind you..." Domitius grinned. "None of you three would wish to meet the man in the arena."

"I've heard Emperor Commodus spends most of the time either in his personal brothel or killing bears like Lucius in the arena. He poisons them first, then, when they're barely able to stand, slits open their bellies in front of the cheering crowds. He's the one we should be getting rid of, not that little snake in Trimontium."

Domitius nodded his agreement.

"If only! But... start small, aim big."

"The other soldiers at Trimontium? Surely they'll not stick with Octavius?"

"There we have a problem. If I've learned one thing, it's that people can easily be bought by false promises. Octavius is evil, but he's no fool. His cunning is as sharp as his *spatha*."

"So... where and when?"

"Lucius?"

"Aye!"

"Follow me."

Domitius stood up and led the three legionaries up to a viewpoint away from the camp. In the distance, on a forested hilltop, curls of smoke rose into the grey, merging with dark, rain-laden clouds.

"The Votadini."

"I've heard about them," the legionary said. "Eat you alive, some say."

Domitius burst into laughter.

"Well, they can mix it with the wine I gave them. Keep you happy in death, right?" He turned to face his soldiers. "But their women would be none too happy if you got slaughtered by the men-folk. They loved the silver trinkets I gifted their elders. And the men love their women up here. They have more goddesses than gods, you know!"

"Don't talk of women, sir! It makes me homesick."

All laughed then returned to the meal around the campfire.

X

Ellen Stevens came downstairs to find the Selgovan boy, alone in the kitchen, crunching handfuls of Cornflakes straight out of the packet whilst staring at worksheets in English that Hannah had prepared the previous day. He stood up and looked at her. She burst into laughter.

"Those kids of mine! Didn't think to give you a bowl? Or a spoon? Or milk?" she said.

"Milk?"

She went to the fridge, took out the milk carton, filled a glass and handed this to Breth. As he peered at the glass in his hand, she sat down and gesticulated for him to do the same.

"Hannah!" she said, folding her arms.

"Adienna," countered Breth.

"Whatever... she's very young. Still a child."

Breth's face lit up. One of the English words on a worksheet was 'child'.

"Breth... Adienna... make child?" he said. "Together?"

His grin spoke volumes.

"Oh my God... No!"

She got up and disappeared, returning with her iPad. Moments later, as her son had done, she was translating into Latin for the Selgovan boy.

'Hannah is too young,' she typed in the 'English' bar.

Breth looked at what appeared as 'Latin', shook his head and said, "No!"

Ellen ran her hands through her hair, like her daughter, then laughed when Breth reached out and coaxed her arms down as she had seen him do with Hannah. He pointed to her, then said,

"Bona Mater[11]!"

---

[11] A good mother!

The woman looked this up on her iPad, smiled then said,

"I try to be. Look, I'll take you to the Trimontium Museum today. Connect you with your past. Or our past and your present." She giggled. "I think I might just be a little naughty and tell them the truth. About you. See what reaction I get."

*****

The more the commander vented his anger on Donia, the more the Votadini woman took it out on poor Adienna. She could hardly wait to be rid of the girl, but she knew she could not kill her. There was value in those blond curls, those blue eyes, and that fresh, young, freckled complexion. One thing she had learned from her previous gentle-hearted master was the value of gifts. She could tease, annoy, and swear at the loathsome child, but to maintain the girl's value, 'Flavia' was to be guarded at all times, well-fed and kept warm whenever the temperature fell below the shivering threshold.

Weeks passed. Donia grew impatient when Lucius failed to return with the hoped-for band of Celtic warriors. Octavius spent all day, every day, supervising the training of his new auxiliaries from the west. His tribal woman-servant had not reckoned on him swelling the ranks of his army with such a force. To attempt to send a messenger to forewarn Lucius would have meant a certain and cruel death if the man were intercepted. Had she had faith in the old gods, prayers might have helped. As it was, the only being she trusted was herself.

Adienna, however, never stopped praying to the gods and goddesses. She had to believe Breth was still alive, somewhere, thanks to them. If not, she would surely have had a sign. She prayed, too, for her father, a gentle soul, like Commander Domitius, but sometimes volatile.

'Why, oh why, did that lovely Roman, Domitius, have to go?' she asked the gods over and over. And what about Aine, Breth's special goddess, the goddess of love? Would

she protect her beloved? The fact that those bullies from Germania had come for her, that morning, without crossbows or slings must surely have been Aine's doing. But the way the Votadini woman, who had been entrusted to keep watch over her, flipped from kind to cruel, in the blink of an eye, made the girl wonder about the gods. Did Aine truly know about love? Could her betrayal have been bought by the Romans with offerings at their own altars? Had that period of peace, with Domitius in charge, been but a fleeting dream? Had Mars been asleep during her years of childhood happiness?

Only one thing prevented the girl from going mad with despair: the image inside her head of Breth's incredible green eyes. They refused to leave her. But what if some other girl should see them for what they were? A girl from another tribe. Or even one of those dark-haired beauties from Italia. Could her friend's eyes be stolen by one of them? Would he then forget her? Oh, if only they were already married everything might have been different. Surely, she would not have been taken away from her home if she belonged to another.

*****

Ellen decided against being honest about Breth. What with all the worries concerning her husband's involvement with SFS, it seemed wiser, for once, to withhold the truth. Besides, she was no longer sure what the 'truth' was. But as she watched the boy's reactions to exhibits in the museum, she had no doubts that he, at least, had been truthful.

She saw him aim a fist at the glass case containing a Roman helmet and grabbed his arm just in time. She shook her head, turned, and smiled at the museum volunteer.

"He's a drama student," she lied. "Practising for an event about the ancient Celts and Romans. Can see which side he'll be on!"

Ellen led the boy away from the Roman artefacts to look at items concerning the Celts. She studied his green eyes as they took in everything concerning his own tribal life. He looked puzzled. Something was wrong.

"No gods," he said before returning to the Roman exhibits. Ellen smiled to herself.

No gods? You can say that again. Oh, if only Jamie would recognize the truth. That if there is an all-powerful God, why should He bother with a tiny country like Scotland? How on earth can this SFS business end well for us? There again, the Romans did finally leave Scotland. Did the Celtic gods play a part in this? Maybe Breth could recommend to Jamie one of those gods he agonizes over? To protect him from himself.

Breth kept returning to the central display to gawp at images of the Trimontium fort as this was his other life. Ellen saw a change in the boy's eyes as he studied the Roman buildings, wondering what on earth was going on in his mind.

*****

Marcus praised Lucius for staying alive at Trimontium, if only for the sake of the other man's children back in Italia. Lucius had found the deposed second-in-command hiding in the woods beyond Trimontium. Both had women and families in Italia, forbidden for legionaries. Not even Domitius knew about this.

"I fear for our families back home," Lucius told his friend. "They say no woman is safe from Commodus. At least his father kept him under some sort of control."

"But surely not if these women stay away from *Roma*?"

"His scouts scour the countryside. If a woman looks pretty enough, she gets dragged off to his private brothel in *Roma*. Married or not."

"The sooner we rid Trimontium of Octavius, the sooner we get back to Italia and help to rid *Roma* of that other monster."

"You'd desert?"

"Not desertion. Duty!"

"So where can we find Domitius? Provided he's managed to evade Commodus's spies."

"Come with me," urged Marcus.

*****

Jamie Stevens worried all day, every day. Unlike his wife, who seemed able to shrug her shoulders and 'just get on with it,' as she kept saying, he would constantly turn things around in his mind, explore every possible path to disaster, retrace the mental steps and discover an even worse outcome. He was probably the most efficient pessimist alive. No potential calamity escaped his consciousness.

As he busily sorted out local waste, he focused his mind on Craig's plan concerning 'the boy.' He could not persuade his brain to use the name 'Breth.' It was a total non-name as far as Jamie was concerned, but his son did have a point. As always. If Craig had been someone else's son, he would have felt angry to be outwitted by a lad turning eighteen, but instead he oozed pride to be the one who would put his son's suggestion to the SFS lads. Of course, they would reckon he was just pulling their legs about having an ancient Celt in the house. But how awesome it would be for 'the boy' to be shown live, on the telly, informing the world, through one of his children (preferably Craig), that Breth was not a distant Polish cousin, as friends and neighbours had been told, but really an ancient Celt, and that creating a military camp on the Trimontium site was both a sacrilege and a crime against the ancestors of all modern-day Celts and Brits alike. Including those in Westminster. As Craig had informed him (and Jamie believed everything his son said) the collapse of Rome, albeit already crumbling within, possibly began in the far north of ancient Britannia where they were outwitted by the guerilla tactics of the Caledonians.

So, where might the collapse of the so-called 'United' Kingdom begin?

Here in Melrose? Yeah! I'll tell Ellen this evening. She'll agree. Taking a day off work, she said, to take 'the boy' to the Trimontium Museum.

*****

Adienna planned her escape in between hours of toil for the woman-servant of Octavius, that Votadini cow who pretended to be her friend. If she could reach the safety of Aine's 'cave', even for a few brief moments, she was sure she would somehow become reunited with her loved one.

For many years they had been so close that their minds appeared linked even when separated by hills, moorland, forest... and Roman walls. He was alive. She knew it. Alive and as desperate to hold her in his arms as she was to be held by him. But it was the thought of any other man doing 'that' to her, gnawing away inside her head, that fired her determination. And Aine would ensure 'that' could never happen with anyone other than Breth... surely?

Behind a chest, containing Octavius's prized silver- and glassware, was a small 'shrine' that Adienna had fashioned for Aine. A secret hiding space where she would leave daily offerings: a flower stolen from the commander's vase, a tiny piece of bread, and, one day, the dregs from Octavius's elegant wine glass which she emptied onto the floor, behind the chest, 'for the goddess's enjoyment.'

The question wasn't so much 'when?' (any day Adienna might be 'given' to some stinking older man to be 'pleasured' till she too stank) as 'how?' This would have to involve Donia, the only person she ever saw apart from Octavius who showed no interest in her body because she was a girl. The answer to her question came when she overheard her master and his minions talking, one evening, about opium. Something that came from the seeds of a poppy flower grown at the other end of the Empire.

"Our physicians use it to cure pain by soothing the spirit, though I warn you, too much might be harmful," Octavius said. "You see, I, your respected commander, have a friend in high places. *Very* high places! So high, you couldn't begin to imagine, but my pain will find no relief, not even with opium, till I find that beautiful, red-haired native boy!"

Breth! I knew it. He's still alive!

Insisting on undiluted wine that evening, the man soon succumbed to the pleasure this brought when sprinkled with opium. Being both drunk and doped, it all came out: apparently inside his cabinet, in a stoppered flask, was enough of this opium to put all the cavalry horses to sleep for weeks. For the commander, a pinch of it in a glass of wine was enough to wipe out all thoughts of Domitius, of annoying women, of the boring wisdom-spouting dead father of their glorious new young emperor, his one-time friend, and of the rebellious Selgovae, leaving only the boy with green eyes to hover in his befuddled mind.

Octavius burped, laughed, then added out loud, "Why do we keep the girl here? Answer: to catch our beloved boy!"

Little did he know that 'the girl' who would one day so change his destiny stood listening on the other side of a thin wooden partition.

*****

"Where's 'the boy'?" asked Jamie Stevens.

He had just arrived home after a meeting with the lads in a wood outside Melrose.

"Our son does have a name," Ellen reminded her husband. "You thought of it. Remember? Something suitably Scottish, you said."

"Not Craig! The other one!"

"Oh, the *other* one. He's with Hannah. Having another lesson in English."

Jamie frowned.

"I really don't think—"

"No, you don't!" interrupted his wife. "Like hiding guns in the loft. What on earth are you up to?"

"How did you—?"

"Oh, come off it! I knew as soon as you said it was 'just a circular'. I have been married to you for nineteen years."

"Now that you know, you might think more about

Craig's plan then. Modified, like. It involves the other boy."

"His name's Breth, for God's sake! And yes, he and Hannah do get on. It's like she's a different girl since he arrived. Like he was sent by..." Ellen stopped mid-sentence. She knew that her husband could not cope with anything remotely connected to religion, so anyone 'sent by heaven' was a no-no. She put down the iron and glanced at her watch. "I'm going to listen to the news. Afterwards I'll ask you and Craig to enlighten me about this bloody plan. Okay?"

Jamie knew only too well that a 'no' after 'okay?' was not permissible. But the thing going on between his daughter and 'the boy' was most definitely not okay. He went to the fridge, grabbed a can of Irn Bru, his beer equivalent, flipped it open and, can in hand, followed his wife into the sitting room like a tailless doggie.

*****

Lucius and Marcus headed for the plume of smoke streaming from the summit of the wooded hill ahead. The 'signal' had been pe-arranged: repeated interruptions in the plume after periods just long enough to say 'Marcus Aurelius Antoninus Augustus' ten times over. Marcus, who had put this in his missive, reckoned Domitius would enjoy reference to the man after whom he had been renamed.

The last stretch was a bit of a scramble, but for Lucius to emerge from the undergrowth to see the old commander, and three able-looking legionaries, was like having the weight of a statue of Mars lifted off his broad back. That is, until, seated around the campfire, after fond embraces, he realized the enormity of the task ahead.

Trimontium was well-defended. And, like the Germanian auxiliaries he nurtured, Octavius was ruthless.

"Must be made from the same cast as our hated new emperor!" suggested Marcus.

"Yes, but how many will remain truly loyal to him?" queried Domitius.

"He went west to raise a rabble tribal army in order to

strengthen his force," Lucius informed his one-time leader. "They're a wild bunch. Not like those living on and around the Three Hills."

"Wild isn't what we do in the Roman army. It doesn't win battles," observed Domitius. "And you say that the fathers of Adienna and Breth have joined us?"

Lucius nodded.

"The tall, skinny one. Adienna's father, Alun. He's a different man. There's a lion inside him, I'm sure of it."

Domitius chuckled.

"And I told Publius I was a donkey!"

"Some donkey!" teased Marcus.

"So... we set off at dawn, then. With all the arms we can carry." Domitius drew his *spatha*, put it on the ground before him, and, when he placed his right hand, palm down over the blade, his friends from Trimontium laid theirs on top of his whilst together they swore, to Mars, that if victory came their way, each would offer up to the god his most prized material possession.

For Domitius, this would be his *spatha*.

*****

"It's like this," began Jamie. "It's all about what's happening at the old Roman fort site."

"It's called Trimontium. Didn't you know?"

Jamie only knew that Ellen was fed-up to the back teeth with the SFS. His wife's touchiness was a warning, and he needed to tread carefully.

"Yeah... well, Trimontium. A military camp. No better than. For the Scottish Special Service, they say. To tame us rebel Scots, no doubt."

"I know, I know." Ellen fiddled with the TV controller till she found the correct channel.

"Well, Craig thought—and I do agree with him—about Gandhi and all that..."

Ellen turned to look at her husband.

"Gandhi? Have you gone mad?"

"No—well, peaceful like. Our demonstration."

"With guns?"

"You still don't get it! That's where 'the boy' comes in."

"So, you plan to use Breth as target practice for those geezers with guns before using the guns you've got hidden in the loft," Ellen barked. Jamie took another slurp of Irn Bru to give him strength to face her obvious anger.

"Not like that at all. We'll use the TV to go international. Tell the whole world we've got an ancient Briton in our midst. See, for the archaeological world, Trimontium is near sacred, and—"

"Shut up! I want to hear the real news."

Jamie felt he, too, was beginning to lose his cool just as an image of the Trimontium site appeared on the TV screen. Ellen laughed.

"She must have heard you," she observed when the newscaster began the broadcast with reference 'an important discovery at the site of the ancient Roman fort of Trimontium.'

"I told you!" Jamie exclaimed.

"Shhh!"

The newscaster appeared on the screen. An attractive young woman, with hair a similar colour to Hannah's, gave the breaking news...

"Recently, a skull was unearthed at the site of Roman Trimontium during excavations for a Scottish Security Service base in the Borders. With a bullet lodged in the bone, the police are treating this as a suspicious death although, so far, suicide cannot be excluded. Any connection with the rumoured disappearances is ruled out, anyone with information about a missing relative within the last fifty years should come forward. It is believed the skull, the only boney remains found so far, belonged to a man, possibly in his mid-thirties, according to the Forensic Pathology Department of Edinburgh University.

PARS SECUNDA

XI

Dr Ranjit Desai watched eagerly as Professor Angela Leckie sent the image of the skull into a slow spin, then after turning it upside down, homed in on the hole where the bullet had been lodged.

"Now, Dr Postgrad, tell me what you notice about the hole."

"Well, it is very round..."

"As it would be. But would you say clean?"

"Not very clean at all. I would not be wanting my pupils to look like that?"

"Your pupils?"

"Eye pupils. Not our beloved medical students!"

"Beloved? What a lovely word. No Ranjit, look at the edge of that hole. What do you see?"

"Not sharp, so... I am seeing it now, Madam Professor! Shattered as if..."

"Force dispersed laterally. And concentrically. Vibration, if you will." Angela swivelled her chair to face the young doctor. The humour was gone from her expression. He knew these sudden changes in his boss only too well.

"Of course! A bullet having got that far should be..."

"A long way from the body. Unless he was standing on his head. Which is highly unlikely. But if our man was wearing a metal helmet, with the bullet's velocity slowed down by..." She fashioned the fore- and middle fingers of her right hand into an imaginary gun which she prodded up under her post-grad student's chin.

"By travelling through skin, muscle, tongue, and... erm... bone, brain, arachnoid mater, dura mater, bone, soft tissue, then..." Ranjit paused.

"BANG!" offered Angela, dropping her hand. "And a

fraction of a second later, another bang. Metal against metal. Dents the helmet and remains in the bone, but..."

"But velocity reduced to zero. Energy dispersed laterally. With a wobble. Further fracturing bone. And the bullet stays there. For nearly two thousand years," offered Ranjit.

"Problem is..." Angela shook her head. "Problem is, this (tapping at the screen) is not a Roman sling-shot but a contemporary police-issue bullet."

"Could it all be fake? Like someone found the old skull, put it in a metal helmet or something equally hard, fired the bullet..."

"That, Ranjit, is for you to find out. But I think you already know the answer."

"That it cannot be fake, but fake is the only sane explanation."

"Precisely! Would you and your lovely wife like to come to dinner tomorrow night?"

She looked up at him. He was reassured to see a return of the mischievous smile.

"May we bring our little daughter? We might be finding it difficult to get a baby-sitter at such short notice."

"Of course. We can talk bones. And my husband can entertain your family. He's quite a magician."

Magician? Ranjit's heart sank. He had but one day to find a logical explanation for the impossible. He badly needed a magician, but not one who was the husband of his boss.

"We must be talking more than bones, I am thinking, Madam Professor!"

"I'm so glad to see I've got you thinking!"

*****

All day, Craig wondered whether he 'should' or 'shouldn't.' Apologies weren't his thing. Particularly when he was in the right. Nothing, and no one, not even Dylan, could prevent him from protecting his little sister.

But Dylan of all people?

For years he had managed to hide something from family and friends. Hide that he was in love with Dylan. But he knew this was an impossible love for Dylan had always made his infatuation with Hannah perfectly clear. Craig had come to terms with this. Hannah's happiness mattered more than anything. At first, he had wondered whether he was gay (he had come to terms with the label) because of his affection for his sister. But no, he loved her in such a different way. His strong attraction for his lifelong friend was most certainly sexual and, until recently, keeping this hidden had been no problem for the ace ruby player over whom younger girls swooned.

But that was the thing. *Younger* girls. Like his sister. The girls in his class all had boyfriends in or out of school. Some had even dated Dylan who repeatedly told Craig of his strong feelings for Hannah, but who was told, in return, 'Wait till she's sixteen, pal.' So far, no one, apart from his father, had questioned Craig as to why *he* did not have a girlfriend, but many would now be wondering, 'Why not?'

Seeing it from Dylan's point of view, clueless as to his friend's sexual leanings, Craig was the bad guy. He had all but promised Dylan he could 'have' Hannah as a girlfriend. 'She's madly in love with you' were his actual words. Dylan's reaction, in the pub, deliberately pissed to kill off his natural shyness, was understandable. But apologize for what? Dylan's behaviour towards Hannah was indefensible. It was lust, not love, that got the better of the birthday boy. Craig was right to defend the red-haired dude who was protecting his sister from his own 'true love'.

How weird!

Craig decided to come clean about everything with his mother. After all, she probably knew. Her excuse to their dad about schoolwork stopping him from having a girlfriend was her way of allowing Craig to delay the inevitable backlash until the man was ready to understand his son's feelings.

Now, he decided, during maths, the time had come.

And Dylan? What if he does inform on Dad? Is this how the disappearances have come about? People grassing on each other? Better see what Mum says. And maybe she'll put Dylan's mum in the picture. Have a wee mother-to-mother chat. That's only fair. But no way am I gonna apologize!

He extended his school day in the library till he had worked out what he was going to say to, and what he would ask of, his mother. However, back home it did not happen as planned. Because of the news on the TV. A discovery at Trimontium. Of a skull with a bullet lodged in the bone. His dad was all fired up, going on about it now being "all-out war!" whilst his mum sat in front of the TV, trying to calm the man down, saying how the skull could be fifty or more years old, possibly a suicide, even if there was only a skull, and, until there was more news, not to go jumping to conclusions.

"Did Dad let on about my plan for Breth?" Craig asked his mother after his hot-headed father left the house to 'talk to his mates' about the skull with a bullet lodged in it.

"Not really. Said it was something to do with Trimontium. Then, hey presto, a picture of the Trimontium site appeared. They even showed a Roman soldier. A dressed-up model of one like they used to use for tours of the Trimontium site before those fascist bastards down south..."

"Did you tell them the truth in the museum? About Breth? When you took him there today?"

"Chickened out."

"Well, my suggestion to Dad is that we *all* tell the truth." But the other 'truth' concerning Dylan hovered helpless inside Craig's own skull. "Come out with it on the telly. Bring Trimontium into the spotlight. Internationally. What it means to folk in Scotland. And the rest of the UK. It's part of our story, Mum. Who we all are, for God's sake! They cannae go building a security services camp there. Bloody sacrilege. But coming from Breth who had to put up with Roman invaders, like we have to put up with—"

"I agree he's bright, but being interviewed on the telly? In English?"

"Doubt whether they could do it in Latin. As for ancient Brythonic!"

Ellen chuckled, then nodded.

"When?" she asked.

"Before Dad and his mates stage their demonstration. Who knows? Otherwise, it could end up with just Dad standing there alone, outside that SSS camp, and a whole bloody squadron of security service zombies in army flak pointing their automatics at him."

"He's got guns, Craig." Ellen wiped her eyes with the back of her hand. Craig had never seen his mum cry. How could he tell now her about that other thing concerning Dylan? "Hidden in the loft. Please do *not* tell anyone else. I was hoping this business would all go away. And that he'd dispose of them somewhere safe. But you heard him banging on about 'all-out war.' He has no bloody idea!"

"I'll talk him out of it, Mum. I think it's his mates who are winding him up."

"Hmm! Doesn't take much to wind up your dad." She smiled through her tears at her son. "Tell you what. Just between you and me, I'll take Breth back to the museum tomorrow. Tell the truth. Ask *them* to put it on the news. Maybe..." A mischievous twinkle played in her eyes. "That Roman soldier's uniform they've got—"

"Legionary, Mum. Roman legionary."

"Whatever! Breth kept going back to look at it. Suppose—just suppose, mind you—but suppose they were to loan it to us. You could dress up in it. For the interview. If they allow it, like." The look of shock-horror on her son's face took her by surprise. "No, no! Stupid of me. Sorry I mentioned it."

Craig's face changed. A grin appeared.

"Dad could do it. Dress up as a legionary, I mean. It

would make him feel more involved. But non-confrontational, like. Have a photo shoot rather than a shootout." Craig paused, then frowned. "Bet he's never held a gun before."

"Oh Craig, he'd not be seen dead dressed up as a... a—"

"Legionary. But alive, yes! Go for it, Mum. I'll tell you the questions to get them to ask me and Breth."

"Questions?"

"Aye! About how it all started. Beside the golf course."

"Will you put it to Hannah? About Breth being on telly? You're the only one she listens to."

"Where is she?"

"In the hut. With Breth. Supposedly teaching him English."

"I'm sure you can trust him. He respects her. Oh, by the way, I'm gay."

Craig was all prepared to rush out of the room after saying this. Give his Mum time to absorb what he had just told her.

"I know," she said straightaway. "Dylan... right?"

Craig nodded. So, she had known all along. He was hugely relieved to know that she knew, but also worried that others might have picked up on his sentiments and spread the word by gossip and in tweets. Then taken it out on wee Hannah. "And I'm so proud of you. Standing up for your sister like that regardless of your feelings for Dylan."

"D'you think Hannah kens as well? About me, I mean."

"Of course she does! But Dad... the silly old bigot? I really think we should wait to tell him after this SFS stuff has all blown over. If your plan works. And I just hope he gets rid of those bloody guns up in the loft."

"He'd never use a gun. Dad couldn't even kill a spider."

"Talking of which... go and check on your sister and Breth in the hut."

*****

Adienna had it all worked out in minute detail. Donia

had become sloppy. She enjoyed using the girl as a personal slave, but this would turn out to be her undoing. The duty of clearing away the mess, after Octavius had wined and dined with his Germanian thugs, was left to Adienna. Before taking everything outside to clean in a bowl of water, the girl would have time to herself to fill a goblet with ground seeds of the opium *papaver* stashed in the wooden chest. Having tidied up and swept the floor, Adienna prepared warmed bread and an infusion for the Votadini woman as requested. 'To soothe her spirit.'

That, from what the girl had overheard, was precisely what would be achieved if a handful of the crushed opium seeds were mixed in with the fragrant herbs. Donia's last duty of the day was to take the food scraps, including bones, chicken guts, feathers, scooped up vomit and the commander's crap, to a heap outside the fort where it would be carried away and spread on the crops growing in long green strips at the foot of the Three Hills. As the muck heap had outgrown its boundaries, because of the additional auxiliaries from the west, Octavius ordered his woman-servant to transfer it to the crops and spread it herself or risk a flogging. If, instead, it was Adienna dressed in Donia's clothes, with a scarf around her head (the nights were still chilly) legless guards might fail to notice the difference on the night in question: the Feast of *Populifugia*. And on the way up the Fire Hills, before surprising her parents, she would stop at Aine's cave to make an offering to the goddess.

If her plan were to fail, and she got caught trying to escape, then Donia, not Adienna, would be flogged to within an *uncia* (inch) of her life. The girl tried not to smile at the thought of this for fear of upsetting the Goddess of Love.

*****

"I'm sorry... so sorry!" apologized Craig. He stepped back from the hut door, and looked the other way, as his sister and Breth, lying on the mattress in passionate embrace, disengaged themselves. "Honest, I won't tell Dad," he added.

Hannah knew her brother too well to think he would. And *he* could tell from the look on her face she was about to come out with something that would change their lives forever.

"What... what is it?" Craig asked.

"We're getting married!" the girl announced.

For a moment, as Craig stood speechless, his mouth agape, he thought he was looking at an angel, or even the Holy Virgin, for his sister suddenly reminded him of a painting he once saw in an art gallery in Florence on a school trip to Italy. The name of the artist was still imprinted on his brain. Sandro Botticelli. *Perhaps I'm not gay,* he remembered thinking whilst staring at the divine beauty of the young Madonna depicted by the artist. Now he realized that the painting had been his little sister all along, but without freckles. The sister whom he would protect above all else.

He looked from Hannah to Breth then back to Hannah. Still his lips failed to vocalize anything sensible. Just a grunt emerged, then...

"But...?"

*****

More 'recruits' appeared from the west to swell Octavius's small army. Younger men, some of whom caught his eye and swelled his staff of Eros in a most pleasurable way. These, he decided, he would personally tutor, in the art of killing, on the parade ground. Those who refused to warm his bed could be used by others as live dummies to practise the lethal thrust of the *spatha*.

The commander's pride also swelled. A missive from the great Commodus himself congratulated him on subduing unrest in the province. His confidence had grown so large it threatened to obliterate the Three Hills and its occupants whom his predecessor had teasingly called *homunculi collis*, the 'little hill people'. But the annoying red-haired boy, who had escaped punishment for defying his trusted auxiliaries, refused to leave his brain. According to *their* story of events, the Selgovans, bearing knives and staves and pitchforks, had surrounded his peaceful soldiers, who were simply carrying out their tax-collecting duty, and were threatening to kill them.

"We were lucky to stay alive and bring back your tax unharmed," Adalfarus told his commander when the man returned.

"But the little boy got away?"

"Because of them, sir."

"And you didn't burn down their houses?"

Adalfarus paused, searching for words that might save his skin.

"We wanted him to suffer when found. He can watch their houses burn and their women and children being killed before you have your way with him."

"Yes, that I shall enjoy," agreed Octavius. Adalfarus and his friend were presented with a small, stoppered amphora of undiluted wine for their troubles. Offerings were made to Mars to ensure not only success in the imminent battle with a rebel-come-tribal army that intelligence scouts informed him had amassed to the east and south, but also time in bed with that beautiful boy who wished to marry the freckled girl he had promised to the Selgovan chief in the west.

Already, he envisaged a victorious parade in Roma, in front of the emperor, his tamed and subdued red-haired slave, the *puer pulcher parvus,* being led, on a chain, by himself.

*****

Jamie found his mates in the Ship Inn. All, except for the police sergeant, were there. This felt wrong. He got himself an orange and soda and sat next to wee Jonny. For what seemed an eternity, he sat staring at his non-alcoholic drink. The lads grinned at each other.

"Fancy something more grown-up, mate?" Jonny asked

in a mock cockney accent.

Jamie nodded.

"Yeah, but I'll not be drinking it. Not now that it's all-out war," he answered.

"What are you on about?"

"On the telly. That poor bastard they shot. Has to be one of the disappeareds."

"Just a skull!"

"Maybe they ate the body. Turned cannibal."

All laughed. Apart from Jamie.

Jonny slapped his friend on the back.

"Sorry, mate. It's not you we find funny. If our only worry was that stupid skull, then we'd not just be laughing, we'd be pissing ourselves."

"Where's Alex?" Jamie asked.

Alex had failed to show up. The bartender, a new SFS member, said he had phoned the sergeant and got no reply. Alex had a wife and two kids. They should have been at home, at least.

"No answer on his phone," he informed Jamie. "Landline or mobile. No text message. Les reckons we're done for if Alex has disappeared."

"They'd never get anything out of him," said Jamie. "Like a bleeding limpod, he is."

"Limpod?"

"He means limpet, Jonny. Limpod must be Polish."

"Shut up! My name's Stevens."

"You're right, Jamie. They'd never prise anything out of Alex. Not even with a cattle prod."

"Perhaps... but no, I can't even think of it."

"Alex a traitor? No way!" reassured Jonny.

"Look guys... this plan of Craig's. Till we know about Alex, it might be our best way forward."

"I'm all ears, Jamie," said the bartender.

No one else entered the pub whilst Jamie, the only sober one, apart from the barman, told them the truth about an ancient Celt in his garden shed, and how he could be used, according to Craig, to stop them going ahead with building an SSS camp in that field where a skull with a bullet lodged in the bone had been found. When he stopped talking, jaws dropped and not a word was spoken.

*****

"Oh shit!" exclaimed Craig.

"Language, brother!" teased Hannah.

Craig sank down onto the floor, back to the wall, in a daze. Their mum already had that other news to contend with. Even though she said that his sister knew, now was not the time to 'come out' about his love for Dylan.

"Have you and Breth already... you know...?" he asked.

Breth looked at Hannah for translation. She shook her head.

"Like I said, we're getting married so that it *can* happen. It has to. His goddess says."

"His goddess or his hormones? Look... you hardly know each other!"

"Marry!" announced Breth, taking hold of Hannah's hand. "My deer."

"Your 'dear'? That's a bit old fashioned."

"No, you don't understand, Craig. See... earlier we went for a walk on the golf-course. Part of my English lesson."

"Like getting married?"

"Don't joke! We were walking across the course. No one out playing golf. I was trying to explain the game. About knocking a little ball into a hole." Hannah grinned. "Breth thought I was mad. Anyway, this orange deer came running from nowhere. Literally! And stopped right in front of me." Hannah glanced at Breth, as if needing his approval to continue. "At first I freaked out. But when it looked at me with those glowing eyes, I knew."

"Knew what?"

"The deer was me."

"Hannah, look... I know you had a rough time with the

ME and all that stuff at school—"

"No one else would have seen it just then. Like it was my..." She looked at Breth again.

"Spirit animal?" the Selgovan boy suggested.

"Spirit animal. I just knew it was coming from me. Then the deer turned and walked slowly away. We followed it. Till we got to a kind of hollow. You'd hardly notice the dip in the ground, but..."

"But it's how Breth got here, right?"

Hannah nodded.

"And it disappeared? Into the hollow?"

Another nod.

"Jesus!"

Hannah grinned.

"I've told Breth about Jesus too. He says he sounds like the emperor who died. The 'good one', he calls him. But the present one is a right bastard."

"Present?"

"For Breth. And the fort commander has taken me, Adienna, as unpaid tax. Just before we were to be married."

"Hannah, we'll have a talk later. About all this stuff. And alone." He looked at Breth whose piercing eyes seemed to bore into truths he had kept hidden for too long. "There's a couple of things I need to tell you."

"Fire away, big brother!"

"They found a skull with a bullet in it at the Trimontium site."

"Where they're building that SSS camp?"

"Uh-huh! And Dad's flipped. Reckons it's one of the disappeareds."

"A skull? Heads don't turn into skulls that quickly, do they?"

"Course not!"

"And they'd keep quiet about it if they'd just shot someone, wouldn't they? We know they censor the news now."

"Aye, that they do! Oh, it'll just be some guy who topped himself years ago."

"A head all by itself?"

"Whatever! Apparently, Dad's so fired up he'll not see sense. So... my plan!"

"Erm... I like *some* of your plans. Not all. Explain."

"Breth goes on telly. We come clean about him being an ancient Briton and—"

"Celt!"

"Whatever! He and I get interviewed. About what happened. Dad gets dressed up as a Roman soldier. Borrows one of the costumes they used to use for Trimontium walks for kids. Mum'll talk to them into it. We could try and sell the public some cock'n'bull shit about it being a message."

"A message. Who from?"

Craig shrugged his shoulders.

"The gods? *Their* gods? Not to desecrate the Trimontium site."

Hannah grinned at Breth.

"She's called Flidais. Must be in with Aine, the Goddess of Love. The Deer Goddess was sent by her to connect me with my other self Adienna. It's why Breth's here. To rescue her. Or me. And that's the truth. Breth told me."

The truth, ay? Craig glanced at the grimy garden tools at the far end of the hut. What a strange place for his sister to consummate her marriage to the red-haired, ancient Celt who bumped into him by the golf course.

"And the other thing, big brother?" questioned Hannah. "You said, 'a couple of things.'"

Craig replied without looking at the girl:

"I'm gay."

"I ken!" she said cheerfully.

Craig kept his gaze fixed on a garden fork. It was all rusty. Is that what his brain was beginning to look like inside his own skull, he wondered?

"What is it about you women? You seem to ken

everything without being told."

"Oh, come off it! No girlfriends. Never had a Valentine card. It's that bastard Dylan, isn't it?"

"We've been friends for so long. Just seemed natural to me. But you changed everything. For him, at least."

"So, it's all *my* fault!"

"Didn't say that. He fell for you when his hormones got the better of him."

"You know, I still thought I loved him till he tried to force me to kiss him in public. Felt like I was just a kinda trophy. To brag about to his mates! If only I'd—"

"That's it!" interrupted Craig slapping a hand to his forehead. "A kinda trophy. The skull. Don't you see?"

"See what?"

Hannah looked at Breth for inspiration.

"Breth, the skull, the Romans. And now a trophy!" explained her brother.

XII

At first, Jamie, after getting home, refused to speak. Ellen, who knew her husband better than he knew himself, also said nothing. Later, in bed, Jamie mumbled:

"Craig's plan. They agreed. On condition."

"On condition of what?"

Ellen rolled over and placed her arm lovingly across her husband's broad shoulders. Her hand travelled up till her fingers touched his lips, which she stroked. He took her hand and kissed those fingers.

"Alex has disappeared. Wife and kids too. Jonny thinks we must come out with everything on the telly. No more cover up. And if they go ahead with that bloody army camp..."

"Scottish Security Services, they call it. Not army!"

"A bleeding army camp. Come out with it on telly and we might get a whole load more recruits. International coverage."

"Recruits for what, Jamie? They're only building that camp because they're scared. Of the likes of Jonny and his mates. Don't let SFS use you. Think of the kids," warned Ellen.

"This business about 'the boy' and Hannah. What d'you make of it?" her husband asked, changing the subject.

Jamie turned over to face his wife. She kissed his moistening eyes then tapped his lips with her forefinger.

"You should talk to your daughter. And to Craig. As for 'the boy', his name is Breth and there really is something quite extraordinary about him. Hannah knows it. Plus, he's cured her ME."

"I'm tired."

Jamie turned over and switched off his bedside light. No way could he let Ellen see his tears.

*****

At the request of Domitius, Lucius took the Selgovan fathers on a reconnaissance before first light. They cut through the woods bordering the river till they came within sight of the Trimontium outhouses. Pigs and chickens were already awake and braving the parade ground beyond. Weapons used for the previous day's practice drill had been carelessly stacked up against the wall. Three guards stood talking in Saxon Germanian. They were laughing. Whilst Alun prayed that Adienna was not the focus of their humour, Gorsedd feared that they had found Breth and were joking about what the new commander might do to his son. In bed!

Lucius left the Selgovans concealed by trees as he crept, like a silent bear, towards the men. It happened so quickly that the guards had no time to cry out. Unharmed and unarmed, one lay face-down, tasting the dirt, with a heavy knee pinning him to the ground, whilst each of his two companions had a head trapped in a massive mould of muscle, their wagging tongues immobilized by the second-in-command's elbow holds. To an onlooker it would have appeared almost comical. Moments later, Alun and Gorsedd emerged from cover to bind and gag the guards. All the weapons were collected and hidden in the woods. Later, at the rebels' camp, truths were extracted from the captive auxiliaries.

Adienna was still guarded, in the commander's house, by the Votadini woman-servant. The girl was to be gifted, after victorious battle, to the Selgovan chieftain in the west. Domitius learned about the Celtic monster with a 'T' carved on his face, renamed Bikkus and now second-in-command in place of Lucius. It seemed that the sacking of the local Roman fort had been due to him. No one challenged the brute on the parade ground and, because of Bikkus, the other Selgovan auxiliaries fought like wild things. Also, they knew that killing their opponents in the coming battle was the only way for them to ever see their wives and children again. As for the wives, the pretty ones would have already been bedded by their hated chieftain. Daughters too, regardless of age.

But it wasn't all bad news. Octavius's superior strength could, it seemed, have been weakened by his brutality. From information supplied by the Germanians, Domitius learned that discontent smouldered beneath the ordered calm of Trimontium. Unrest fired by the commander's cruelty... a man killed for failing to inform on Lucius, beheadings of any villagers who claimed to know nothing about the whereabouts of the missing *puer pulcher parvus*, and an auxiliary flogged senseless for sleeping on duty. The three captives begged *not* to be returned to Trimontium.

"He'll not only kill us but think of ways to do this in front of everyone to make sure no one else is taken unawares."

"I know enough," Domitius said. "I'm still your commander. Octavius has disregarded *Pax Romana*. Like Commodus in Roma, he's shown the world he is unfit to be a leader of men. Join us. We must rid Trimontium of this beast!"

The Germanians returned with Lucius and several others to gather the weapons hidden in the wood.

*****

"A trophy? Yuk!" exclaimed Hannah.

"Like a stag's head stuck on a wall. In the old days, outside towns, castles... forts. They'd stick heads of decapitated victims on spikes," Craig explained. "Personal enemies, whatever. Gave 'em a sense of power, ken! A reminder to others to behave, I guess."

Hannah would have gladly seen Dylan's head on a spike but said nothing. She knew about her brother's feelings for his best friend, and she was immensely proud of him for having stood up for her despite this.

"Yeah, but with a bullet in his skull? Unlikely he was shot back in the Roman times."

Breth winced visibly at the word 'Roman'.

"It's okay," Hannah whispered, stroking his cheek.

"Okay not!" the boy replied. Hannah frowned then shrugged her shoulders.

"I'm going to bed," she said, standing up. "Have to be up early to give Breth another lesson before school. I've got him reading English already."

Craig, too, stood up.

"Tomorrow with Mum and Breth are going to the museum. To tell the truth, this time. And about the Romans too."

Breth shook his head.

"Romans... no!" he called out just before the brother and sister left the hut. At the entrance, Hannah turned and saw a tear trail the cheek of her Selgovan fiancé. She couldn't bear to think what her other self, Adienna, must be going through because of the Romans.

On her way back to the house, with Craig, Hannah said more about the deer:

"It shone. Honest it did. Sort of orange. That's how I knew it wasn't for real. I mean, not outside of me real. Different sort of real."

"Get some sleep, Sis."

Hannah gave her brother a hug.

"I'm so sorry about Dylan," she said. "But you have to know the truth. He really *is* a bastard."

"It's made me realize what a very special sister I have."

"Could you call me 'Adienna'? I need to get used to it."

"You won't disappear if I do?"

Hannah hesitated, for the question made her wonder, then replied,

"No way! Poor Dad, though. Alex the police sergeant disappearing like that. He's kinda key to the whole SFS thing here in Melrose."

"Guess so. And with it all being so secretive, Dad'll feel pretty isolated now. Him and that English gun-junkie Jonny and the rest of their bunch here in Melrose."

"I'll have a word with Dad before going to bed," Hannah

said. "Work out how and when to tell him about me and Breth."

"What are you two *really* planning?"

"I told you. We're getting married."

"How? Gretna?"

"Na! On the golf course somewhere. G'night!" Hannah hugged her brother again then ran up the stairs. Never since their last holiday abroad six years back had he seen the girl so full of life.

*****

All night, Breth tossed and turned on that mattress in the garden hut. Dreams of his parents, wise old Domitius, and the evil newcomer, Octavius, opened and closed like doors to another world. Some included Craig and Dylan and Ellen Stevens, but Hannah was always Adienna. The final dream, from which he was thankfully awakened by three gentle knocks on the door of the hut, hit him like a punch from one of Dylan's drunken mates. Adienna was being pushed, reluctantly, into a large Selgovan roundhouse he had never seen before. Inside stood a grey-bearded old man, naked from the waist up and painted with animals, including a deer. He removed the tunic covering his body from waist down. Adienna screamed at what she saw. Then Breth awoke.

"Old man with grey beard, no! With Adienna, no!" he shouted when Hannah appeared in the doorway clutching an iPad. The girl was in tears. Moments later, as they fondly kissed whilst lying in each other's arms on the mattress, her tears blended with the boy's.

"I had the same dream," she whispered.

"You and old man with grey beard?"

Hannah nodded. She took hold of his hands and placed them over her breasts.

"I would rather kill myself than let him take me," she said. "Please. We *must* get married. Today. After school. I get back early. Being Friday."

"Friday?"

"Sorry. We haven't done the days of the week yet. I'll go over them with you right now!"

She wiped her tears and picked her iPad up off the floor. Over the hour before breakfast, whilst Breth wrote out repeating lines of the days of the week and the months of the year, Hannah tried to decide on what to wear for their 'wedding' on the golf-course.

The registry office stuff could come later.

*****

Ellen hardly got a word out of Jamie as they sat together over breakfast.

"Did she say anything about Breth?" Ellen asked. "Last night? Hannah said she was gonna have a word with you."

"Nope! Only told me not to worry about Alex. She reckons he's been seconded to another area. There's trouble in Edinburgh as well. Apparently."

"SFS?"

"Dinnae ken."

"I'll take Breth to Trimontium today. See if they can be persuaded."

"Aye! That telly thing." He stood up, leaving half of his food uneaten. "Back late tonight."

"The lads?"

"What's left of us."

"Are you sure about Alex. I mean, could he be a spy working for *them*? And with you hiding those guns... Jamie, this might be a trap."

Jamie kissed his wife and, without another word, left for work.

*****

"Wake up, you lazy little bitch!"

A vicious slap on the face jolted Adienna out of her nightmare about being forced into a strange roundhouse where she was confronted by an ugly, old, grey-haired Selgovan chieftain. He was daubed in blue from the waist up to the cheeks with Celtic twirls and whorled creatures, including a deer. When he lowered his tunic to expose what only a wife should see, she screamed. At that moment, Donia woke her up.

"It's today!" she said. "The Feast of *Populifugia*."

"Already? But... you never told me."

"I'm telling you now. The table, the stools, the food, the wine... not to forget the bowls for all their vomit."

"Will you not help me with so much to do?"

The girl's question prompted another, even harder, slap across the cheek.

"I'll forgive you your impudence if you get everything prepared before the sun starts to fall. Otherwise, a flogging. To work, now!"

Knowing that it was *she* who would be flogged if things didn't go to plan, the woman-servant, for a change, did help the Selgovan girl, unaware that in Adienna's mind a plan was forming. One that would change everything...

*****

"Sergeant Alex Laidlaw? Never heard of him."

"But he's bloody been with the local bloody police for bloody years!"

Jamie struggled to smother the seething anger in his brain whilst muffled asides to someone at the other end of the phone line crackled on his mobile. The woman's voice returned and asked him to identify himself. He turned off his mobile, then realized they might have already traced the call.

"Shit!"

He could hardly focus on what he was doing for the remainder of the day.

"Okay, Jamie?" one of his mates asked.

"Na!" he responded.

"That pretty little daughter of yours, is it?"

In a flash, the man who said this was up against the wall, on his toes, lifted in the grip of a bear-like left hand whilst Jamie's clenched right fist pushed up against his fellow refuse worker's chin.

"If you even mention my daughter again like that, I'll... I'll smash you through this wall like Corky the bleeding Cat!"

The foreman came over and pulled Jamie away.

"We'll have none of this, Jamie. Danny meant no harm."

For the rest of the morning, Jamie's mates avoided him. But they were none too surprised when a police van drove up to the council tip at lunch time. All stood and gaped as Jamie Stevens immediately ran to the back of the building. The van drove off.

"What the heck?" queried Danny.

*****

That afternoon, Hannah and Craig walked home together up the hill from the bus stop.

"We could ask Mum to see about getting permission for him to come to school with us," Craig suggested. "The rate he's going with your lessons, his English will be up to it in a week or so."

"Hmm!" grunted his sister.

"Look, if you're not happy with my idea about having Breth on the telly, just say. I thought it might help Dad. God knows what he plans to do with that stuff in the loft."

Hannah stopped.

"What stuff in the loft?" she asked.

Craig realized he'd not yet spoken to her about the hidden guns. Maybe now was not the right time.

"Just stuff. Stuff on his mind, too. I'm trying to get him and his lads to do the Gandhi thing. Peaceful demos, like. So maybe having it out on the telly—"

Hannah halted and folded her arms.

"What stuff in the loft, Craig?" She knew her brother was a hopeless liar, and he knew that she would not budge until he'd told her.

"Guns."

"Oh shit!"

"Language, sis!"

"Bloody idiot! It'll be those SFS cranks' fault."

"Not cranks. They care about what's happening since those bloody fascists took over in Westminster, that's all."

Hannah carried on walking. "Craig, you have to understand. What I said last night. About me and Breth. It's gotta happen."

"In time, Sis. For God's sake, you're only just sixteen."

"Juliet was fourteen!"

"This isnae a play, Hannah. It's for real."

"So was that deer. I honestly am Adienna. As well as... as me. Hannah."

"We'll talk again when Mum gets back."

Hannah said nothing more. Back home, Craig buried himself in work. Latin, this time. Because of Breth, he had suddenly become interested in Latin, having dropped it in S3. It seemed to open doors to so many languages. He now fancied becoming a translator of sorts. Or an international journalist.

On their return, Hannah ran to the garden shed to find Breth on his knees and praying to Aine. She knew why. Later, after changing into a long purple dress, which she hoped would please the young Celt, and now holding hands with him, she told her brother they were going for a walk.

"Nature stuff. Breth's gotta learn English words about nature."

"Ad proximum!" said Craig, grinning. Breth appeared puzzled. "Latin for 'see ya soon'! I think."

But he didn't. At least, not in twenty-first century Melrose.

*****

Whether or not they believed her, Ellen Stevens could not make up her mind. But 'the boy' certainly made an impression. In English, interspersed with Latin. For him to have become so fluent within two days should have been enough to convince even a hardened sceptic that this was no ordinary young man, but his detailed knowledge of life in the ancient Celtic fort on the northernmost Eildon Hill, and what went on in the nearby Roman fort back then, would have made even the most blinkered academic wonder whether the impossible could, indeed, be true.

"I'll put it to our supervisor later today," said the woman at the museum.

"No time. Please do this now," begged Ellen.

The supervisor was called and told her it would be raised at the next committee meeting under AOCB.

"When's that?" she asked.

"Next month."

So, instead, Ellen called the local television network herself. They were very responsive. Even excited. Indeed, they *would* put pressure on the museum to cooperate. And *yes*, having someone dressed as a Roman legionary was a great idea. They would interview Breth and Craig together at the edge of the Trimontium site, now cordoned off with crime scene tape, and Jamie, as yet unaware of her plan, would appear as a Roman legionary.

If only she had known that 'they'—the same people who were desecrating the old Trimontium site—had infiltrated all media networks.

That evening, Ellen and her son sat together in the living room, waiting and waiting. Jamie failed to return home after work. As for Breth and Hannah, according to Craig they had "gone for a walk" after she got back from school. Hannah was "wearing her best dress," he told his mum. A long purple one, birthday present from Dad and only to be worn for special occasions, she had said. Craig had assumed it was just a ruse to allow them to sleep together without feeling guilty, but by eight pm his sister and Breth had not returned. Craig, racked with guilt, finally summoned the courage to tell his distraught mother about Hannah's crazy notion:

"Maybe we should phone the police in Gretna," he suggested.

"What are you talking about?"

"Hannah. Told me she and Breth were getting married. Going on about also being 'Adienna'. After seeing a deer that came from herself. But the funny thing is—"

"Funny?!"

"She seemed totally normal. And happier than I've ever seen her. Look, Mum, just stop worrying. She'll be fine. They're probably sharing a lemonade in a pub."

XIII

Jamie Stevens never got as far as the pub. On his way down the hill, past the golf-course, a figure sprang from nowhere, slapped a sack over his head, yanked his hands back and snapped his wrists into handcuffs. Cursing and shouting through the musty-smelling sackcloth covering his face, he was quickly bundled into a van which sped off out of town and onto the by-pass.

*****

"Are you certain?" Breth asked when he and Hannah reached the golf course.

"Never more certain!" the girl answered. "Oh my God!" she gasped. Holding back, she grabbed the boy. "Look!"

On the grass, away from the road, motionless, stood a female deer. The light given off by its silken orange coat far exceeded that of reflected evening sunlight.

*****

Whilst preparations were under way for the Feast of *Populofugia*, Adienna proved to be the perfect slave. Even before the merriment began, she kept the commander well filled with undiluted wine, his preference. The food was put out on the long table, nothing spilt, and no fuss made when Donia told the girl to rearrange everything to "please the Italians". Apparently, colour was important to them. The wrong colours juxtaposed on the same platter might spell disaster for the battle ahead.

For Adienna there was only one battle that mattered: the one between the opposing gods who would map her future. Aine, the Celtic Goddess of Love, would soon be pitted against the Roman God of War, Mars. An unequal fight? It might seem so, but the girl prayed that forces neither the Romans nor her own people knew about would give Aine power over the brute strength of the Roman Army. But what, she wondered, of Lucius, the Roman giant who had vanished from Trimontium? Could he, too, be with Aine? Whenever she served him at mealtimes, he had been respectful. There was no lechery in his eyes. And he had not taken her, as had been Donia's intention, before selling her on as a slave to be used by the Votadini chieftain instead of the old Selgovan in the west.

Such thoughts gave Adienna the courage she needed to open the chest and steal the sealed jar of *Papaver somniferum* seeds. These she ground into a paste which was stirred into her mistress's drink whilst the commander, his officers and Germanian friends shared jokes and drunken ribaldry in the room next door. The woman-servant even thanked the girl for the warm concoction that promised to pitch her into an untroubled sleep after Adienna had returned an empty jar to the chest. Later, when Octavius finally stopped flogging the corpse of the Votadini woman (Adienna honestly did not know a jarful of those seeds would prove fatal), he told his legionaries that the amount of poppy seeds consumed by 'that foul thief' was sufficient to stupefy a whole legion. But it wasn't so much the loss of the mind-distorting contents of the jar that angered the man but the disappearance of the priceless virgin with blond hair and freckles. Although Octavius preferred boys as bedmates, he did have an eye for beauty and an understanding of its worth. Because of that stupid woman's curiosity about the effects of poppy seeds, an item of inestimable value now walked free.

There was only one place where the girl he called Flavia could have gone to: the Fire Hills as the Celts called the hills that loomed high above the fort. For his new Selgovan auxiliaries to see this ablaze, after slaughtering all its inhabitants, would be a warning to all that no one could subvert his authority without paying the price. Recaptured, the girl would be taken, by himself, to that Selgovan beast of a chieftain in exchange for every remaining male and all the corn that he still possessed. Octavius felt sure the man could come up with some suitable punishment for the little vixen after exhausting his desire.

But Adienna never did reach her village.

*****

Craig looked at his watch. Ten-thirty and Hannah had still not returned home with Breth. He felt guilty for forgetting about his sister, having lost himself in the structural mysteries of Latin. Researching 'how to shoot a gun' in that ancient, yet still alive, language had been both a challenge and an antidote to what had been on his mind, particularly after his punch-up with Dylan and what Hannah had told him.

Nevertheless, his sister was now sixteen and, in Scotland, legally entitled to marry. As for his dad, probably still matching pints downed by Jonny and the others in the Ship Inn with glasses of orange juice whilst they planned their next move should Alex fail to show up.

Unable to find a suitable Latin word for 'gun' ('crossbow' did not seem right), Craig went downstairs. On seeing her son, Ellen Stevens turned off the television. She appeared distraught.

"Hannah and Breth are still not back and it's already dark," she said.

"I'll go get Dad."

"He'll be livid!"

"Mum... just check the hut first in case they came back and never said. There's something I need to get."

"We all need to *get* a little peace again. Your dad's got himself so worked up with SFS. And now this!"

Whilst his mum went out to the empty shed, Craig ran upstairs and retrieved the gun he had hidden in his bedroom. Earlier, in between translating what he read on Instagram and WhatsApp into Latin, he had been thinking about his loss: a lifelong friendship with Dylan which, of late, had transformed into an impossible love.

They had such fun as kids, and he would always insist this should include his shy little sister if she happened to be around. When their voices broke, and Dylan began to press him about Hannah, asking what she was up to whenever she failed to appear, Craig thought nothing of it. Even when his friend's enquiries were laced with sexual innuendo. Comments about her forming breasts, her shapely legs. Hannah was pretty. That was all. Craig hoped. And the other boy's threat to kill the girls who teased his sister, three years back, made him feel closer than ever to Dylan.

It seemed natural that Craig should find Dylan attractive when, almost overnight, his best friend turned into a fine young man. Hannah, whose own sexuality had blossomed like an opening flower, described Dylan as 'gorgeous'. Craig's brotherly love was, for three blissful years, in perfect balance with his love for his friend, but he knew all this would have to change after Dylan said he wanted to date Hannah. It was not jealousy that needled him, but the knowledge that he, Craig Stevens, was somehow 'different'. The macho, rugby-playing high school star, over whom younger girls swooned, was 'queer'.

He hated that term. It sent a shiver down his spine when cruelly used by lads referring to other, weaker, boys with homosexual tendencies. But instead of 'coming out' about his feelings, he joined in the boobs-and-bums banter at break time when pimpled teenage males compared carnal thoughts about giggling gaggles of teenage girls. He even, for a while, invented a fictitious girlfriend. A girl called Helen whom he had supposedly 'met on the internet'. When Helen reached the ears of Hannah, who challenged her brother about the desirability of an internet romance, the truth emerged.

"They just bang on all the time about the girls they're having sex with, so I—"

"I know," interrupted Hannah. "No need to tell me. You're different. All work, no play, right?" Not the whole truth, but big brother nodded his agreement.

That was the week before her sixteenth. Already, in her

mind, Hannah had worked out how this landmark could change her from an eager child into an experienced woman. And in her embryonic novel, she had already fast-forwarded to the bit where her heroine, just sixteen, is taken to bed by the Dylan-lookalike hero.

Now, just weeks later, Craig was about to kill *his* hero, the real Dylan. If his dad had gone missing because of his best mate's jealous rage over Hannah bringing Breth to the pub, he would shoot Dylan. Google had told him how to load the police-issue Glock 17. With the magazine in place, he slotted the gun into his belt. On the landing, he heard his mother sobbing in the sitting room. Hannah, whose room was empty, and who was not in the shed, was gone. What if she and Breth had suffered the same fate as his dad? In a flash of anger, his love for Dylan flipped into hatred.

On the landing, peeping out from under wraps, was the Roman legionary's costume on loan for Jamie to wear on the telly in an interview that Craig now knew could never take place. He recalled his and Dylan's school visit to the Trimontium Museum the previous year.

"Might suit you, dude! A Roman suit!" Dylan had joked as they stared together at the Roman military regalia worn by soldiers pictured on display.

Craig mistook the joke for admiration. A Roman soldier's 'suit' became special for him. *Well,* he thought as he slipped out of his jeans and top and donned the Roman uniform on loan, *it can be special for Dylan too before I blow his bloody brains out!*

A perfect fit!

"Oh my God!" exclaimed Ellen Stevens when her son came downstairs dressed as a Roman legionary. In between wiping away her tears, she erupted into fits of giggles. These reminded Craig of bursts of machine gun fire in a crap, late-night Hollywood movie he had recently watched. "My son a Roman legion thingummy... Oh God... Oh my God!" The tears took over. "What's happening, Craig? Please tell me!"

Craig cradled his mother in his arms, his anger intensified by her distress.

"He's gonna pay for it this time, Mum," he said on stepping back.

"No fighting. Please. Just talk to Dylan. See if he knows anything about the..."

She could not even say the word...

...*Disappearances.*

*****

Adienna halted when she saw the deer, an unreal, orange colour, glowing like the eyes of the Fire Goddess with whom the hills, where she had lived for all her sixteen years, had, according to legend, been created by an embrace with the Land God. The deer's eyes were her own. Ever since Breth had called her his 'little deer' for running as fast as him, the girl had known this was how her animal spirit would appear to her. She followed the spirit deer to their 'special cave' where she and Breth would often lie together and pray to Aine, the Goddess of Love. Part of her feared she might find her beloved's body there, butchered by the Romans, but the deer knew better. Knew that her would-be lover was strong.

Once inside, she heard voices outside. Breth's and her own, although out there *she* was speaking in a strange tongue. Was it the language of Aine... or even that of the great Fire Goddess herself? She bit her lower lip, as always when unnerved, and she waited.

Not for long. The deer, whom she had followed into the cave, now appeared in the entrance. She saw Breth beyond the magical vision and wanted to call out, but her mouth remained open and speechless as the deer shrank into a girl. A girl with a face and hair identical to her own and wearing a beautiful dress of purple. Adienna closed her eyes as the girl turned around and edged backwards till her body touched Adienna's foot. At that very moment they merged, like two beautiful, identical petals pressed together to make one...

*****

Hannah knew it was no ordinary deer. Its colour, and the strange orange glow, told her this, but it was the animal's eyes that confirmed her fear. Fear that she and her other self, Adienna, were both fragile and frail and in mortal danger. But she also understood, now, why Breth had come all that way, across nearly two thousand years of other peoples' history, to seek her out. Through the deer, she and Adienna would, at last, become 'one', and together they would overcome whatever it was that troubled her other self.

Breth, however, saw nothing when he followed Hannah onto the golf course.

"Wait!" he called out as the girl suddenly ran after the deer ahead of him. Hannah stopped and turned. He caught up with her. She held her hand out for Breth to take hold of.

"I have a feeling..." she began. "A feeling that soon I'll be able to speak your language better than you speak mine."

Breth laughed. He had understood and nodded.

"Yes!" he agreed. "Adienna is good with words."

"I'm writing a novel," Hannah said.

"Novel?" the boy queried.

"Never mind. She's waiting for us."

"Adienna?"

Hannah's turn to nod.

"But...?" She looked down at her dress... her wedding dress. "May I keep this on? There? In that other place?"

"Ask Adienna!"

Hannah kissed her husband-to-be.

"Adienna says, 'Yes!'" she replied. And hand in hand, they followed the deer to the hollow from which Breth had emerged only three weeks before.

"Adienna first," said Breth. "On hands and knees."

Feeling rather silly, and hoping no one was watching, Hannah pulled up the hem of her dress, not wanting to spoil it, dropped down onto all fours and crawled into the grassy hollow. Only it was no longer grassy but covered with scrub and heather and bracken fronds. And very dark. She turned around to see the evening sky partly shut out by broken-off branches and bracken. Breth's silhouette obscured the entrance to the 'cave'. She shuffled backwards to make room for the boy and came up against something warm. She reached back. It felt alive.

Should I feel afraid? Afraid of my other self?

Breth lowered himself and crawled towards her till his face was inches from hers.

"Am I really Adienna?" Hannah asked.

Gently stroking her freckles with the back of his hand, he spoke in ancient Brythonic. Adienna understood every word.

"I knew you'd return to me," she said in that language. Her hand reached back again. Nothing there.

*****

Craig had been gone a good hour. It was now well past eleven. The phone rang. Initially reluctant to answer, Ellen Stevens finally picked it up.

"Yes?" she said, then held her breath.

"Ellen?"

She recognized the voice of Jonny's wife, Morag.

"You too?" she asked.

"Me too what?"

"They've disappeared, haven't they?"

"What are you talking about?"

"Jamie, Jonny and the others. Because of what those bastards sent by Westminster are doing at the site of the old Roman Fort. Trimontium. Must've got wind of what we'd planned to do on the telly. About the Celtic boy..."

She stopped. Morag knew nothing about Breth being an ancient Celt. For the Glaswegian woman, the 'Celts' were a football team. News had got around that a 'distant Polish relative' called Breth was staying with the Stevens family, and now was not the right time for Ellen to spill the truth.

"I've no idea what you're on about, Ellen. We're all here. In Hawick. Outside the police headquarters."

"In Hawick?"

"Like I said. Have you not seen the news?"

"News? About the skull?"

"Skull? No idea what you're talking about. Look, Jamie says he's sorry he didn't phone earlier. Sort of got tied up talking to the reporters. This is big, Ellen."

"What the hell's going on, Morag?"

"We'll be here all night. Jamie told me to call you. It's like half of Scotland's bloody joined us. For the sit-in."

"Is Craig with you? Dressed as a Roman legionary?"

"What?"

"Never mind."

"Didn't recognize him, ken. Hair dyed black, no beard. Looks years younger."

"Who?"

"Alex!"

"I don't understand. So, he hasn't disappeared? You're all at the police headquarters in Hawick, you say?"

"Look, Jamie can explain. The reporter's just finished with him."

Ellen heard shouting and jeering at the other end of the phone before Jamie's voice cut in.

"Sorry Ellen. Meant to call earlier but—"

"Craig. And Hannah. Where are they?"

"What?"

"Our kids, Jamie. They're not here. What's happening?"

"I've no idea what you're on about!"

"Craig went to look for you at the Ship Inn. Over an hour ago. Because Hannah and Breth didn't come back from their walk."

"Oh my God, Ellen! This changes everything!"

*****

After being bundled into the back of the van, kicking and thrashing about, Jamie recognized the laughter. Jonny's. His hood was removed, handcuffs unclasped. Jonny ruffled his friend's hair whilst Jamie, frowning, sat, squashed in the van with ten others, rubbing his wrists.

"You have to ken what it's like!"

Alex?

It was Alex's unmistakable voice emerging from the mouth of a clean-shaven man with weirdly styled black hair who, only on closer inspection, resembled the missing police sergeant.

"What the—?" began Jamie.

"He escaped," prompted Jonny. "The others are all holed up in the police headquarters. Awaiting deportation south of the border, we reckon. What they're planning to build at the old Trimontium site's nothing compared with..."

"We dinnae ken for certain, Jonny," interrupted Alex, "But things are happening that would make your blood run cold, Jamie. Science bloody fiction stuff. Playing with our minds. The SSS have taken over a wing at police headquarters in Hawick. It's where they've been keeping the disappeareds. Some got taken away from the cells and returned—later, like—kinda different. Freaky zombies!"

"How did you get out?" asked Jamie.

"I... I..." Alex hesitated, as if trying to recall something that struggled to break free from a hidden nook of his brain.

"They nearly did for Alex," added Jonny. "But whilst they were out of the room he smashed a window, clambered through and made off with a police van."

Jamie stared at the sergeant as he rolled up a torn bloodied sleeve where a sliver of glass had gashed a groove in his hairy forearm.

"So, it was you came who to the council tip for help? From me?"

Alex nodded.

"Reckoned you bunch would always be injuring yourselves."

"And I ran off."

"I couldn't risk chasing after you," replied the sergeant.

"Your wife and kids?"

Alex looked away. He shrugged his shoulders. Jonny answered for him:

"He knows nothing about their whereabouts, Jamie. It's why we're actually doing something now. Not only for them. For everyone. In Scotland, at least!"

"But you're English, Jonny," someone remarked.

"Shut up!" snapped Alex. "He's one of us. This isnae about the Scots and the English, Hamish, but about those who care for others and those far-right fascists in Westminster who only care about themselves."

"Did *they* make you look funny? Hair dyed and all?" asked Jamie.

"Funny?" Alex ruffled his hair. "No, Morag did this. Being a beautician, I thought she could help with the disguise."

"Hmm! Keep your mouth shut, Alex, and it might just work," someone remarked.

"But what d'you mean by, 'doing something', Jonny?" asked Jamie.

"There must be thousands there already in Hawick. Plus, teams of news reporters not in the pay of the Westminster Government. Morag too, of course. With more women than you could fit into the Murrayfield stadium," replied the Englishman.

"Craig was right, then. Gandhi!" said Jamie.

"Gandhi?"

"Peaceful demonstration, like."

"For now. Maybe," responded Alex. "But I'm telling you, if I don't get my wife and kids back unharmed, I'll—"

"W*e* will, Alex. Just you see," reassured Jonny.

Jamie decided to wait till they got to Hawick, and he could be sure that this was not a trap, before contacting Ellen. Once there, 'big' turned out to be 'super big'. It quite blew his mind. He forgot all about Ellen. That is, until later, almost midnight, when Morag asked why Ellen hadn't shown up.

"Shit!" he exclaimed.

*****

"I see my training has paid off," observed Octavius as he watched Bikkus instructing the Selgovan auxiliaries about battle formation in the fields beyond the fort. Less tipsy than the legionaries and the Germanians, as their wine rations had been well diluted, they would be a formidable force. He and his Selgovan second-in-command acted as one: he the brain, Bikkus the mindless brawn. He just prayed that the infantry with their *pila,* crossbows and slings would be clear-headed enough to aim true. Hopefully, his promise to personally disembowel any soldier who failed to kill enough of the enemy would sober them up.

'Why not wait till the wine and beer of the Feast of Populifugia has all been peed out into the sewers that drain into the river?'

This was the question remaining in the detached head of a drunken legionary who had dared to undermine his authority with such a ridiculous question. The answer was simple. All the training weapons had been taken. Those empowered to keep watch had obviously defected, otherwise the Celtic natives would have left behind their headless bodies. More auxiliaries might follow suit. Whatever sort of an army Lucius and that fool Marcus had mustered, it would still be easily defeated in open battle. The cavalry would see to this. And Octavius yearned for a parade of victory in Roma. Maybe Commodus would make him governor of all Britannia. How many more beautiful boys (and he truly did fancy the Celtic lads) might he bed then? But before any of this, something else had to happen. Something that would involve the *puer pulcher parvus*.

A runner appeared from the direction of the Three Hills. The man stopped and stooped forward to catch his breath. Octavius's hand clutched the hilt of his *spatha*. He had only spared the rest of those annoying Selgovans on the hill to provide bait for that runaway girl he called Flavia, but if this native messenger came with bad news...

'I'll creatively kill him and all his Selgovan cousins to give me a little amusement in these dreary times!'

"So?" demanded the commander.

"She... seen..." came the breathless reply in broken Latin.

"'She' being?"

"The girl. Flavia."

A grin slowly took shape on the Italian's clean-shaven face. His hand left his *spatha.*

"You are indeed my friend, good man."

"There's more, sir."

"Do I need more?"

"The boy. With red hair. Looks different, but—"

"The boy? You mean the *puer pulcher parvus?*"

"The one who escaped from Adalfarus and his friend. Who made them look like..." The messenger, seeing a dangerous change in those reptile eyes, fell silent.

"Look like what?" pressed the commander.

"Like heroes, sir. Alone they had to fight off hundreds of armed Celts."

"Well-trained by me. That's all. Where are the boy and the girl?"

"Down by the river. They didn't see me. Don't know they've been spotted."

"Well done. When I've slaughtered Lucius and his rebels, I'll see to it that you are rewarded. Take Bikkus with you and bring the little tearaways back here. To the battlefield. Alive!"

Neither Octavius, the messenger nor the Selgovan second-in-command saw the camouflaged faces at the far side of the battlefield. Brown as donkey shit, silent, static, these peered out at the battle formation that had flattened the crops grown to feed hungry mouths. Seemingly, Octavius cared not a jot about the hunger of others. His personal larder and wine barrels would always be full, whatever the cost to his minions.

*****

"*This* is where we must marry," said Breth. "No priest, no village elder. Just us and..."

He paused. The girl laughed.

"And Aine?" she added. "You know, that other me—the one in that other world... the world where my other brother is still alive—she would have simply called Aine 'God'. So much easier."

"Your brother, he's good," said Breth. "But that drunken boy, the one who tried to take you by force in front of all those people..."

Adienna frowned, trawling her brain for memories from another world.

"My other brother is very brave," she announced. "But I can't seem to remember his name."

"Craig?"

"Yes! That's it! Craig!"

Breth led Adienna by the hand along the path beside the river. Having passed the fork in the path where, the last time they were there, Octavius and his Germanian bullies had intercepted them, he felt strangely relieved. He had advised Adienna against visiting their families on the Fire Hills. Either there would be Roman spies waiting for her there, or they would never make it up the hill. On open ground, they would be easy targets for Roman slingshot and crossbow bolts.

Beyond the fork, overhanging the river, was the tree.

"Here it is!" announced Breth.

He supported Adienna as she clambered over tree roots exposed by the river after flooding its banks the previous autumn.

"There!" he said, proudly pointing to a deer beautifully carved into the trunk of the tree responsible for the roots.

“Me?” the girl queried. Her face was aglow with admiration, with happiness and with love.

“You are mine, as I, Breth of the Fire Hills, am yours. Adienna. This must be our marriage. Here and now. Aine would have it no other way. Wait...”

The boy scrambled down the bank and pulled up a reed caught in the flow of the water. Returning to Adienna, he placed his right hand over hers, then wound the reed around their wrists, holding them together. Then, in the place of the village elder who would normally speak the marriage vows, together they chanted the words they had often heard on the very top of the middle Fire Hill...

“We are now one with Aine, the Goddess of Love. Only death can separate us. This, we both promise.”

Alarmed by a cackle of laughter from close behind, Adienna stumbled. She stepped back from her self-pronounced husband. The reed dropped to the ground. Had Breth not caught hold of her arm, she would have toppled into the river.

“A sweet but empty promise!” chuckled a gravelly voice in Selgovan Brythonic.

*****

“Jamie... please come home,” begged Ellen.

“But Craig and Hannah might be in there. In the police headquarters. Having their brains scrambled by whatever’s going on in that place.”

“I don’t think so. I’m their mother. I’d know. I’d feel it. They’re not in Hawick.”

“Well, where the heck—?”

“Jamie, I think it’s something to do with Breth.”

“The boy?”

“No, not ‘the boy’! Breth! Listen, I think...” Ellen paused. She glanced at the window, hoping against hope to see her son, daughter and Breth coming up the front drive together. “I think they’ve just vanished. All three of them.”

“Not them too! No one messes with my kids’ brains,

Ellen. We're going in. Now!"

"Jamie, please don't! I'll ring for a taxi. And come and join you. Just don't do anything stupid. And they're not in Hawick."

"Taxi? No way. Morag must've told you. They're all here in Hawick. All the taxis in the Borders. And those fascists will not dare shoot at us with the whole world bloody watching. This is the beginning of the end for them, Ellen. And if Craig and Hannah are in there, I don't mind telling you—"

"You're not listening to me! Come home, Jamie! I beg you!"

"Stay put. In case the kids do come back. Just watch the breaking news on the telly. You might see me."

A loud bang and a series of screams slammed, like hammers, into Ellen's eardrums, making her drop the phone. When she picked it up, it was dead. She reached for the television controller. Moments later, she was watching frantic live action erupting in a seething mass outside the Hawick police headquarters. Spotlights were trained on one particular group. She saw Morag, her hands clenched, and then... Oh, thank God, then Ellen spotted Jamie. Standing beside Morag, and alive.

XIV

The grisly, decapitated head of the Votadini woman-servant grinned an opium smile from the top of a post at the entrance to the fort whilst Octavius's two favourite Germanians scaled the northernmost of the three hills in a hunt for the fair-haired girl promised to the Selgovan chieftain in the west. Further heads were added because she could not be found. Those of the girl's mother and the mother of the missing *puer pulcher parvus*. Neither could provide a sensible answer when asked where their men were, so they were beheaded on the spot. Their heads were delivered to the commander soon after he got news that the girl and the boy were down by the river.

Something for their children to look at whilst I work out fitting punishments, he decided after the heads had been added to that of Donia outside the Trimontium entrance.

Octavius paced up and down across the parade ground, on edge, periodically stopping and flicking his vine stick, whilst Adalfarus and his friend went from barrack to barrack rounding everyone up. With half of them barely conscious, their brains addled with alcohol from the previous day's festivities, all legionaries and auxiliaries were unceremoniously gathered *en masse* on the battleground in front of the fort. The Selgovan giant with a T-shaped scar on his forehead stood in front of Octavius's small army, his hands resting on the handle of a huge broad-headed battle axe. Behind him were the Roman officers, each secretly seething at the way their new commander had treated them. Octavius's Germanian bullies headed the ranks of tipsy auxiliaries.

"Look carefully at the heads of the woman who betrayed me and the mothers of the boy and the girl who defied me. Regretfully, my woman-servant's greed killed her before I could slit open her foul belly whilst still alive, but that, I warn you, is nothing compared with what I have in store for anyone who disappoints me."

He stopped pacing and poked with his stick at one of his legionaries who was having obvious difficulty in keeping his eyes open. The man snapped to attention.

"My spies inform me that the traitor, Lucius, has teamed up with the dishonoured Marcus, and that together they have joined forces with a rabble of Votadini."

His reptilian eyes focused on the rows of cowering Selgovan auxiliaries.

"Once again, it will be native against native in this bleak and desolate place called Britannia. But we, my friends, will win. Because I am a true Roman. I fight for our beloved Emperor Commodus. So Mars will be on our side." Octavius stepped forwards and approached Bikkus. "Plus, the giant that he's given us," he added. A delicate finger reached up and traced the T-shaped scar on the Selgovan's face created with the point of its owner's *spatha*. "I shall enjoy watching this man reduce that traitor Lucius to a heap of butchered meat."

He turned to face his troops.

"Today!" he bellowed.

A gasp of disbelief spread through the ranks. One of his most able legionaries dared to show his surprise:

"But commander, why today? Are the men truly ready and prepared? After—?"

Octavius slow stepped towards the man who had dared to speak out. He turned to look at Bikkus whose expressionless eyes watched every move and gesture made by his new master. It was as if the two men were joined in evil by an invisible thread. Octavius nodded. The giant stepped forwards, raised his axe and carried out the unspoken deed. Moments later, Bikkus shouted in Brythonic to two of the new Selgovan auxiliaries. Their job, he told them, was to remove the unsightly body and detached head of the legionary who had spoken out of turn.

"Thank you, Bikkus," said Octavius. "Now, each and every one of you listen, and listen carefully. I'll only tell you once..."

*****

Domitius agreed with Marcus. His one-time second-in-command had learned the ways of the Celts after, following demotion by Octavius, he deserted his post in Trimontium. Despite having confidence in his fighters, Roman and Celtic—men brought together to rid the land of the silken-tongued lover of boys—he knew that to confront Octavius in the open field would be suicide. Years of peace under his command meant that there was still a large stockpile of weaponry in the strongholds of Trimontium. One that far exceeded what his men had to offer on the battlefield. Also, spies watching the Selgovan auxiliaries practising on the parade ground testified to the formidable fighting skills of these desperate men. But should Octavius be foolish enough to send soldiers into the woods to rout the rebels, these could be quickly dispatched to face Orcus in the land of the dead. Nearly every tree, all the ditches and even the lowly bushes concealed death in the shape of a *spatha*, a crossbow or *pilum*. Several archers had climbed the trees, and now hidden, trained their weapons on the ranks of cavalry, legionaries and auxiliaries under Octavius's command. Too far to kill from where they sat perched like owls at dawn, but any attempt by the Trimontium commander to approach the woods would have considerably diminished his fighting strength well before his soldiers could reach the trees.

Octavius, unfortunately, was not stupid. Cunning and evil, he was a formidable adversary. Domitius could see this ending up as a long and drawn-out siege, the outcome of which would be uncertain. Not only did they have enough food and provisions in Trimontium to last for months but, after raiding local Celtic settlements, including the one on the Fire Hills, perhaps years. And long before this could happen, the governor of Britannia, appointed by Commodus, would send an army to crush any resistance to the authority of the new commander. In the long and eventful experience of Domitius in Germania, tribal alliance with Romans could be very short-lived. Overnight, his Votadini fighters might vanish, preferring to return to their families than face certain death.

It was whilst Domitius and Lucius were planning their next strategy—to create a diversion by sending a unit of crossbowmen, led by the Publius's three legionaries, up the rear flanks of the Three Hills, in order to descend on Octavius's army from above—that a shriek cut through the silence and changed everything.

*****

Neither Adienna nor Breth recognized the voice, although it spoke in their tongue. Out of the scrub appeared a giant, double the size of anyone Breth knew. Although dressed in Roman military uniform, his ugly face and the whorled birds adorning his dirty tree-branch arms were Selgovan. An encrusted T-shaped scar decorated his face. The man's eyes reminded Breth of the elegant Trimontium commander, not only devoid of humanity, but positively oozing evil.

"The problem, my short-haired, little friend, is that Flavia here already belongs to our chieftain back home. As a gift for the new auxiliaries doing their work so well. Destroying those rebels."

Towering above the young lovers, he stepped forwards and drew his *spatha*. Breth held his ground and fixed the evil in those Celtic eyes with the inner strength he felt now united, in the eyes of Aine, with the love of his life. The giant hesitated, briefly, but when Adienna tried to run from him a hand the size of an eagle's wing, with nails like talons, grabbed the girl and pulled her back. As she fought and tried to bite him, he laughed, then yanked her arms up behind her back.

"Ouch!" she cried.

Breth struggled to remain calm.

"She is not Flavia," he said. "You've got the wrong girl. Her name's Adienna and she's now my wife."

"And you, little boy, belong to my master, Commander Octavius. He wants you both alive, so do not make this difficult for me." He glanced over Breth's shoulder. "Seize him!"

Breth turned around just as another Selgovan in an auxiliary's uniform appeared from nowhere and took hold of him. The self-declared bride and groom, each held in a human vice, were dragged backwards along the path, then up the slope towards the chosen battleground: a field of trampled cabbages, beans and turnips. Octavius stood legs astride, his vine stick in one hand and *spatha* in the other. When Bikkus's paired quarry showed above the brow of the riverbank, a chorus of cheers erupted from the troops, now, in appearance at least, less drunk and more threatening. The commander raised his vine stick above his head. A signal for complete silence. Not even a whisper emerged from any of his soldiers. Only the muffled quack of a duck on the river.

"Take the girl back to *praetorium*," ordered Octavius. With one arm, Bikkus lifted Adienna off the ground, face down, and headed for the fort. "Wait!" Bikkus halted. "Others can also enjoy her body, and without that silly purple costume on, whilst you flog the boy. Seems your chieftain's not too fussy whether the girls he takes to bed are virgins or other men's whores."

"Nolite, nolite!" cried Breth. "Do what you must with me but—"

A cry from the woods cut him short. "No!" yelled a tree. Octavius laughed, but he stopped laughing when a lone figure ran forwards from behind the tree. It was Breth's father. He, too, held a *spatha* and ran like a mad thing towards Octavius.

A scout had just returned from the other side of the Fire Hills. He had been sent by Domitius to ensure the coast was clear to send his best crossbowmen to the Selgovan fort, and, from there, mount a distracting attack on Octavius's forces. Instead, he had returned with news of the brutal slaughter of the wives of Alun and Gorsedd. Normally the calmer of the two men, Gorsedd flipped. He snatched a weapon from a nearby Roman, dodged those, including Alun, who tried to intercept, and sped like an enraged lion across the field. Octavius calmly handed his vine stick to Bikkus, grabbed a crossbow from one of his auxiliary guards, slotted in a bolt, and took aim...

*****

It was getting dark as Craig walked away from their house. He felt the Glock 17, slotted into his belt, press against his belly, and he looked back. The light in the sitting room, where he had left his mother, remained on. Never had he seen her in such a state. The anger this aroused blended with the sadness of knowing he was about to kill a friend he truly loved. As he walked, fingering the gun, he recalled the times he and Dylan had as children. But looking after Hannah was always his number one priority, his duty as her big brother, back then and even more so now.

He reached the road fringing the golf course. Five minutes at the most to Dylan's house. His head had already formulated a plan. He would chuck a stone at his friend's bedroom window.

'It's me, Craig!' he would call out as soon as Dylan opened the window. *'Came to apologize!'*

He knew his friend very well. Dylan could never refuse an apology. He was, after all, a conceited bastard. Craig would then lure Dylan down to the river. That's where he would do it. The place where they used to create a harbour, as children, with stones and rocks, using sticks and leaves for the boats. Pirate boats, destined to set off around the world, via Kelso, Coldstream and Berwick-upon-Tweed, their invisible occupants doing what all pirates do. *Good* pirates, of course. Killing the bad guys.

Is Dylan now the bad guy? Craig was asking himself as he neared the spot where, three weeks earlier, an ancient Celt called Breth had bumped into him and knocked his phone to the ground. *No doubt about it,* came the answer. *But Hannah married to an ancient Celt?* He halted and, as his mother might have done, suddenly found this extremely funny. He laughed and laughed till tears filled his eyes, and only stopped laughing when, from nowhere, a large female deer, emitting an unearthly orange glow, came running towards him. She stopped just yards away.

"Hannah?"

It had to be his sister. No one, and nothing else, had eyes like that. He recalled what she had told him about seeing a deer that was also herself.

Maybe I'm wrong about Dylan informing on Dad? he wondered. Also, he desperately needed an excuse not to kill his friend... like following a deer who was also his sister.

The deer turned and ran towards the Eildon Hills, or, as Breth called them, the 'Fire Hills'. Craig chased after the magnificent creature until, on reaching a dip in the ground, it suddenly vanished. The boy stood there, feeling a right dumbo dressed as a Roman legionary, looking around, whilst seeking out what had to be an illusion, yet he knew it was for real. Gradually, the hollow changed. It became deeper and, after he sank down onto his knees, the grass turned into heather, moss and bracken. A hole appeared. The entrance to a cave? He crouched down and crawled into the space. Inches away was the head of the deer with the glowing eyes of his sister. He heard shouting. The eyes and head of the deer vanished. He sprang upright, knocking down a roof of branches and bracken fronds.

"Oh my God!" he exclaimed.

It was now daytime and, exactly as described by Breth, a large settlement of Celtic roundhouses sat perched on the top of the northernmost Eildon Hill. A snake of dark smoke curled upwards from the ancient fort, merging with a leaden sky.

No road, no houses. Only heather, bracken and gorse. Further down the hill, towards the river, fields had been marked out. Beyond, in the distance, was the old fort of Trimontium, surrounded by ditches and, outside these, three distinct fortified clusters of buildings. Slowly, Craig approached the Roman fort. It was as though he had stepped into an artist's impression of the ancient site as on display in the museum in Melrose. He stopped. Between the fort and the woods beyond, on trampled crops of vegetables, stood rows of both mounted and foot soldiers resembling the little plastic figures that he and Dylan, as children, once used for mock battles. Feet astride, standing away from the main force, was a man wearing a crimson-crested helmet, like one display in the Trimontium Museum. He held a raised crossbow. Behind him, Hannah, in her purple dress, was held mid-air, face down and struggling against the grip of giant of a man in a Roman unform similar to what he wore. Beside them, Breth was trapped in a headlock by another freak who looked as though he had just walked off the set of a Hollywood horror movie. But it was the lone figure running from the woods, waving a *spatha* and shouting, who caught Craig's attention. The lad from Melrose wanted to stop the man, wished he would duck for cover... anything to prevent him from being shot with a crossbow bolt...

Shot? I've got a bloody gun, haven't I?

Realizing in that instant he could never have killed his soulmate Dylan anyway, whatever the other boy had done, he had the Glock 17 out in a flash. In rugby, he had never once failed to convert a try. He pointed the gun at Octavius whose crossbow was aimed at the running man but, just as his finger was about to squeeze the trigger, his target reeled. The crossbow and bolt fell to the ground and the man with the *spatha* continued to run as the Roman commander staggered forwards before dropping to his knees.

*****

"There's some sort of disturbance out there in the crowd. So much noise here in front of the police headquarters, it's difficult to know exactly what happened but... wait a minute..."

The reporter, a young woman, turned as the camera focused on a man breaking through the jostling crowd. Despite the disguise, Ellen recognized the features of her husband's police sergeant friend.

"Make way for the ambulance, for heaven's sake," Alex called out.

"Could you give us some information for our viewers? Is someone hurt?" asked the reporter.

"Shot. By a sniper. Get these people away from here."

"Do you have—?" the young woman began.

"I'm the police. Clear the area!" yelled Alex.

The screen went blank. Moments later a newscaster appeared, in the safety of her newsroom.

"I'm afraid we appear to have lost our live transmission from outside the police headquarters in Hawick, the scene of a public demonstration in protest against what have been called the disappearances. We'll return to Laura as soon as we can. Meanwhile, we have an update on the skull found at the site of the old Roman fort of Trimontium. Ashok, over to you."

An Asian man, holding a microphone, appeared against a backdrop of wire netting beyond which stood a dozen or so temporary buildings.

"Here, at the site of the ancient Roman fort of Trimontium, near the tranquil little town of Melrose in the Scottish Borders, the grisly discovery a skull..."

Ellen turned off the telly. Not knowing whether to scream, shout, cry or even laugh, for everything had become so bizarre that laughter seemed to be her best escape from the nightmare, she got up, went through to the kitchen, took out a loaf from the bread bin, cut two slices, each thicker than her long-dead gran's well-used Bible, spread them with industrial quantities of low fat margarine, placed a week's worth of sliced cheese between the pieces of bread, looked at what she had created... and *then* she laughed. She laughed till her sides ached, when, in tears, she took the sandwich, on a tray, into the sitting room, sat down and waited. The sandwich remained untouched.

Craig always fancied a cheese sandwich when he came home after a rugby match.

XV

Domitius, whose battle sense, in Germania, had been honed as sharp as a butcher's knife, saw, in an instant, that there was no need to dispatch his best crossbowmen to the Three Hills. The distraction, caused by Gorsedd's insane anger and Lucius's skill with the sling, was enough. Behaving like a histrionic child who has stubbed his toe, Domitius shrieking like a *dialobus*[12] rolled onto his back and clutched at his right forearm, embedded in which was a sling shot. Bikkus let go of the girl who ran off towards the entrance of the fort where she stopped and stared in horror at what were impaled on blood-spattered posts: the sightless head of her Selgovan mother together with that of her new husband's mother and of the evil Votadini woman who had so tormented her. Meanwhile Bikkus offered to help his wounded Roman master to his feet. Instead, Octavius grabbed the Selgovan giant's tunic, sprang upright, and, with blood oozing from his injured arm, pulled out his *pugio*[13].

"You fool!" he yelled. "Get the girl!"

But Bikkus was now more concerned with what had emerged from the woods. Already, Lucius, as fast as he was large, had caught up with Gorsedd. Close behind, hordes of Votadini warriors kept on appearing like waves of water from a burst dam. Showers of bolts, shot from trees, prevented Octavius's army from intercepting, whilst the Trimontium infantry sling-bearers and crossbowmen, caught unawares, either fell or fumbled with their own weapons.

Bikkus pushed Octavius aside. Grinning like the god Bacchus, and holding his axe with both hands, he ran to meet the Roman giant. Breth, on seeing his beloved new wife alone

[12] devil

[13] dagger

and staring in terror at their mothers' spiked heads, stamped on the foot of the auxiliary holding him. The man, aching for a real fight, lost interest and let go of the boy. After drawing his *spatha*, he shot off towards the tsunami of Votadini warriors. It was to be a trial of strength between the Selgovans and the Votadini. The Romans seemed almost incidental, although the auxiliary had been personally trained by Octavius's best legionaries and felt certain those savages from the East would be no match against superior Selgovan military strength. That, however, was the last thought that entered the auxiliary's mind. A second later, he fell forwards with a bolt driven through his right eye into his brain. Overconfident, he had not reckoned, like others who ran to meet the foe, on bolts, delivered from on high, where experienced sniper crossbowmen sat perched on branches, travelling further than those shot from level ground.

Lucius and the Selgovan slammed together like enraged bulls. No one dared come near the pair. The Selgovan's axe and the Roman's *spatha* were soon discarded in favour of hands, knees, feet and any other part of the body that could inflict injury. Meanwhile, Domitius and Marcus led the few legionaries under their command forwards in an orderly formation. Like a knife with butter, they cut a clean path through Octavius's disordered throng. All attempts by the Selgovan auxiliaries to put into practice their newly acquired skills were frustrated as the Romans supporting the Votadini ducked, dodged, then thrust their *spathae* with lethal effect.

Above the noise of battle, Domitius heard a shriek from where the new commander stood well away from the battlefield. Breaking through the melée, he saw Gorsedd on his knees before Octavius. Breth's father, out of his mind with anger, and desperate for revenge, had lunged at the Roman who skillfully dodged the blade. The silken-voiced commander's right arm, still clutching a *pugio*, dangled, dripping blood, whilst his other arm held Breth in a headlock.

Octavius kicked the boy's father backwards. "Just finish him off!" he shouted to his guards. "I have a job to do. To teach this miserable little boy a lesson."

With difficulty, for his right arm was giving him hell, he touched the boy's forehead with the point of his *pugio*, intending to carve a deep 'O' to establish ownership of his *puer pulcher parvulus,* when a legionary he had never seen before grabbed his wrist.

The young man, whose grip was strong, held something that looked like a metal finger.

"Who are you who dare challenge our Emperor's commander of the fort of Trimontium, huh?" he sneered. The legionary, who did not appear to understand one word, jammed the metal finger underneath his chin, pushing his head back. "This *puer pulcher parvulus* is my—"

The last words ever spoken by Emperor Commodus's brutal commander. The bullet had done its job before the word 'prize' emerged.

*****

"For God's sake, man, say something!"

Jamie Stevens knelt on the ground beside Jonny. Face down, his friend remained motionless. A dark red hole on his blue tee-shirt grew, as did the pool of blood in which he lay motionless. Jonny's lips quivered slightly, then went still. Morag screamed and screamed. Alex pushed Jamie aside and rolled Jonny over. A mere glimpse of his friend's face was enough to tell him that Jonny was dead. Weeping, the police sergeant attempted resuscitation until Jamie pulled him away. Nothing could bring the Englishman back to life.

"For God's sake call an ambulance!" begged Morag. "He can't die."

"I'm afraid he's gone," affirmed Jamie. "Did this for all of us. For Scotland. And for freedom from the fascists."

Alex fought his way to the front of the crowd and held up his hands. "This is it, guys! We're going in. I'm the police and I'm gonna get my wife and kids outa that building.

Anyone with guts can join me!"

Jamie stood rooted to the spot as Alex and all the others, apart from Morag, stormed the building. Whilst the dead man's wife knelt, cradling Jonny's head on her lap, and stroking his hair as the angered horde swept past, Jamie dialled 999.

They say a crowd on the move behaves like flowing water. The huge wave that engulfed and poured into the police headquarters in Hawick would have needed far more than machine gun fire to halt it. Windows were smashed, doors broken down, as the crowd flowed on into the building to seek out whoever was responsible for the shot that had killed an innocent man. A man who had only been there to find out the truth about the disappearances. An Englishman with a Glaswegian wife and a keen sense of what is right and what is wrong.

In no time, an ambulance arrived. They allowed Morag to stay with her husband whilst Jamie followed in his car, now worrying about Ellen.

She had not answered calls from his mobile. At the Borders General Hospital, he dialled home over and over, in between trying to comfort the grieving Morag and repeating the story of what happened outside police headquarters to everyone they saw. No one would answer him when he asked, "Why?" After all, mere words could now get a person shot. Or made to disappear. But the horror of what had happened in Hawick clearly showed in their faces.

"Who do you keep phoning?" a nurse asked.

"My wife. She's not answering. Makes no sense at this time of night. She was at home only half-an-hour ago."

"Nothing makes sense anymore. Look, I'll stay with the dead man's wife if you want to get on home. I'm sure you'll find your own wife fast asleep. Dreaming about times before all this awful business began."

But the house was empty.

He checked on the guns in the loft. Together with a

bullet magazine, one was missing. He loaded two and slotted these into his belt.

*****

Because of temporal quantum entanglement, at the same time as the gun that killed Jonny Aveyard was discharged in the twenty-first century, in AD 180 a twenty-first century police issue Glock 17 released a bullet that travelled through skin and soft tissue, silencing forever a tongue that spoke reptile words in a silken voice, then on through bone, brain, the three maters (pia, arachnoid and dura), bone again, soft tissue, skin... before BANG! It hit metal. The echo of this was the last sound to be heard by the owner of a helmet that prevented the bullet's onward journey into the world of ancient Britannia.

*****

"Craig?" queried Breth, stepping back as Octavius fell forwards. "You? A Roman?"

Craig, staring at the body of the man he had just shot, shook his head.

"I was going to kill the bastard who said those things to my sister in that pub. Back in Melrose. Or forward. Then... this deer appeared and..."

He looked up at Breth.

"Where's my sister?" he asked in English.

"There!" Breth turned and indicated the lone figure in a purple dress staring at the heads stuck on a post at the entrance the fort. "My wife. Adienna."

"Hannah!" Craig called, but his voice was drowned by a burst of excited shouting. The fighting had stopped, apart from Lucius and Bikkus who remained locked in an unwinnable tussle between giants. They were being urged on by shrieking legionaries and warriors from both sides, now encircling the pair. News of the death of Octavius had spread rapidly, and on seeing their beloved old commander, Domitius, others, apart from a few mindless Selgovan auxiliaries, had no wish to fight on, and Alun soon dissuaded these from continuing a senseless conflict. Laughing, Domitius pulled Lucius and Bikkus apart. He approached Craig, halted and stared at the boy.

"Num Romanus es[14]?" he asked.

Craig, still staring at the body of Octavius, shook his head. "English," he replied. He pointed to Adienna. "Her brother."

Breth ran to fetch Adienna. Craig showed Domitius the gun.

"I just killed a man. With this," he said.

Craig fired the Glock 17 into the air. Domitius jumped back in alarm. A crowd, including the giants whose fight had become pointless, had already congregated around them. Frozen in shared disbelief, all stared at the young man from Melrose with the exploding metal finger. Domitius, realizing he was no ordinary legionary, hesitated before stepping forward again. Craig shrugged his shoulders.

"I had to do it," he said in English. "Breth gave my sister back her life. Couldn't let that..." He looked down at the lifeless figure of the commander. "...That bastard harm him."

"Brother?"

Craig turned around. Behind him stood Hannah wearing the purple dress their dad had bought her when she turned sixteen. 'Sweet sixteen' he had called the occasion. It was his fatherly attempt to help the girl out of the doldrums that threatened to jeopardize her grades at school.

"It's not a dress she needs, Dad. She needs understanding. Don't go on at her so!" the boy recalled saying. Then, "Viruses can do that to you. Make you feel half-dead." But Craig, who knew his little sister better than anyone, was not thinking about the glandular fever virus. Rather, the virus of jealousy that had infected a gang of spiteful girls.

Now, here in a different Scotland, during the Roman

---

[14] Are you a Roman?

occupation, she was strong and defiant, yet tearful, and all because of Breth. She spat on the body of Octavius then held her arms wide for a hug from Craig.

"I just knew you hadn't been killed by that boar," she said, but her brother understood not one word.

"Adienna, speak in English. I don't think he understands Selgovan Brythonic," Breth pointed out. The girl frowned, as if trying to remember something.

"Why not?" Adienna asked in English.

"He's your other brother."

"*Other* brother?" enquired Craig. He felt a pinprick of jealousy at the thought of the girl having had someone else to guide and protect her as a child. Adienna gripped her hair with both hands. Just like Hannah. She looked from Breth to Craig to Breth.

"I *do* remember," she finally said in English. "That dream. A deer. Another place. Just grass." She looked back at the gruesome entrance to the fort, then nodded up at Craig. "Your mother too?" she added. "Alive?"

"She was. Or will be! Not so long ago. And I think you should get back to her."

Domitius, who had been watching in silence, held out his hand. Craig looked at the gun, snapped out the bullet magazine, and handed it to the Roman.

"It's useless now," he said before flinging the magazine into the crowd. "I could never have killed Dylan, but that animal down there..."

Holding the gun, Domitius knelt to unstrap the helmet from the dead commander. He wiped away the blood spattered on the inside, then studied, with curiosity, the dent created by the bullet before placing the helmet on Craig's head.

"I don't know who you are," he said in Latin, "but you must take this as a trophy. Will you return with me to Rome?

*****

"Leave him to me!" shouted Alex.

In one of the rooms, the human surge had discovered a lone firearms officer, holding a semi-automatic, crouched below the window which was open a mere crack but enough for the man to have shot Jonny. As Alex approached, the figure shrank down, terrified. For several tense moments, no one spoke. No one moved. No one dared to move, for anything could have happened. And one thing was certain. But for Alex, the man would have been lynched alive by force of numbers.

"They've all gone," the officer said, as if this might vindicate him. "Out the back. Went for reinforcements, they said. Left me alone. Honestly, I didn't mean to do it. It just bloody happened. Because of all you lot out there. 'They're armed,' someone shouted. 'Plan B. Out the back!' another yelled. 'Before they get into the building.' Then that guy down there pointed his hand. I saw something. I swear it was a gun."

"Wasn't! Just a hand." Alex's steely gaze held the other man in its grip.

"'Take him out, you dozy bastard,' someone else screamed," continued the firearms officer. "I pulled the trigger. Never killed anyone before. Only shot at targets, like. Then it hit me. What I'd just done. Kinda froze. The others... they all left the room. 'Keep 'em away from us!' were the last words I heard. Already we were surrounded. In the front, anyway. I heard windows break. Then that awful noise. Of hundreds of people on the move. Did my head in. I knew I couldn't escape."

Alex held out his hand. The tearful man handed over his semi-automatic. One police officer to the other. They just happened to be on opposing sides.

Someone shouted from along the corridor,

"They're gone! The prisoners!"

"Where are they? The disappeareds? My wife and kids?" Alex asked the other officer. He felt surprisingly calm.

"Tear him apart till we get to the truth, Alex," a woman

suggested.

"No one touches this police officer," the sergeant told the mob. "Not until I find my wife and daughter. So, you lot can clear off and search every room. Every corner and cupboard." He sat down beside the firearms officer. Staring at the semi-automatic that had just killed his friend, he turned to the face the man. "You and I need to talk," he said. "The truth. Where are they? My wife and daughters? Did those bastards take them away? And what about all the other disappeareds?"

*****

Ellen Stevens could no longer alone doing nothing. In case the whole evening had been a ridiculous dream, she went upstairs to her kid's bedrooms. Empty. She returned to the sitting room, turned on the TV, hoping to see Craig appear, on screen, wearing that stupid Roman armour, with Breth holding forth, in Latin, about where he came from. And Hannah. Adorable little Hannah. But... only the usual late-night rubbish appeared on the screen. Rubbish from another life, another world.

Another world? Hannah? Of course! This is all about Hannah.

After focusing on her daughter it seemed to Ellen that a curtain had been pulled back and sunlight now filled every space of the living room. Everything became as clear as the cut crystal Polish decanter inherited from Jamie's grandfather and which had stood proudly on the living room dresser for almost eighteen years, regularly cleaned but never used. This always reminded her of her son for it had been a gift for his christening from a distant Polish relative, now dead.

Ellen suddenly felt so very proud of Craig, for *he* had always known about Hannah being special. Also, although they had never spoken of it before the previous evening, she had known that Dylan was the love her son's life. It was as obvious to her as the three Eildon Hills that loomed over the golf course at the top of their road whenever she went into town to go shopping. But protecting Hannah was her son's self-proclaimed duty, and that evening in the pub, when he defended his sister's honour, Craig put duty before selfish love. Wherever they were, Ellen Stevens prayed that Craig would be with his little sister.

And Breth?

Who Breth really was remained a mystery, but Ellen enjoyed mysteries. She could laugh about them. And if Craig had accepted Breth, this had to be all right. As for Jamie, he would come around to his son's way of thinking. In the end, he always did. Alike in many other ways, father and son were poles apart when it came to making the right decision which came so naturally to Craig. Had Ellen's son inherited this particular trait from his mother, she wondered? Or hoped. And one day, she reckoned, Jamie would accept his son's sexuality.

But Hannah?

Ellen stood up, turned off the TV and fetched her coat. Although dark outside, inside herself her daughter had illuminated everything, for everything was about Hannah.

Ellen—normally bright, bubbly and unbothered about what happened outside her household—had changed. Her father, a local roofer, fell to his death when she was but three. A loose tile, some said. Others, less forgiving, blamed the booze. Whatever the true reason, Hannah's grandma, attractive, like her daughter and granddaughter, soon found another fellow. Or two. Or, at times, three. Being a waitress gave her ample opportunity. She kept the (monetary) tips in an old jam jar on the mantelpiece. 'Our special jar', she called it.

Nevertheless, the woman doted on wee Ellen. At the end of each month, if funds allowed (unlike her deceased roofer husband she was canny) she would treat Ellen to something special. When the girl, aged sixteen, told her that she was going out with the 'Polack', as Jamie was called behind his back by jealous rivals, she was curiously happy. Ellen never knew that her Irish mother had once enjoyed a fling with her amusingly serious boyfriend's uncle.

Although Ellen had inherited her mother's looks and sense of fun, she was fiercely loyal to Jamie. No way would it have occurred to her to have a 'fling', for it was *her* job to guide her husband through his dark moods. Although he was clever, and should have ended up as a doctor, a lawyer or a company director, she never once criticized him for wishing to remain, as he called himself, a 'working man'.

But his attitude towards his children she found hard to endure. Why did he go on at Hannah about focusing on her schoolwork when he had opted out of academia? Craig, until recently, had been the easier of the two for Jamie Stevens. Brilliant, like himself, this showed in everything the boy applied himself to. But the boy's sexuality was a different matter. Although they had never spoken about it, she knew that he also knew their son was gay. Every day she tried to bring it up in a roundabout way...

“I've heard that some kids who are really bright, like, are also... you know... kinda gay... like.”

“Oh, really?” Jamie’s way of killing the discussion.

Poor Jamie had, of late, been so intense, so wrapped up in SFS business, each day she would reckon that it was not the right time to have that proper discussion. Besides, it was Jamie's insistence that Hannah should be an academic superstar, like her brother, that really upset Ellen Stevens. She blamed her daughter's ME on pressure from Jamie as much as teasing at school.

"Just give her a break," she begged the morning after he had reduced Hannah to tears by saying, "Enough is enough!" when the girl said she wasn't up to going to school that day. If Craig hadn’t stood up for his sister, Ellen might have screamed at her husband.

The gene that had bestowed both Ellen and her mother with a sense of humour—something that gave everyone with whom they came into contact the strength to soldier on—must have been suppressed in both Hannah and Craig by the Szczepański gene. A dark one, shaped by millennia of cold Polish winters and sad Polish songs. But their mother had somehow kept brother and sister going until Breth arrived.

Breth came from the past to seek out her daughter. Ellen had never questioned that he was genuine. Nor her daughter's need for the love the boy showed the girl. It was as she sat alone in their living room, fearing her own children had also become disappeareds, that it suddenly became clear. The whole thing was about Hannah. Not about herself, Jamie, Craig, Alex or any of the others now protesting outside the police headquarters in Hawick. Breth knew this, and now, so did she.

Dylan, too? He worships Hannah.

With the intention of speaking with Dylan, if the lad's mother allowed, she left the house in the dark. All she took was her house key. Dylan lived on the other side of Melrose, beyond the old abbey. Ellen chuckled to think the abbey, nearly a thousand years old now, was almost a thousand years from being built when Breth was conceived. Did that make him two thousand years old?

How's that for the Guinness Book of Records?

She was walking down the hill towards the town and the abbey, alongside the golf course, wondering how to get Breth into the Guinness Book of Records, when she spotted an orange glow halfway up the side of the Eildon Hills. She stopped and smiled, for it seemed almost comical the way the point of light hovered, darted and danced. Soon, it became apparent that the light was speeding down the slope towards her, dodging dips and gullies, running swiftly. Running to meet her. Someone carrying an orange torch, perhaps? Craig?

Oh my God, it's a deer! Sprinting this way. To meet me. I know it. Wait a minute...

When only yards away, the deer stopped. Only one

creature in the universe could match her for beauty. Hannah. And when the deer allowed Ellen to approach and peer into her eyes, blue, not brown as a deer's should be, she knew this was Hannah.

"Where are you?" Ellen asked. "And is Craig with you? Breth too?"

Instead of replying in words, the deer turned around and took off again. Ellen ran after her. Suddenly, the ethereal animal seemed to get sucked into the ground until, when closer, Ellen saw that she had dived into a hollow. A kind of cave in the middle of the golf course. It was covered with branches and bracken fronds. Ellen could no longer see the deer, but the entrance glowed orange.

"Wait, Hannah. I'm right behind you."

On all fours, she crawled through the entrance. Pitch black until...

It was as if someone had switched on a light outside. Sunshine streamed in between the leaves and branches above her head. At the same time, she heard shouting. She crawled out backwards, stood up and giggled. She only stopped giggling when tears clouded her vision. She wiped her eyes and stared. There, down towards the river, and where the village of Newstead, a residential extension of Melrose, should have been, stood the Roman fort of Trimontium. It looked just like a movie set. In front of the woods, beyond the fort and its outbuildings, it seemed as though an ancient Murrayfield had just disgorged its spectators, all dressed like ancient warriors. They were shouting and pushing at each other and, even from a distance, Ellen could see that they bore weapons, but it was a scene unfolding close to the fort that focused her attention.

Hannah stood there in the purple dress Jamie had bought for her on turning sixteen, together with Breth and Craig who wore the Trimontium Roman legionary costume, plus others in similar dress.

Wish I'd brought my mobile with me, she thought.

Maybe the guy in the museum would believe me if I texted a picture.

Ellen's jaw dropped when she saw one of the Roman soldiers remove a helmet from the body of another lying face down on the ground. He gave it a wipe before placing it on her son's head. Overcome with pride, she called out!

"Craig! Hannah!"

Craig turned and gawped at his mother.

"Mum?"

XVI

Jamie halted on seeing Dylan approach up the hill from Melrose. The lad appeared to be alone but, after what Craig had told him, Jamie was taking no chances. He cupped his right hand over the Glock 17 slotted into his belt. Dylan also stopped.

"Is Hannah at home?" he called out.

"Why d'you want to know?" shouted Jamie.

"To say sorry. To Craig as well."

If Dylan has anything to do with their disappearance, he would not be saying this, reckoned Jamie.

"Both vanished. Their mum too," he responded. From the shock horror distorting Dylan's features, it seemed unlikely that the lad was involved with what was going on in Hawick. His hand relaxed. Like Ellen, Jamie had, over the years, grown fond of Craig's best friend. He walked on to join Dylan. "I came to look for them. Because of what's going on in Hawick, I—"

"Me too," interrupted Dylan. "Saw it on the news. That poor guy getting shot."

"That 'guy' was my friend. I followed him to the hospital."

"Is he...?"

"Aye! The bastards killed him."

"Look, Mr Stevens—"

"Jamie, please! You're eighteen now. Grown up. We can be friends."

"Jamie... I really didn't mean what I said to Craig. About telling the police. My dad's with you lot every inch of the way."

"Why didn't he join us?"

"Oh... he will now! We all will. But I'm worried about Hannah. And that red-haired weirdo. Who the heck is he really?"

"Wish I knew. Look, I was on my way to the old Trimontium site—"

"The military camp they're building?"

"SSS… whatever." Jamie pulled his jacket apart to reveal the guns. "I know I shouldn't be asking you this, but would you—?"

"Yes," replied Dylan before Jamie finished his request. "And my mates will, too. I'll text them. And they'll text their mates. Hawick will be nothing compared with what we'll assemble together there in Newstead."

"No. Just your dads. No young'uns. Ken, I've a hunch I might find my kids there. Being held by the SSS."

Dylan held up a clenched fist.

"Like you said, Jamie, I'm eighteen. No one messes with Hannah or Craig. And what happened in that pub was all my fault. Because I was pissed. I just hope she can forgive me. If you find them, please say 'sorry' from me. Whatever, I'll see you at the camp."

"Here, take this," said Jamie. He slipped his hand into his pocket and took out his front door key. "My house key. In the loft. Bring all of them. No idea what we'll be facing."

Dylan took the key, glanced admiringly at Jamie, then took off up the hill. He wished he, too, had a dad with guns and guts. But perhaps not enough to…

*****

"If you help me find my wife and kids, I'll let you live," remarked Alex.

No sooner had he said this, than his wife and daughters appeared in the doorway. He leapt up from the floor. The two girls, shrieking with delight, ran to hug their dad. He held them together, at arms' length, and looked them up and down, as if to reassure himself there wasn't a single blemish on their fresh young faces, otherwise he would have killed the man who shot Jonny.

"This is such fun, Daddy," announced the younger girl. Alex looked at his wife. Her smile reassured him that she, too, was unharmed. He turned to look at the firearms officer still crouched by the window.

"Name?" he asked.

"Sergeant O'Brian. Don O'Brian," answered the other man.

Alex left his wife, Fiona, and their two daughters, and walked over to the crumpled wretch.

"Sergeant Don O'Brian, I'm arresting you for the murder of Jonny Aveyard and the wrongful imprisonment of my wife and two daughters. You do not have to say anything, but anything you do say may be taken down and used as evidence in court."

He produced a pair of handcuffs, taking no pleasure in towering above the wimp who had so mindlessly killed his mate.

"Can *I* do that, Daddy?" begged the younger child. Her father shook his head.

"Have to draw a line somewhere, Erin," he replied, turning to address the child. "Wish this bastard here had done the same."

*****

"How the heck did you get here, Mum?" asked Craig.

"I should ask you and Hannah the same question. But..." She looked at Hannah who, still staring at the entrance to the fort, had not yet seen her. "But I think we both know the answer, don't we? It all makes sense now. The deer. And that..." She pointed to the body of the Roman commander. "...That creature down there, right?"

"I had to do it, Mum. He was gonna kill Breth. And God knows what he'd have done to poor Hannah."

"Adienna," corrected Breth.

"Those heads?" Ellen asked.

"Her other mother. Plus that of Breth's mother, apparently," offered Craig. Hannah-Adienna turned around, paused then shrieked,

"Mum!"

Ellen held out her arms for her daughter. As they embraced, the girl sobbed, “We were too late to save them, Mum. I feel so awful. Will Aine ever forgive me?”

“Who’s Aine?” Ellen asked her son. He shrugged his shoulders.

“Our Goddess, Mum,” answered Adienna.

“That orange deer?” queried Ellen.

“That’s a different goddess. Flidais. But we got married in Aine’s name. Down by the river.”

Ellen frowned.

“Married? You and who?”

Adienna, her eyes still wet with tears, giggled.

“Breth, of course! It’s why he came for me. And I brought Craig back here. To save us both. And you as well. I knew you’d come. But what about...?” The girl broke free from her mother. She was looking over the woman’s shoulder. “What about my other dad? Is he all right?”

Followed by Gorsedd, Alun strode towards the strange gathering. Adienna ran from her mother to hug him, then pointed to the entrance of the fort.

“I’m so sorry,” she sobbed in Brythonic. “I came too late to save her.”

*****

Jamie stepped aside as a TV crew van, speeding from the direction of the SSS camp, shot past. Further on, he halted at the crime scene tape. Barely discernable, in the dark, were a few armoured vehicles flanking a cluster of temporary military huts. A cold blue light showed in one of the windows.

Jamie did not have to wait long. A grinning Dylan soon reappeared, carrying a holdall, and returned the house key.

“Found these, no bother,” reassured the boy. “Backup’s on the way!”

Sure enough, in almost sacred silence, others began to appear, singly, in pairs or groups. Women too. A human wall, several deep, formed around the site of the ancient Roman fort. No one spoke as Dylan handed the guns to those who knew how to use them. Everyone remained still, partly through fear and partly from the shock of what they had seen on the television news. Like cattle, they watched as Jamie, on his own, crawled under the crime scene tape and headed for the hut that had a light on inside. He stopped, turned and beckoned to Dylan. The boy seemed only too eager to join him. Perhaps he hoped a display of bravery might win him back Hannah's precious young heart.

Had he truly 'seen the light' and now wished to put a stop to what was going on? Or was he still driven by jealousy? Moments later, he and Hannah's dad stood together, outside the hut, guns at the ready. Jamie, who had just whispered instructions on how to use the gun, raised his free hand. A sign for Dylan to remain as motionless as the Borders reiver statue in Galashiels. Were they both prepared to die? As far as Jamie was concerned, 'Yes'. A small sacrifice for rescuing those whom he loved. And 'Yes', Dylan still loved his long-time friend, although not in the same way that he ached, all the time, to be with the boy's sister.

*****

Domitius called out to Lucius and Marcus. Craig understood little of what was said, but Breth enlightened him in broken English:

"Commander Domitius says our gods sent you to save *Pax Romana*. Now we must feast to thank the gods. In Trimontium. With Lucius and Marcus. But first our commander must talk *'pax'* with all the soldiers. Then..." Breth paused. He glanced at Adienna who had just introduced her mother from one life to her father in another. "Then... *Decernere quid facturus*[15]."

Craig shrugged his shoulders. '*Decernere*' wasn't in his Latin vocabulary, but the word *'festum*[16]*'* appealed. He was

---

[15] Decide what to do

[16] Feast

ravenous. Together with his mother, sister and Breth, he followed the Roman legionaries through the gruesome gateway and on into the ancient fort. They were taken to a free-standing building. Adienna knew it well, for it had been her home and prison for many weeks. The *praetorium*. Inside, she led her mother from the future, still dazed, to a seat and told her 'other brother' and Breth to make themselves comfortable. The girl disappeared, soon returning with food and wine.

"The water's rubbish here," she said. "Best to stick with diluted wine." When her brother frowned at the word 'wine', she added, "It's okay. Honest. You won't get pissed. The alcohol helps to kill the germs."

The local legionaries, maintaining a respectful distance, eyed Craig with suspicion until their old commander reappeared, accompanied by the Selgovan giant bearing a T-shaped facial scar, and the three legionaries from Roma. He placed his *spatha* on a table where Adienna had spread out the food... bread, fruit and cheese, folded his arms, looked meaningfully at Craig then uttered only three words:

"Dic vere! Veritas![17]*"*

*****

Still holding the automatic weapon that had killed his friend, Alex Laidlaw took the prisoner down to a 'cell'... a room with a bench, a lock and no window. By then, Don O'Brian, wracked with remorse, would have done anything the other sergeant told him to do. If were ordered to tie weights to his shoes and jump into the River Teviot, he'd have obeyed. Alex felt almost sorry for the man, but there was no space in his heart for sentimentality. It had turned to stone. Nevertheless, before contacting Jamie and taking his wife and children back home, he was determined to revisit another room, originally a sort of storeroom.

Alex stared in horror. In the room—or 'lounge' as 'they'

---

[17] Tell me the truth!

preferred to call it, and from which he had escaped only hours earlier—men and women sat in silence on benches. Some he knew, but their blank faces told him they had no idea who he was. Nor, indeed, about anything. *Bloody zombies!* On the wall was a large head and shoulders photo of the monarch. This most certainly had not been there before. Nor the large Westminster Government propaganda poster bearing an image of the prime minister on a bicycle sporting that familiar crocodile smile with a caption:

OUR BELOVED WESTMINSTER GOVERNMENT WILL PROTECT YOU!

"Is there anyone here who can tell me anything? Where are the bastards who did this to you? The bastards who scrambled your brains!"

Empty eyes followed Alex as he approached the nearest man.

"Your name?" he asked. "I'm the police."

"Kev," came the reply. "Kev Crombie."

"You frae Hawick?"

Silence.

Alex noticed they all had greasy blobs on their hair, or, for the hairless, their bald pates. He recalled one of the so-called police officers squeezing jelly from a tube onto the heads of others in the room before he made a run for it.

"Where *are* they? The arseholes who did this."

Zero response.

Alex took out his mobile and keyed in Jamie's number.

*****

Jamie was about to kick open the door of the hut when his mobile rang.

"Could be Hannah," whispered Dylan. "If so, I think I should—"

"Shhh! It's Alex. Our sergeant," replied Jamie, raising his hand... a sign for Dylan to stay quiet. "Thank God!" he exclaimed, throwing a glance at Dylan. "They've been found?" he questioned. "In Hawick?" Craig's friend fizzed with excitement. Jamie covered the phone.

"Quiet!" he cautioned again. "Not Hannah and Craig! Alex's wife and daughters."

"But what about Ha—?"

"Shut up!"

Over the next few minutes, Jamie explained everything over the phone to Alex. How Jonny had been pronounced dead on arrival at the Borders General Hospital, how Ellen, Hannah and Craig had gone missing "together with 'the boy'", as he still insisted on calling Breth. He suspected they might be held captive in the SSS camp at the old Trimontium site and told his police sergeant friend, "We have the place surrounded. Was about to go on in when you rang me."

"Wait!" warned Alex. "Dinnae do anything stupid. For God's sake dinnae get yourself killed too. How d'you know they're in there, anyway?"

"Just do!" replied Jamie.

"Wait for me. I'm the law. Remember?"

Jamie smiled to himself to think that the law of Scotland as they knew it was now in the hands of one lowly rural police sergeant.

"Okay," agreed Jamie. "There's no sound coming from inside this hut anyway. Could even be empty. But there's a light on."

*****

Veritas was one of the few Latin words that Craig did recognize—truth—but with what had been happening over the previous few weeks, he failed to understand it. In any language. The only truth he could get his head around was that he cared. Cared about his mother, his sister, her new husband (*Hannah married? Now that cannot be true!*) and even the Roman commander called Domitius and his legionaries. He cared about what was happening to the old Trimontium site back (*or forwards?*) in the twenty-first century, and about what was happening to Scotland, to Britain and to the world. He cared about Dylan. But was there *truth* in any of it?

He pointed to Hannah, seemingly here known as 'Adienna'.

"Veritas!" he said, meaning she was the reason he was there. Nothing to do with the gods, as far as he was concerned. Only love for his little sister. Love that so many felt. Domitius glanced at Adienna, grinned, nodded, fetched a *sella*[18] and sat beside Craig.

He curled a finger at Breth, a sign for the Selgovan boy to sit beside them and translate.

"Surely her goddess sent you?" he asked.

Through Breth, Craig replied, "A deer. That deer," pointing again to Adienna.

Breth translated, then told Craig and the commander about Flidais, the Celtic deer goddess, and how she would always wish to help Aine. Domitius was correct, he pointed out. It was the gods who had brought him to the Fire Hills, and all four of them back to Trimontium. Craig shook his head. He suggested it was his anger. Breth laughed.

"Ira?" the Selgovan boy said.

"Ira?" questioned the commander. Then he made Craig an offer. It was long and complex and involved many tricky translational pathways being traversed between Breth and Adienna, and Breth and Craig, then back to Breth and Domitius, but when the message finally got through to the Melrose boy his eyes lit up. There was, however, one problem:

What about Dad back home?

*****

Some had brought sleeping bags and others, provisions. As Jamie and Dylan waited for the sergeant to appear, the expanding 'camp' outside the new SSS site at Newstead

---

[18] chair

began to look more like a haven for refugees from somewhere in the Middle East, only peopled by Scottish Borderers. Dylan had gone up in Jamie's estimation by leaps and bounds. The boy's rival in love, the so-called Selgovan who claimed to have lived in an ancient Celtic fort on the northernmost Eildon Hill, had no hiding place in the man's brain. Not if he had anything to do with his daughter's disappearance. Having retreated to the crime scene tape until the police—viz Sergeant Alex Laidlaw—arrived, he sat on the ground, beside Dylan, and started to talk. Or, more accurately, ramble.

XVII

"You what?"

Ellen Stevens' eyes nearly popped out of her head as she, her two children and Breth sat together, a while later, after Craig returned from a tour of Trimontium with the old commander.

"I have to, Mum. Don't you see? I've just killed a man," replied Craig.

"No, a monster!" insisted Adienna.

"Still a man. Look, I know my Roman history, Sis, and now I'm a part of it. Plus I ken what happened to Commodus. Or *must* happen. These guys don't. And *he's* the real monster."

"Don't," said Ellen. "Your father—"

"Dad might be proud of me. For once. Help him accept me as I am."

"We'll talk when we get back, Craig," suggested his mother.

"I've made up my mind, Mum. They need us here."

"Us?"

"Christians. The Polish Catholic of my grandpa is still inside me. Somewhere. In Dad too, if only he'd let that particular gene do its job."

"Also in my Irish grandparents' genes," added Ellen.

"Craig'll come back, Mum," Adienna reassured her mother after a period of silence. "Flidais will see to it. There's Irish in all of us. Like her."

"Who?"

"The deer goddess. Flidais. Irish Celtic. My other granny came from Ireland as well."

"Other granny? Oh, if only I could laugh off this whole business and be back home with your dad, but—"

"Believe in me. And in Craig."

"I do, sweetheart, but how do we get back home? All

three of us."

Adienna looked keenly at her mother.

"Four," she corrected. "Don't forget Breth."

"Four then. How?"

Ellen Stevens looked at her daughter, saw Flidais and got her answer.

"Three, not four," observed Craig. "Not yet anyway. And Breth's not staying here. Look, I've already arranged things with Domitius. The commander and I will travel to Roma. As Christians. Got it all worked out. And I know what I have to do. I will be okay, Mum. I'll help make history that hasn't yet happened, here and now, come true. I promise."

"What do I tell your dad?"

"Tell him... no, *just say* that what I'm doing back here might help Scotland of the future. If he asks. Who knows what could happen if their emperor doesn't get strangled? And something's telling me I must play a part in that. The whole of history could change if I don't. The butterfly effect."

"The what?"

"Never mind! First, I think Breth will want to take Hannah—or rather, Adienna—to his place on the top of the Eildons. What's left of it. Their gods are important to them."

"And afterwards?" Ellen could hardly make out her son's features through her tears. Adienna comforted her mum with a hug.

"Flidais will look after him," she reassured. "And he'll take the Eurostar back from Rome, won't you, Craig?"

"Too expensive," joked Craig. His mother laughed and cried like never before.

*****

Ellen Stevens had to believe in her daughter.

Later, after the feast (*would've preferred a Chinese takeaway,* thought Ellen) to thank the gods for their victory over the despot sent by Commodus to terrorize the Celts, Adienna, together with Breth, took her mother back up the northernmost Fire Hill to the Selgovan village. There was nothing habitable left. The boy knelt and said prayers to gods whose names were mere meaningless words for his new mother-in-law. On their way back down, Breth and Adienna stopped at the hollow out of which Ellen had entered this alien world of the past. No deer, no orange glow. Just a hollow in the ground over which two 'children', now married, had placed branches and bracken fronds to contain their love.

"How are we—?" Ellen began but got no further with her question. Instead, a shriek from Adienna exploded in her ears...

"Dad!" she yelled.

Before Ellen could ask what was going on, her daughter took off down the hill towards Trimontium, followed by Breth.

"What now?!" she exclaimed. Then she saw the answer. Down by the river, where Trimontium should have been everything was aglow. Not on fire, but an intense orange light, the same orange as the deer who had led her back in time to where she now stood.

The Trimontium site in the twenty-first century? Turned into a military camp? The SFS and...

"Dad? Jamie? Oh, my God, no!"

She ran to catch up; ran faster than at any time since her childhood; ran to save Jamie...

*****

It began to rain. Pinpoint spots cooled his forehead and hands before turning into a drenching downpour.

"Curses!" muttered Jamie who, seated on the ground, had been boring the pants off Dylan with his frustration over Hannah's poor performance at school since being labelled with ME, and her ridiculous notion that she might become a writer. Dylan already knew from Craig that *he* had been the focus of amorous interest in the girl's budding novel. His mind was elsewhere whilst Hannah's father jabbered on. She would—no, she *had* to—lose interest in that red-haired freak.

Jamie stopped and looked at his son's friend, aware that the boy hadn't taken in anything he'd said.

"Look, just get yourself home, lad. Cannae have you catching pneumonia on my account. Your mum'll be going berserk with worry. Dunno what came over me."

Dylan, still clutching the gun, pulled his top down over his bent-up knees and shook his head.

"I'm not a kid. Whatever happens, I want Hannah to know I've got guts."

"You'll need more than just guts when their troops appear."

"Have you read it?"

"What?"

"Hannah's novel. Craig told me that—"

"She'd never show it to me," Jamie chuckled. "If, indeed, there is one!"

Dylan went quiet.

If there is one? All a sham? Na! Cannae believe this bastard sitting beside me. Hannah's mine. Always was and always will be! And her novel will prove this.

Jamie broke the silence by going on about how he wished Hannah would, like Craig, focus on her schoolwork, and how Craig should think about getting a girlfriend, like other lads of his age, and that what everyone was saying about the boy with red hair made no sense. On hearing a grumble of heavy vehicles approach from the direction of the Melrose bypass, he stopped mid-sentence.

"The bloody army!" someone shouted. Another screamed. Everyone hurriedly scrambled to their feet, scattering in all directions. Jamie sprang upright and helped Dylan up. Sure enough, a row of heavy, khaki, army vehicles, headlights full beam, groaned slowly towards them from out of the gloom. The engine noise ceased. In the drenching downpour, and in the dark, it was difficult to make out what exactly was happening in the scurry of activity. Jamie had to hold his arm up against the glare when a searchlight suddenly turned everything incandescent.

"You're not here," he told Dylan. "Run behind the huts. And get rid of your gun."

But the lad remained where he stood. The door of the hut that they had been about to enter opened. Out stepped a man in army flak holding a semi-automatic, followed by another and another. Soon, what had seemed a vast horde of SFS supporters had become a pathetic huddle of men and women of all ages, teenage upwards, totally surrounded and terrified out of their minds.

One of the soldiers, grey-haired, without a beret, holding only a handgun, approached Jamie and Dylan, unaware that these two were the cause of the whole annoying affair.

"I'll deal with this," whispered Jamie.

"No," replied Dylan, turning to face his friend's dad. He held his gun up against Jamie's chest. "I will. Drop it!" he said, indicating Jamie's weapon.

*****

"Bloody rain!" cursed Alex, switching on the windscreen wipers.

"Alex! No swearing, please. Not in front of the girls."

"My teacher swore once," announced Erin. "When she stapled her finger in class."

"Stapled her finger?" queried Caitlin. "Why did she do that?"

The younger girl shrugged her shoulders.

"Dunno! Daddy, can you see that funny light?" she asked.

Alex Laidlaw did, indeed, see it. A mysterious orange glow hovering over the land, in the direction of Melrose.

"What is it?" asked the elder daughter.

"Looks like a fire," replied her father.

The car shot forwards after Alex slammed the accelerator. Caitlin giggled.

"It's not a fire," announced Erin. "It's a goddess."

"Don't be so stupid!" rebuked her sister. "It's a fire. Might be our house.

"Or Jamie's," added Alex.

"Those nasty people could have started it," said Caitlin.

"I know it's not a fire! It's a goddess," insisted Erin.

"Oh, please take care," Fiona begged her husband when centrifugal force swung her sideways as the car curved a bend at speed.

"Jamie's in trouble, whatever's causing that strange light. I know it. We all are."

Erin began to cry.

"Why won't anyone believe me? It's a goddess. It really is."

Alex had to agree that the orange colour was wrong for a fire. But a goddess? He did not even believe in God, let alone goddesses.

*****

That same evening, Craig headed south from Trimontium in the company of Domitius, Marcus and the three Roman legionaries, guided through the forest by their Votadini friends. The commander reckoned open roads might still be dangerous. Craig had no qualms about having made the right decision and removal of the gruesome spiked heads decorating the fort's entrance seemed to make his departure easier. As did killing the man responsible for that gory display, for he knew his penance was to spread the Christian Gospel plus ensure that things changed forever in the Scottish Borders, and not only AD 180. What might happen if Commodus were to live on beyond AD 192? His Christian duty, he felt, was to help rid the planet of that monster. Denying himself self-pity over Dylan, he had agreed to Domitius's suggestion: that Hannah and Breth should return, with his mother, to the 'land of the gods', as twenty-first century Scotland had become enshrined in the mind of the old commander, whilst Craig, who seemed to know so much about the new religion that often occupied the

Roman's mind, would help rid Imperial Rome of the evil tyrant Commodus. The boy who appeared from nowhere, dressed as a legionary, even seemed to know how this would happen: strangulation.

Craig was relieved that those ghoulish heads had not been replaced with the severed head of that other, hated, commander whom he had shot with the Glock 17. The Selgovan giant, renamed Bikkus by Octavius, had wanted to take the head back to his village as a trophy, but Domitius insisted they bury it within the fort as a gift to Mars. This way, the torment of Octavius's failure would follow him into the afterlife even when Trimontium had been totally abandoned, as surely it soon would be. Meanwhile, Lucius, it was decided, would stay on to oversee the gradual dismantling of the Roman settlement, starting, ironically, with the construction of an observation station in the ruined Selgovan fort atop the northernmost of the three hills.

As for Breth's dad, Gorsedd, he had always known there was something special about Adienna. He now believed, without reservation, she was in allegiance with one of the gods or goddesses. But the deer? He knew of no god in Selgovan legends that fitted the description of a deer with blue eyes that emitted a strange orange glow. Alun went quiet when pressed about this. Did he know something about his daughter which he wished to keep secret? Or about her dead mother's ancestors?

*****

"I don't like this," muttered Alex slowing down as he drove out of Melrose through Newstead on the way to Trimontium. He knew the road at the far end on the village was blocked for maintenance works. He also knew there was no 'maintenance' going on. Only army trucks going back and forth off the by-pass.

"Stay with the girls, Fiona. I'm going through."

Erin was in tears.

"It's a goddess, it's a goddess, it's a goddess!" she

persisted. “I keep telling you, Mummy. You’re half-Irish too. So, you should know.”

Alex got out of the car, then, holding on to the door, peered in at the younger girl.

“I do believe you, sweetheart,” he whispered. “Because of the silence.”

True. Apart from the sound of the rain, it seemed eerily quiet beyond the end of the village from where that strange glow emanated. No crackle of fire.

“My jacket, please, Caitlin. On the floor there, under your feet.”

The elder daughter handed her father his bullet-proof police jacket, then hugged Erin close. Their mother remained speechless as she watched Alex swagger, like the police officer he was, and always would be, around the corner and down the hill towards the eerie light.

It was only after, in a burst of engine noise, a fleet of army trucks trundled passed the sergeant, away from the SSS camp, in a hurry, that he suddenly realized how right wee Erin was...

XVIII

"Ranjit, how good to see you. And your lovely wife, Radha." Professor Leckie kissed the Indian woman's cheek, then that of her post-grad student. "And what a beautiful daughter you have." The little girl beamed up at her. "Celandine, isn't it?" She reached down and stroked the child's sleek black hair. "Oh, what lovely hair. Wish mine was like yours." She looked at Ranjit. "Celandine doesn't sound very Indian," she added.

"Oh, it isn't!" the girl said. "It's a flower. Yellow. When she was pregnant with me, Mummy saw some in a wood down in the Borders. That's when she decided to call me that. And I'm going to marry a man with yellow hair, see!"

"Are you now? Not this evening, I hope."

"No. When I'm grown up."

"Oh, don't grow up too quickly. Being grown up gives a woman so many headaches."

"You could take pills for them!"

Angela Leckie laughed. She led the Indian family into the sitting room.

"My husband does the cooking when we have guests. Doesn't have much confidence in my ability to avoid culinary disasters."

Later, after one of the best meals Ranjit and Radha had had during their five years in Scotland, one which had wee Celandine squealing with delight at everything she tasted, and asking if Jimmy Leckie could cook for them too, Angela suggested, on their return to the sitting room, that Ranjit should sit next to her whilst her husband practised his magic tricks for the child.

"Oh please. I love magic!" begged Celandine.

"Me too!" exclaimed Jimmy, making the girl giggle by widening his eyes till they almost popped out.

"So, Doctor Postgrad, what more do you have to say

about the skull with a bullet lodged in it?" Angela asked Ranjit.

"Indeed, very puzzling. But I'm thinking we have to leave the biology of this behind! Enter the realms of non-biology."

"Non-biology? I love it, Ranjit. I just knew you were someone rather special when I agreed to take you on as a post-grad student. Explain!"

Ranjit glanced anxiously at his wife, as if to first seek her approval, but already Jimmy Leckie had the young Indian woman distracted, and their little daughter enthralled, with disappearing and reappearing eggs.

"Erwin Schrödinger," the doctor said, as if this explained everything.

"Yes. I've heard of him, but physics has never really been my thing. He was the cat man, wasn't he?"

"No, this is very much not about cats."

"Good. We don't get on, me and cats."

"His cat was only to show you can't transfer literally what happens inside atoms to the real world."

"Which includes cats."

"Very much includes cats!"

"So, where does he fit in? That Schrödinger fellow."

"Where Einstein doesn't. This is very much the point."

"You've lost me, Ranjit. What on earth has all this got to do with an ancient skull with a bullet in it."

"The skull and the bullet we know are not possible. And neither is their non-existence."

"Non-existence? Doesn't sound very scientific, Ranjit."

"Mr Schrödinger was telling the world that the impossible exists, but we don't even know what existence means. I'm thinking the skull with the bullet could be explained by entanglement. Non-biologically."

"Now you've really got me!"

"When subatomic particles are entangled, they behave as being linked together. Like at the very same time.

Wherever they are in the universe."

"We're not talking the same time. We're talking two thousand years apart."

"Precisely! So now we must ask Mr Einstein. Space-time continuum. Entangled in space, time becomes immaterial."

"You mean...?" She paused whilst turning over in her mind what Ranjit had just said. "Brilliant!" she shrieked.

"Yes!" agreed an excited Celandine. "He just magicked an egg from behind my ear. Can you magic a rabbit, Mr Leckie? I so love rabbits!"

"Rabbits are all right," agreed Angela. "But cats aren't. So, Doctor Postgrad, you're telling me either the Glock 17 bullet is entangled with an ancient Roman bullet, or...?"

"Yes, Madam Professor. Very much 'or'. The murderer."

"Magic a murderer, Daddy? No! I prefer rabbits. Please, Mr Leckie."

"Now who on earth could refuse such a request coming from a girl called Celandine?" Angela asked of her husband. "A rabbit, Jimmy. After all, her Daddy's just solved an impossible conundrum. Surely you can magic a rabbit for wee Celandine!"

"Please," begged Celandine.

The Indian doctor's deep-set eyes, staring at nothing in particular, lit up. It was as if an unseen celestial hand had flicked a switch and turned on something; something behind those eyes and beyond Life itself.

"Magic!" he announced.

"Yes, Daddy!" agreed his excited daughter.

"It doesn't exist because..." He paused as an impish humour danced on his face. Celandine frowned. "Because it's true! But we call it by another name."

"Which is?" asked Angela.

"Science!"

"Oh Daddy!" The girl now targeted her frown at Jimmy Leckie. "He can be so annoying, you know!"

"Can he really? So, Celandine, how do magicked rabbits

usually appear?"

"Out of hats!" the child replied, offering her father a daughterly pout.

"But I do not have a hat," said the professor's husband. Celandine's pout was now directed at the table. She folded her wee arms and her frown darkened. "But I do have a chair!" A grin broke through the girl's pout as Jimmy Leckie reached down under his chair. Moments later, held in the magician's hands, a large white flop-eared rabbit was staring at the little Indian girl, its twitching pink nose savouring the childish scent of, quite possibly, its new owner.

"A rabbit!" shrieked the girl. "See Daddy! I just knew magic existed. It made this rabbit!"

"Which proves my point, sweetheart. Billions of years of evolution also made that rabbit. So, science and magic are the same."

Celandine's large brown eyes, still moist, sparkled at Jimmy the magician.

"Can I keep the rabbit, please?"

Ranjit winked at his professor.

"Only if you treat him well," replied Jimmy.

"Oh, I will, I will!"

The girl gently took the rabbit from her host, placed it on her lap and began to stroke it.

"I'll call him Jimmy!" she said, grinning up at Jimmy Leckie.

"So, Doctor Postgrad..."

Professor Angela Leckie leaned forwards, fixing her brilliant student with grey eyes that had seen so much that could not be explained during their fifty-eight years on Planet Earth. "It's not the bullet that was entangled, as you say, but the murderer. Like a time-ghost, he appears to do his dastardly deed, then vanishes without a trace. Nothing for forensics to sink their teeth into. Such behaviour makes our work doubly difficult, do you not agree, Dr Postgrad?"

"Very much I agree, Madam Professor!"

*****

After several weeks of journeying in a strange world, for which no erudite history book or historical fiction novel could have prepared him, Craig stood with his companions, a small band of cloaked men on a hill overlooking the Tiber plain. There, spread out like a museum display, was ancient Rome. Imperial Rome. The city whose power affected every human from North Africa to the Scottish Highlands, and yet the largest building it had to offer, the Colosseum, was barely visible. This brick and stone many-times-great-granddaughter of Romulus and Remus looked so small and frail, but the boy from Melrose knew that the evil lurking within the Servian Wall that encircled ancient Rome was greater than anything his dad back home would have to face in the SSS camp they were building near Melrose, in the future, and where Trimontium now stood. The internet had informed him of this.

Domitius came over to Craig, saw fear in his eyes and placed a comforting arm across his shoulders.

"You, a servant of Mercury, should feel no fear. Mars is with us."

It was strange how quickly Latin had replaced English in the boy's brain. He had understood every word as he turned to face the old Commander.

"Credo in unum deum," responded Craig.

"Yes, yes. This thing the Christians talk about. And the second coming of their 'Lord' whom we Romans crucified. You truly believe this?"

Craig did not know what to believe beyond that he had a destiny to fulfil. To help rid that ancient world of an evil tyrant called Commodus.

"First," announced Domitius, "we must take you to the emperor. For his praise. Remember, to say that you are the one sent, through Mercury, by Mars, to defeat, with his magic finger, the rebel Celts who had killed Octavius. The *veritas* remains our secret. Together we shall head a triumph through the city. As a result, you might gain access to the Imperial household."

"Triumph?" Craig felt far from triumphant.

"No doubt the emperor will reward you. With a *puella pulchra*. One he's grown tired of." Craig shook his head.

How can I hide the truth?

"That *puella* will be someone's sister," he replied. "I can't. My God wouldn't allow it."

"Well... just as long as you raise no suspicions as to what your true intention is," responded Domitius. "Come. We mustn't dally. Have to meet up with my old soldier friend, Publius. Old, but a lot younger than me. You see, we go back a long way in Germania."

With cloaks wrapped around their tunics, they headed off down the hill towards a city where, in the twentieth century, European countries once got together to sign a treaty in an attempt to stop senseless wars that not only killed millions but had the potential to destroy human civilization.

"One of his mistresses, Marcia, tries to do it..." began Craig, pausing as he tried to recall details about what he'd read concerning the demise of Emperor Commodus.

Domitius halted and looked at the Melrose lad.

"Do what?" he asked.

"The right thing. Kill him. When Rome cannot take any more. Calling your city 'Commodiana', claiming to be the God Hercules, son of Jupiter. The bastard flips. Completely. Marcia tries, but the poison doesn't work. They have to get a wrestler to strangle him in the end.

"Soon, I hope. Publius will—"

"Not for twelve years, I'm afraid," interrupted Craig.

"The gods tell you this? I mean, your single Christian God."

"History books," the boy replied. "And the internet..." he added in English. *Internet? Here? he wondered looking down at ancient Rome. "Sanctus Internetus.*" He explained.

"We Christians have saints, not multiple gods and goddesses. Saint Internet can tell us many things. Look, I have to make sure it happens. And you must protect me."

They continued on down the hill to a hopefully known future in what was, for Craig, a totally unknown past.

"Tell me more about your sister, Adienna. I always knew there was something very special about that girl. I've known her since she was little."

In perfect Latin, and grinning, Craig told his new friend how delightfully cheeky she had been as a child, how sensitive she had become, and, yes, how special she had *always* been.

"I don't think Dad truly understands her," he added.

"Alun?"

"Her other dad. Always going on at her. It got on my nerves."

"Breth will take care of her."

"He'd better!" Craig's mind flashed back to that pub in Melrose, to the skirmish with Dylan and his bullies outside. He nodded. *He will,* reassured his brain.

Of course, Craig made no mention of Dylan. Why should he?

Because I love him, was the answer. *That's why I'm bloody here. Couldn't kill Dylan. Cannae go back to Melrose. But here, in ancient Rome, when we Christians are being persecuted, I can help spread the 'Word'. And make sure the devil lurking in Commodus is destroyed.*

*****

The first explosion of orange light was so blinding that Dylan had to cover his eyes. Jamie knew the safety lock was still on and saw his chance. Pushing the boy into the soldier holding a handgun, the two collided, slipped in the mud and both ended up in a struggling heap. All were too concerned about the mysterious glow to stop Jamie from hotfooting it behind the huts and down the bank towards the river. If he were to swim to the other side during the chaos, there was a chance he might escape. But he tripped on an exposed root, banged his head on a stone as he fell and when he came too, he was underwater, his foot trapped by an overhanging branch, struggling to reverse the 'up' and the 'down' whilst desperately suppressing the urge to cough for water had already found its way into his lungs. His arms and his free leg frantically sought something solid but seemed trapped in a watery hell. Above, through the dark swirl patterned by rain, he glimpsed movement. As he hovered between the consciousness of life and the blankness that awaits all of us beyond death, a shadow plunged down into the water. Limp and almost lifeless, he felt himself lifted by an unseen force, unseen because everything was black. Then... air and a strange, rhythmic rasping noise... himself... somewhere in his throat.

"Dad?"

A voice from heaven?

XIX

Ranjit Desai, carrying a hutch, paused on the doorstep as they were leaving. Wee Celandine lovingly hugged the large white rabbit which she had refused to let go of until they were in the car.

"Madam Professor, do you remember telling me about a rumour concerning a curious orange light appearing in the Borders after they found the skull."

"I do indeed, Doctor Postgrad. And we wondered why there was no mention of it on the news."

"The same night as the protests in Hawick."

"Of which there has been no further mention."

"Cover up?"

"Dr Desai, you are surely not implying a connection between our beloved Westminster government and the disappeareds?"

The hutch rose up and down as the Indian doctor shrugged his shoulders.

"Careful, Daddy," said Celandine. "That's Jimmy's home!"

"No, sweetie, our home is Jimmy's home from now on. He'll be a house rabbit. As for the disappeareds, Professor, perhaps we shall never know. But that orange light? Could very much be our old friend Erwin Schrödinger again."

"What orange light, Daddy? I do like orange as well as yellow, you know."

Ranjit nodded his head as if something had just occurred to him.

"Tomorrow, Madam Professor. Tomorrow we will very much be talking about orange lights."

"Yes, I do believe we will," his boss agreed.

Celandine was too busy stroking her rabbit to notice the wink that the professor gave her father.

*****

Things became clearer...

First, he was alive. The rasping noise coming from his larynx, as he fought to get air into his lungs, told him this. Second, he had been rescued. 'The boy' they called Breth, his rescuer, was peering down at him. Then the voice of his daughter,

"Are you all right, Dad?"

How wonderful to again hear Hannah's voice. Gasping like a frog turned inside out, he held on to the strong young arm that had pulled him free from that liquid trap, and he sobbed and croaked at the same time,

"Is... Mum... okay?"

"She's fine, Dad. Here with us. But first we'd better turn you over. Get the water out of your lungs."

Lying face down on the riverbank, chewing on mouthfuls of earth, Jamie coughed, spluttered, gasped and wept, feeling more alive by the second. He felt an arm across his shoulders, then saw a face, Ellen's, as she knelt beside him and stroked his hair.

"You silly, silly boy!" she scolded. "What *have* I been trying to tell you about this SFS business?"

She turned him around and helped him to sit up. Above them stood Hannah in the purple dress Jamie had bought for her on turning sixteen, and beside her stood 'the boy', his arms dripping.

"So, it was you who saved me?" Jamie said to Breth.

"No. It was Flidais."

"And who the heck is Flidais?"

Breth turned and pointed to the orange glow above, beyond the bank.

"You'll not believe me if I tell you the truth, Dad. But just now we must all get the hell out of here. We'll help you along the bank till we reach Melrose. Can't have you falling in the water again."

"What about Dylan?"

Hannah looked at her mother, as if to ask who should

tell her father the truth.

"He's dead," said Ellen. "You shot him. At least, that's what they're saying up there, though it's difficult to get much sense from anyone. That light's driven everyone crazy."

"It's a lie. For God's sake, it was Dylan who was about to shoot me. Before that Flidais thing happened. The orange light."

"I knew they got it wrong." Jamie saw relief in his wife's face. "You, Jamie Stevens, couldn't even harm a flea."

"What about the army? Special forces or whatever? Dylan was with them after all, I'm sure of it."

"Not so sure of anything, myself," said Ellen. "We found him just before he died. He said he was trying to protect you. Wanted you to give yourself up rather than get yourself shot by them. Those were his last words. Guess we'll never really know what happened."

"And those bloody soldiers?"

"They left. Terrified of the orange light. Of Flidais. But we can't take any chances. Better stay beside the river. Can you stand?"

Breth stepped forward.

"I help," he insisted.

The Selgovan boy supported his new father-in-law as they made their way up the steep bank.

"Thank you, Breth. So, it was you who saved my life."

Ellen laughed.

"Finally, you admit he's got a name!"

She wanted to explain their new relationship with the boy they had only known for a few weeks, that of parents-in-law, but now was clearly not the right time. Nevertheless, she reckoned this was one step forward for the stubborn man whom she loved to distraction.

Hannah's marriage was one thing, but how on earth was she going to explain to Jamie about Craig, now on his way to ancient Rome as an early Christian.

Back in Melrose, as they headed for home, with Ellen

supporting Jamie, a police car pulled up beside them. Alex stepped out. For a while, the two men simply stared at each other.

"Fiona? And the girls?" Jamie finally asked.

"All fine. In the car. But *you*, Jamie? You look bloody awful. What the hell happened? Did those bastards—?"

"No, they didn't. I fell in the river."

"You what?"

"Trying to escape as soon as that orange light..."

But the eerie light was gone. Like the soldiers. Everything seemed to have returned to normal, whatever 'normal' was.

"Will you join us, Alex? At our place?"

"Looks like you could do with a lift, Jamie. Get in the back of the car with the girls."

In the car, wee Erin told Jamie about the goddess responsible for the orange glow.

"She's Irish, you know," the child informed him.

"Don't be silly," retorted Caitlin. "What do you know about gods and goddesses anyway?"

"A lot. We did them in class. Our teacher's Irish if you must know! She told us about Flidais. We did Irish mythology. She said she's like Earth Mother. Protects nature and everything. And she's very beautiful and rides a charry thingy—"

"Chariot?" suggested Jamie.

"Mmm! Pulled by a deer. But sometimes she looks like a deer herself."

"How do you know that strange orange light was—?"

"Just do!" affirmed Erin, glancing at her sister with an expression that discouraged the older girl from offering any further opinion on the matter.

Later, back home, it felt safer for Alex and his family to stay with them until things became clearer. The Laidlaw girls were bursting with excitement, and, unaware of who Breth was, or where he came from, immediately took to 'the boy' and showered him with all sorts of questions, including, from Erin,

"Did Flidais bring you here?"

Breth smiled, looked at Hannah then nodded.

"So... I can hug you then!" the child announced, and she did.

*****

Breth shared a bed with his new bride. And 'it' took place. The following day, with their marriage consummated, as should have happened on the Fire Hills nearly two thousand years before, each felt strong and reborn into a strange new world.

Yes, a new world. Ellen, Jamie, Alex and Fiona sat around the kitchen table the following morning, each with their hands around a mug of coffee, all fearing the news after Ellen switched on the radio. None could believe what the newscaster said...

"Plans to develop the site of the ancient Roman fort of Trimontium, near Melrose, in the Borders, have been put on hold after peaceful demonstrations outside the police headquarters in Hawick last night. A Scottish Government spokeswoman said that it was agreed, in the early hours today, that the site, where a skull was unearthed, is of overwhelming archaeological importance and that the Westminster government acknowledged public concern, although denied the so-called 'disappearances' had anything to do with the proposed development as rumoured.

And now, the weather. Storm Saoirse, which hit Scotland last night, after crossing the Irish Sea, has moved away eastwards, and today we can expect glorious sunshine everywhere."

"The bastards!" exclaimed Alex. "No mention of poor Jonny. How can they just hide the truth without any qualms whatsoever?"

"What about Craig?" asked Jamie. "I really couldn't make sense of what you told me, Ellen, before I drifted off last night. Gone to Rome, you said?"

Ellen looked from Jamie to Alex to Fiona. Three pairs of eyes remained fixed on her. As she tried to work out how to break the truth to her husband, she listened to squeals of excitement coming from Caitlin and Erin in the living room. Everything seemed so normal. Somehow, she knew she would be seeing Craig again, and that this would be soon. How she knew this, she had no idea. Meanwhile, what should she say to her husband?

"History."

"History?" queried Jamie.

"Like I said. History."

"I do ken what history is, Ellen, but what's this got to do with our son going to Rome. Another Treaty of Rome? If only! I never wanted us to leave Europe, anyhow. Not with Polish genes in me."

"Perhaps..." Ellen twirled a spoon in her coffee mug and stared at the mini whirlpool she created. Nothing compared with the whirl of thoughts in her head. "Perhaps we should ask Breth and Hannah. They're awake. I heard them."

"This marriage thing?" asked Alex. "I really don't understand—" he began.

"The lad saved my life," interrupted Jamie, as though this explained everything.

"We're going to the registry office today," explained Ellen. "To book an appointment."

Jamie looked at Ellen, then at Alex and Fiona. On the face of each hovered the unspoken word... *pregnant*. Before the word could pop out of anyone's mouth, the doorbell rang.

*****

Hannah and Breth were in no hurry to get up that morning. The girl lost count of the number of times she had been entered by her husband during the night, each more blissful than the previous. She truly felt like a goddess. As she lay sideways with Breth's gentle fingers tracing the outline of a deer on her back, she giggled. Two lives, merged into one. Two sets of memories, but clearly distinguishable, not jumbled. She turned around to face Breth.

"I was writing a novel," she said. "Before I met you."

"Novel?" The word registered nothing in the Celtic lad's mind.

"A story. Like..." Hannah tried to think of a piece of writing that someone from AD 180 might know about. "Erm... like *The Odyssey?*"

Breth's eyes informed her that he hadn't a clue what she was on about.

"Perhaps not! Never mind. I was creating a world with words. Written down. And things were happening. I was there, see, but as someone else. Facing demons within me. Because of what was happening at school. Being bullied and that."

"Bullied? Dylan?"

"That's just it. I thought I loved Dylan. And in my novel, he was going to rescue me. But I couldn't have been more wrong. As for all that fantasy stuff—"

"Fantasy?"

Breth stroked his wife's face, she took hold of his hand and kissed it. Several times.

"Nothing is more fantastic than the truth, Breth. So now..." She paused.

"Now?"

Hannah laughed.

"Make love to me again, husband!"

As Breth drew Hannah close, the doorbell rang. The girl sprang up.

"It can't be!"

"What?"

"At the front door. Already?" Hannah leapt out of bed and ran to put on her dressing gown.

XX

"How's Jimmy today?" Angela Leckie asked her post-grad student the following morning. He appeared bleary-eyed and a little puzzled by the question.

"I believe, Madam Professor, that you will be knowing better than me how your most esteemed husband is," he replied.

The professor laughed.

"The rabbit, Ranjit, the rabbit! Has he taken to his new home? Seemed he and Celandine were getting along very well together last night."

"They are like peas in a pod. But that got me thinking. All night."

"No wonder you look like death warmed up."

"That's it, Madam Professor. How can death even exist?"

"What?"

"Lavoisier. 1785. The Law of Conservation of Mass. This I very much believe."

"Stood the test of time, I'll grant you."

"Death, we know, happens when life leaves living matter. Which has mass. But we cannot define life in absolute terms. So how can we define death? If we cannot, how do we know it exists?"

"What's this got to do with death and that skull with a bullet in it?"

"Like death, time may not exist as something we can define."

"Ranjit, I, too, am tired. Please get to the point."

"Our killer is alive. Somewhere."

"Hmm. And his victim is nearly two thousand years old?"

"Precisely. But..." He performed his intriguing little head wobble that always made her want to laugh. Sometimes she would practice doing this herself in front of a mirror and could not get it right. Nor could her magician husband, Jimmy. "But I am thinking that those in government who are telling us so many lies do not need to know the killer's whereabouts. Not if the victim is old enough to be their sixty-times great grandfather."

"So?"

"Target practice."

"We withhold the truth and say in our report that the ancient skull we've puzzled so much over has been used by the army for target practice?"

"Did we ever seriously consider another possibility, Madam Professor? Anything else, and the skull would have been discovered during the excavations of Trimontium by James Curle."

Angela Leckie shrugged her shoulders.

"I do hope you have plenty of rabbit food for Jimmy. My husband tells me he's a rather hungry rabbit."

"Our kitchen is very much like a vegetable shop."

Another little head wobble sent the professor into fits of laughter.

"By the way," she added. "I just received an e-mail. Seems the Scottish Security Service is to be disbanded."

"That, Madam Professor, is indeed good news. Would you like a coffee?"

*****

On their way through the vineyards and orchards carpeting the Tiber valley, passing farmsteads and clusters of labourers' dwellings, Craig thought how peaceful it was compared with twenty-first century Scotland. Wearing long cloaks that concealed their weapons, the small band of soldiers, including Craig, attracted puzzled looks. Workers downed tools and stared at the young man who wore the ornate helmet of the dead Trimontium commander but was clearly too young to be a military leader of any description. Domitius was to personally present the helmet to Emperor Commodus, who was not much older than Craig, for ridding

Rome's northernmost province of a 'traitor who had colluded with the Celtic natives, even making one of them second-in-command'. Domitius would inform the *Senatus Romanus* that Octavius had cherished plans to set himself up as emperor of those islands of the North. Instead, because of Craig, whom Domitius had renamed Caracigus, 'sired by Mars and a Celtic goddess', the legions of Commodus now remained in control of Britannia, even in the distant desolate valleys of Caledonia. Not strictly true, but the old commander did believe his prayers to Mars had delivered him the God of War's son, Caracigus, for the things the young man came out with were quite remarkable. His abilities, too.

Whilst travelling down through Britannia, Gallia and Italia, Craig received tuition in hand-to-hand fighting, in the art of military warfare and, most importantly, in the use of the *spatha*, a skill for which one of the legionaries displayed exceptional talent. All were amazed at the speed of the boy's learning, his lightning responses, although his attempt to explain, in fluent Latin, that this was due to his passion for a game called 'rugby' only added to their belief in his connection with the immortals. Rugby, such a strange word, was surely a sport of the gods?

Approaching *Roma*, Domitius halted and held up his hand as they passed outcrops of buildings spilling from the city and lining the *Via Salaria* on the approach to the *Porta Fontinalis* through which they would cross the *Murus Servii Tullii*, or Servian Wall, to enter *Roma*. Before crossing the threshold into the city, high-pitched, feminine screams emerged from one of the rickety houses made of wood jumbled outside the city wall. Male laughter alerted the old commander to what was happening inside the humble abode. He turned and beckoned to Craig.

"That'll be some poor woman destined to earn someone a few silver *denarii* if her body pleases the young emperor, unless we do something. She might scream now, but she'll be beyond screaming when forced to share the monster's bed.

Wait here."

Craig, standing apart from the others, watched as Domitius entered the hovel. Abruptly, the laughter and the screaming ceased. Two horror movie ruffians emerged, followed by the commander, his *spatha* drawn, and a girl no older than Hannah. Although gay, the boy knew feminine beauty when he saw it, and, like Hannah, the girl was as perfect as a Botticelli angel. The look of sheer terror on her face made his blood boil.

*****

"It's Craig. I know it is," Hannah told Breth. "Mum'll open the door for him."

"But Craig will be on his way to Rome by now."

"Was. Nearly two thousand years ago. Oh, you men! You know nothing about reality. The deer, Breth! Flidais. Don't you understand?"

"You are my deer."

Hannah returned to the bed. She sat down and took hold of her husband's hands.

"The deer that brought you here. She's called Flidais, but her name really doesn't matter. She's all about love, you see. Like Aine. Connecting us. You and me. Me and Craig. Our parents to both of us. So, you've no reason to feel jealous. Craig has always been special for me. And the other way around. But it's because of you and me that he's doing this thing in Rome. To make sure."

"Make sure?" Breth appeared uncertain.

"Make sure that all of this..." Hannah gesticulated between herself and her husband. "All of this happens. Like a reverse butterfly effect."

"Butterfly?"

Breth looked totally puzzled.

"I'll explain later," said Hannah. She leaned forward, kissed Breth on the lips then got up to leave the bedroom.

*****

"Him?" questioned the larger of the two ruffians,

peering at Craig. "The son of Mars? Aren't all Romans the children of Romulus? It's why we're called Romans. You trick me, old man. I will take this pretty little thing to The Palatine Hill. Her reward, a proper bed in one of Commodus's brothels and the pleasure of his rod of Eros. Mine will be a handful of silver denarii."

"What's the girl's name?" Domitius asked.

The ruffian shrugged his shoulders.

"Lucky Cow, maybe?"

The man's accomplice laughed. Domitius grabbed his tunic and pressed the point of his *spatha* up against his throat. He looked at the girl and asked her name.

"Julia," she replied.

"Julia, the young man over there is the true son of Mars and a goddess of the North. He will defend your honour." Domitius glanced at Craig who tried to conceal his mounting anxiety. "By fighting these two men who would take her, against her will, to become yet another plaything for our debauched new emperor."

The larger ruffian guffawed, slapping his chunky thighs with delight.

"Delighted to oblige," he announced. "And may I keep his helmet when it's over? As a corpse, he'll not need it."

Domitius let go of the smaller man, approached Craig and held out his hand.

"Your *spatha*, Caracigus," he said. "This will be a fair fight. The son of Mars and a Celtic goddess versus two men who shamefully claim to descend from Romulus."

After taking Craig's sword and cloak, Domitius stepped back.

"I know about your Christian story of the man called David and the giant called Goliath," he said. "And you've already shown me what it means to believe in one God. This is where it all begins again for us Romans. Here outside the gate to *Roma*." He nodded, pensively, then told the larger ruffian, built like an ox, to stand in front of Craig.

Craig glanced at the tearful girl called Julia, saw Hannah, and immediately had no fear. He waited.

His opponent, over-confident and furious at the thought of losing that handful of denarii, sprang forward, but Craig was gone in a flash, catching the oaf's foot as he twirled sideways causing the larger man to stumble forwards. Before he could steady himself, Craig trapped his legs in a flying rugby tackle, bringing him down face forwards onto the dust. Moments later, two brawny arms were held back in a full Nelson with Craig's knee pinned into the small of the ruffian's back, not that there was anything particularly small about the Roman. With his free hand, Craig pressed the man's face into the dirt whilst Domitius sauntered over to them.

"Davidus et Goliatus!" he calmly remarked. "And now your friend, huh?"

Neither Craig nor Domitius were too surprised to see the other man take off at a sprint and disappear between ramshackle buildings further up the road, away from the ancient metropolis.

Craig stood up as Domitius helped the ruffian to his feet.

"Next time..." began Domitius, completing the sentence by miming slitting the throat of the Roman oaf who then took off like a terrified rabbit.

The girl, in a state of shock, stood staring with feminine admiration at Craig, as though he were truly immortal. He was reminded of the mini-skirted girls from Earlston High who would whoop and shout and jump about whenever he scored a try. He smiled at her.

"Come over here," Domitius said to Julia.

Slowly, the girl approached, not taking her eyes off the boy from the twenty-first century. Halting a few feet from him, she bowed respectfully.

"I think you can help us," Domitius told her.

XXI

Julia, in between long pauses when she simply looked up at the young legionary who wore the distinctive helmet of a commander, explained how her mother had died of the bloody flux when she was a child, and how her father, sometimes a labourer in the vineyards, other times employed in repairing the roads in the city, and, when lucky enough, finding work tending the gardens of wealthy villa owners, had recently vanished. For Romans, this usually meant murdered. She had an elder brother who had left home, but who kept an eye on her whenever possible.

"You stay alone, then?" questioned Domitius.

Julia shook her head.

"With my uncle."

The girl hung her head in shame. Craig could see what was coming.

"The one who ran off rather than fight Caracigus?"

Julia nodded.

"And he was going to sell you to become one of Commodus's whores, right?"

Julia looked up. In Craig's eyes, she became Hannah. After he opened his arms wide, she ran into his embrace and he thought she would never stop crying. Domitius winked at him, but Craig knew this was for the wrong reason. He felt no carnal desire for the girl. Only compassion.

"Do you know where your brother is?" asked Domitius.

Julia nodded. She broke free from Craig's hug.

"He's in hiding. Joined a group of Christians. Uncle threatened to inform on him. I think..." the girl paused and looked again into Craig's eyes as if trying to work out why she found them so comforting. "I think he cut a deal with that ox of a man to save his skin. If my brother is caught by the local proconsul for worshipping a single God, they'll also take it out on our uncle. He probably hoped that gifting me to

Commodus would buy them off."

"Makes sense," figured Domitius. "Save him from ending up in the gladiators' arena to be slaughtered with other men by the emperor himself after first being poisoned."

"Your brother's a Christian?" queried Craig. "In hiding?"

"Yes. Marcus Aurelius asked the senate to stop persecuting the Christians, despite their reluctance to recognize the old emperor's divine authority. Apparently, a Christian prayer by one of his soldiers dying from thirst on the eve of a battle was answered when the heavens opened up and it simply poured with rain," Julia said.

"I heard Commodus, too, is tolerant of Christians," added Domitius.

"Only because he's too busy murdering people who get in his way to even think about Christians. The local proconsul has it in for them, though, so my brother's gone into hiding. But I do know where he is," Julia offered. "Near the *Forum Boarium*[19]. It's so smelly that no self-respecting official would go anywhere near the place. I'll take you there."

Domitius, Craig and the three legionaries who had faithfully served the old commander, after leaving *Roma* to travel to Britannia as instructed by their general, Publius Petronius, followed the girl through the *Porta Fontinalis* and on into the old capital. For the first time since leaving Melrose in the twenty-first century, Craig was overcome by a curious sense of unreality, as if he were wearing an invisible virtual reality headset. He was there, in ancient Rome, yet he wasn't. He couldn't be. Common sense told him this. Unless he was a ghost. From the future.

Like a ghost, he walked side by side with Domitius through narrow streets teeming with folk who, in twenty-first century reality, would be movie extras... yet they

---

[19] Cattle Market

weren't. This was no movie. They reached an open space. Passing the Capitol Hill to their right, he saw the Palatine Hill ahead, crowned with the magnificent buildings of the Imperial Palace. They followed Julia along a narrow street opening out into a forum, alive with flies, that stank of cow shit. A one-legged beggar, wearing a brown tunic soiled with excrement, sat, back against the wall, his outstretched single leg complemented by a solitary sad eye that fixed on Craig. He held out his hand. Craig halted.

He was reminded of a time when he and Dylan, two years back, had taken the train from Tweedbank to Edinburgh. In Princes Street, he stopped to put a fifty-pence coin into the hat of a beggar who sat at the top of the Waverley Station steps with a small spotted black and white dog lying curled up beside him.

"What are you doing, Craig?" asked Dylan "That lazy sod can afford to keep a dog and your dad's an impoverished council tip worker! Are you mad?"

Craig dropped the coin into the hat. Ignoring his friend, he patted the dog and asked the man what its name was.

"Misery," grunted the beggar.

"Hmm. Nice name."

They walked on. Dylan's sour expression said it all.

"You could've given me that fifty 'p'," he said. "I mean, why the hell did you do that, you freaky weirdo?"

Craig shrugged his shoulders. "'Cos I'm a freaky weirdo. Anyway, I bet Misery is the only friend he's got. C'mon, race you to the top of the Royal Mile." He took off, into Princes Street Gardens, at a pace that Dylan struggled to keep up with.

Again, here in Ancient Rome, Craig, or Caracigus as Domitius insisted on calling him, stopped beside the beggar. He felt a tug on his elbow. It was Domitius.

"Not here, Caracigus," the commander warned. "Our beloved city is a hornets' nest of thieves and murderers. If an onlooker thinks you have enough wealth to give to the poor, he could fleece you of everything you've got before you're able to say *'Pax Romana'*. Just say a prayer to your Christian God for him." As they walked on, Craig reckoned the difference between Domitius and Dylan was that the Roman cared about others whilst Dylan thought only about himself.

In the *Forum Boarium,* a cacophony of shouting mingled with the bestial noise of cows being herded about and pushed into pens. As for the humans, it seemed to Craig that everyone was arguing with everyone else. Just like Italy in the twenty-first century, he imagined.

Julia halted. She pointed to a young man, standing by himself, garbed, as were other cattle workers, in a short tatty tunic.

"My brother!" she exclaimed, raising her voice above the din.

The young man looked up, saw his sister and gesticulated wildly. Julia ran to meet him, and they embraced fondly before Julia explained to her brother what had happened.

Craig thought of Hannah. Had he been right to leave her with Breth because of a sudden notion that he had to make this mad journey into the past to secure the future? Or was it truly a form of penance for killing another human? If so, a rather strange penance with the goal of ensuring that the young Emperor Commodus was murdered in AD 192. But when Julia's brother came over to where Craig, Domitius and the three legionaries stood in their Christian cloaks, and when their eyes met, the lad from Melrose knew *this* was why he had come back in time to the ancient capital of the Roman Empire.

"My brother, Petrus," Julia said, turning to introduce Craig to her brother. "The name the Christians have given him. Petrus is one of their saints, he says. A disciple of Jesus."

Craig paused, staring at the young cattle market worker before offering his hand. Rather than shaking it, Petrus firmly grabbed Craig's hand and smiled. In that brief moment, Craig realized that he had never actually loved Dylan. Only fancied him. As did his sister. Once. But this was different. The connection between the two young men was immediate. And unique, as was the relationship between Breth and Hannah. Plus, he sensed that the closeness between the brother and sister standing before him mirrored that between Hannah and himself.

"Petrus works here with the cattle, Caracigus," Julia explained, "but he prefers to think of himself as a Christian priest."

"Caracigus?" Petrus looked puzzled. "Julia says you are also a Christian. Why such a strange name?"

Craig felt embarrassed. Names were clearly important in this alien place.

"Craig is my Scottish name," he explained, "only you guys can't pronounce it properly. So... I became Caracigus."

"Like that great leader from Britannia, Caratacus, who dared defy the might of Rome and was brought to speak before the senate," added Domitius.

So that's where it comes from! thought Craig.

Petrus's keen, brown eyes studied the cattle workers within earshot to reassure himself none might be imperial agents.

"And you? You too wish to defy Rome?" he asked. There was a mix of amusement and concern written across his face. Craig could see from those handsome features how closely related Julia and Petrus were.

"We must talk," Domitius urged. "Away from imperial ears."

"Follow me," Petrus said. As he led them across the forum, Craig tried to avoid squidging cowpats, whilst dodging frisky cows, until they reached a narrow street of hovels, one of which the young Roman entered after pulling aside a dirt-encrusted curtain. No door, and, inside, no furniture. Only mats and straw. The legionaries remained outside, on guard, whilst Julia, Craig and Domitius joined Petrus in a circle on the floor. Whilst Domitius explained the purpose of Craig's presence—to fulfill a prophesy concerning the imperial fiend sired by the great Marcus Aurelius, and of which the boy from Britannia had certain knowledge—Craig felt himself slide from that earlier unreality into a sharply focused new reality. The reality of love.

XXII

Ellen knew before she opened the front door. Knew that it would be Craig.

As she hugged the 'Roman legionary', she swore to herself she would never again let go of him as had happened in AD 180. Not even for a Celtic deer goddess. After they separated, her son asked what day it was.

"The day after yesterday," grinned Ellen. "Were you expecting anything different?"

"I just..." the man, no longer a boy, began. "Oh, never mind. Is Hannah okay?" His mother grinned.

"Your sister and Adienna are still in bed with Breth."

"And Dad?"

"Ask him yourself. But say nothing about what happened. He's still in a state of shock."

"Aren't we all."

"I take it you didn't come back by Eurostar. Only left us under twelve hours ago. But..." Craig's mother felt the muscles bulging her son's arms. "You're twice the size. Muscles like your dad. He'll be right proud!"

"Twelve years, it took, back then."

"You don't look thirty!"

"I'm not. Not even eighteen. Not here, at least."

"I'll ask you gain. How did you get back?"

"Same way as I left."

"The deer? On the Eildons?"

Craig nodded. His mother sighed.

"What do we tell your dad, then?"

"That I spent the night saving Europe. And that's the truth. He'll just accept it as SFS business. No need to explain."

"Things are changing, Craig. Fast. Heard it on the news."

"I'm not going to school today," Craig informed his mother.

"Nor is anyone in Scotland," she responded. "Just before the doorbell rang, an e-mail popped up on my iPad. Schools are closed throughout the country. Something big's happening."

"Oh, talking of iPads, Mum, I just need to check something on the internet. Before I do anything else."

"Wait here. I'll get mine. Oh, by the way, Alex and his family spent the night with us. Dad will explain. The military have left. They've disbanded the SSS."

Craig shrugged his shoulders and peered with curiosity at everything in the hallway: the mirror on the wall, the photograph of the Eildon Hills, the coat stand.

"All looks the same to me," he said. "So, history must've happened as they said it did before yesterday."

"What are you talking about?"

Craig glanced at his mother but said nothing. Whilst she returned to the kitchen to fetch her iPad, he sat down at the foot of the stairs. Jamie told his wife that he overheard her and Craig in the hallway. "To Rome and back overnight? Nothing makes sense to me anymore," he griped.

"Craig will see you when he's had a shower and a change of clothes. Still wearing that ridiculous Roman soldier's costume which he seems to have outgrown overnight. First he wants to check something on the internet. Ah... there's my iPad."

"Alex, you just wait till your girls become teenagers!" remarked Jamie. "It's like they have you in a spin dryer all the time. Turned up to full speed!"

Ellen took her iPad out to Craig and watched as he checked something on Google.

"Thank the Lord!" he announced. "Emperor Commodus, strangled in the bath by his wrestling companion, Narcissus, December 19th AD 192. After vomiting up the poison his mistress Marcia had given him. So, it actually happened! Took all those years, but we got there. I told them the poison we mixed for Marcia would make the beast puke. But our backup plan worked... so!"

"Our?"

"Oh... just me and the lads! Lasses too!"

"You and the lads? Don't only look like him with all those muscles you've grown overnight, but you even sound like your father! Go have a shower and come down decent. We'll return that ridiculous costume to the museum later. I'll go with Breth."

"No need for an interview on TV, then? Now that they've gone? Those SSS guys sent by Westminster?"

"Things have moved on so fast since we got back, Craig. Oh, and please do *not* disturb the newly-weds upstairs."

Ellen Stevens returned to the kitchen to proudly announce the safe return of her son to their friends. Craig, meanwhile, smiled at the thought of his little sister being someone's wife. Somehow this took the pressure off him about coming clean with his father regarding his sexuality. Then, as he stood up, Hannah appeared at the top of the stairs. Decidedly the best moment in his life to date. At least, his twenty-first century life. They met and embraced halfway up the stairs.

"Hello Mrs... erm... Mrs Breth?"

"Bit of a bugger that, big brother!"

"Language, little sister!" At the top of the stairs They halted and hugged again.

"Actually, 'Hannah Breth' sounds perfectly okay to me," said Hannah. "Not so sure what others will make of the 'Breth' bit, though."

"We need to talk."

"Yeah, yeah, yeah!"

"No. Seriously."

"Mum's taking Breth back to the museum today. She thinks he should become a volunteer there. Knows a thing or two about the real Trimontium, she says. Plus, the Celts. I suggested he offer classes in our native language for children—"

“Our?”

“I really am Adienna as well as Hannah. Anyway, they can make use of that funny costume you’re wearing.” Hannah looked her brother up and down, then grinned. “You’ve outgrown it already. Overnight! Look, when we’re alone, big brother, we can talk... and talk and talk.”

“Sounds good.”

*****

Jamie had no problems at all with his son’s revelation about his homosexuality. Still in a state of shock following his near drowning experience the previous evening, Dylan’s behaviour and his death, plus the news that their sixteen-year-old daughter was married to an ancient Celt, when Craig announced his sexual preference, Jamie merely said,

“I ken. Care for a coffee, son?”

Later, with Jamie back at work, Ellen and Breth returned the Roman legionary suit to the Trimontium Museum where they were informed the Trust would be delighted to accept Breth as a new volunteer. Ellen thoroughly enjoyed explaining how the young red-haired man, who had married her schoolgirl daughter, was really an ancient Celt on the run from the Romans who had behaved just like the SSS. Meanwhile, back home, and alone, Craig and Hannah sat together and talked.

“So... Dad agreed to the marriage?” asked Craig.

“Didn’t get the chance. We were married already, poor Dad. Breth saved his life you know. Pulled him out of the Tweed.”

“What on earth was he doing in the river? And how did you get back from Trimontium?”

Hannah played with her long blond curls as she wondered how and what to tell her brother.

“It’s complicated,” she said, finally. “All I know is that Flidais called us as we were coming down the hill from Breth’s and my place on the top of the Eildons. We’d just found out that bastard Octavius—”

"The man I shot?"

"Him! He'd slaughtered most of the inhabitants and burnt our homes. Anyway, I kind of sensed that a weird orange light coming from the Roman fort was her. Flidais. Somehow, I knew our dad here in the twenty-first century was in trouble. Like, *real* trouble."

"You knew he was drowning?"

"Boy, I've never run so fast. As soon as we got there, at the fort, everything seemed different. There was a sort of modern prefab hut thing bursting with orange light. But outside it was dark and pouring with rain. There were soldiers in flak and ordinary people charging around. Blind panic! Oh, you've no idea what that light was like. And the effect it had was totally weird. Then I saw Dylan and..." Hannah paused and looked away from her brother.

"And what?"

"I knew Dad was dying."

"How?"

"The light. Somehow it led us to the river. Dad's foot had got caught in a branch, and there he was, hanging upside down with his head under the water, thrashing about. Then went still. Breth clambered down the bank, grabbed Dad and pulled him out." Hannah's face was aglow with pride. "He's incredibly strong, you know."

"Is he okay? Dad, I mean. Like now. Just that he didn't even seem interested when I told him I'm gay."

"Oh, you know Dad! And he's definitely okay. He'll have more lives than a frigging cat! And we all knew about your feelings for Dylan, Dad included."

"What about you and Breth? Not a Neanderthal, I presume. In bed, like."

Hannah appeared embarrassed to be reminded of her initial reaction to the ancient Celt.

"That was so horrid of me! Breth's incredibly gentle. It was like..." The girl paused and took hold of her brother's hand. "No one could have been a better brother for me than you, Craig. You are awesome. But I always had a feeling there was another me. Whose brother died."

"Adienna?"

"I guess those catty girls at school also sensed there was something different about me. And gave me hell for it. But when Breth made love to me last night, for the first time in my life I believed in heaven."

"Your marriage? Where did it happen?"

"Yeah... well, almost exactly where Dad almost drowned, only nearly two thousand years ago. The Celtic way. Our marriage, that is. Blessed by Aine, the Goddess of Love. Not long before you showed up and saved Breth from that fiend."

"I'm afraid nowadays you'll need a piece of paper. It's called a marriage certificate."

"Yeah, yeah! The registry office. Mum and Breth are going there today to book a slot. If they're open. Everything's gone a bit pear-shaped since last night, Mum says."

Craig grinned.

"Nothing wrong with pears," he said. "Or their shape. Look, you still haven't told me what Dad was doing in the river."

"Dylan. Maybe. Look, I've always known how you feel about—"

"He's a bastard?"

"Was!"

Craig looked quizzically at his sister.

"You're telling me he did the dirty on Dad?" he asked. "Because of what happened in the pub on his eighteenth."

"He's dead, Craig," Hannah said quietly. She took hold of her brother's hands again and gave them a gentle squeeze. "And I'm so sorry," she added. "Died shortly after we found him. I'd like to believe he was trying to save Dad to allow him to escape, whatever Dad says. It all happened at the same time, apparently. Dylan turning his gun on him—"

"One of those bloody guns in the loft? Like the one I used to shoot that Roman bastard outside Trimontium? Whose skull they unearthed at the Trimontium site?"

"Uh-huh! Seemingly, he'd kind of changed allegiance and pointed the gun at Dad after those SSS monkeys came out of the same hut that we found ourselves in later. It was pissing down, and when we came out of the hut in a blaze of orange light, it was like everyone went mad, rushing around and screaming. We saw Dylan lying there. He'd been shot. There was nothing we could do. He slipped away so quickly. And I just knew Dad was in trouble in the river. Trying to escape, I guess, either from Dylan or the soldiers. He must've slipped and fallen into the water, catching his foot in a branch. As for Dylan, we'll never know what was going on inside his head."

"He never loved you properly, Hannah. Only himself. You would have been like a possession. That's a fact!"

"I know. But enough about me. Look, it's lovely day now. How about us going for a walk together on the Eildons and you telling me what happened after you left for Rome with Domitius. And why you've turned all muscley!"

*****

Celandine sat fondly stroking Jimmy the rabbit stretched out across her lap.

"Why isn't there any school today, Daddy?" she asked her doctor-father.

"I am no wiser than you are, my little daughter, as to the reason for this."

Ranjit Desai scooped out what remained of his boiled egg and popped this into his mouth, followed by a generous bite of toast and butter.

"Does that mean you won't have to go in to work today?"

"Indeed, it does, mistress of the house. Mummy's gone to work already, and I cannot leave a beautiful young woman like yourself all alone. Not even if guarded by a rabbit."

"So, the professor lady won't mind if you take me to see the Eildon Hills in the Borders."

"Now why would you be wanting to go there?"

"Because it's near where they found that skull with a bullet in it that she and you were talking about when *her* Jimmy magicked *my* Jimmy for me."

"Those little ears of yours aren't just for decoration, then?" teased Ranjit.

"Daddy!"

"Well," began the girl's father, "it is a lovely day and we're both in need of a little exercise."

"So is Jimmy. Can he come too?"

Ranjit Desai said nothing but frowned at his daughter. Celandine giggled, for she knew this meant, 'yes'.

"He will behave himself," she promised.

"Tell him that if he doesn't, the foxes might eat him."

"Oh Daddy!"

"I think, very much, that he will fit into my sports bag, sweetheart. Come on. Get dressed and ready before I change my mind."

"Did you hear that, Jimmy? We're going to see the Eildon Hills. Near where they found that skull."

And so, within the hour, Dr Ranjit Desai, his daughter and her pet rabbit were on their way, heading down the A68 towards the Borders town of Melrose.

XXIII

Unable to fit into his jeans and T-shirt, Craig had to borrow his dad's clothes before he and Hannah set off beyond the golf-course, past Bowden Loch and on up the middle Eildon. Not a word was spoken until they reached the summit where they sat with their backs against the stone triangulation pillar, absorbing the view. Hannah pointed to the Cheviot Hill squatting, like a beached jellyfish, on the hazy horizon.

"That's in England, right?" she asked.

"Uh-huh."

"Will they listen to Dad and his mates in SFS now?"

"They'll have to."

"So, tell me, then. What really happened after you left with Domitius and his mates? And why do you look so different? I mean, you were pretty sturdy before, but even Dad now looks like a weakling compared to you."

"First, not all the Romans were bad. Like the English. Dad's really cut up about Jonny getting shot, Mum said, and he was English. Anyway, Domitius the Roman was a great guy—"

"I know," interrupted Hannah. "Remember, I'm Adienna too."

"—As were his legionaries. It's the system that was wrong. Corrupt. Like Westminster. I know Dad would agree. Anyway, I learned so much as we travelled across Europe to Rome. Particularly how to fight properly. Meaning you always *have* to win. Rugby helped me a lot. I think I rather amazed them."

"I know you did! But what actually happened? When you got there."

"I fell in love."

"Good! About time!"

"I met him through his sister whom I saved from Emperor Commodus in a fight that was over in minutes."

Hannah patted her brother's knee.

"I hope you didn't kill the other guy."

"Na! Went off with his fat Roman tail between his legs. The irony is the girl became a servant to the emperor's mistress. Or rather, his concubine."

"And the brother?"

"A Christian called Petrus. We lived together in a hovel barely fit for pigs, but it was..." Craig paused and looked at his sister. She finished his sentence:

"Heaven?"

"You'll not believe how happy we were."

"I know already, big brother. Me and Breth, we're the same."

"At first, we had problems with a proconsul called Quintus. He had it in for the Christians like a lot of them did. Because we were different. Refused to worship their multiple gods. I lost count of the number of temples dedicated to different deities. Anyway, he fell afoul of Commodus and..."

Craig mimed the slitting of his throat.

"Yuk!" exclaimed Hannah. "I saw what Octavius did to my other mother. And Breth's."

"Domitius introduced me to his one-time general. A guy called Publius Petronius. High ranking in the Senate. Guess he was like a double agent. Supposedly on the Emperor's side, at the same time looking for every opportunity to get rid of the bastard. It was he who secured the downfall of Quintus."

"D'you think Dylan was also a sort of double agent?"

"I really don't care about Dylan anymore. As I was saying, Petrus's sister changed her name from Julia when she escaped from the clutches of their uncle after their dad disappeared, presumed murdered. It was a Roman thing, constantly changing names. As well as murdering people. Like the bloody Mafia, they were. Anyway, she became Aurelia."

"Hmm! Not a bad name. I like it. Aurelia!"

"Things got really complicated. You see, she hated the squalor of our place near the cattle market. I mean, imagine living with smell of cow-shit invading your nostrils every minute of the day. So, Publius arranged for Aurelia to meet high ups in the Senate. Being beautiful, she became a servant girl to a highflyer called Marcia, mistress of one of the emperor's cousins, Marcus Ummidius Quadratus."

"Don't tell me. He was not only Ummidius, but odious!" chuckled Hannah.

"Whatever, Marcia also had eyes for the man's servant, Eclectus! I'm telling you, it was like musical beds in ancient Rome. Whatever, Petrus's little sister, she was in with the top knobs of the Imperial Palace on the Palatine."

"Palatine?"

"It's where we get the word 'palace' from. The hill where the emperor and his cronies hung out."

Hannah laughed.

"I like it. So, our Royals 'hang out' at Holyrood, ay? Even if we go independent?"

"*When*... not *if!* Back to ancient Rome, though. Nearly everyone hated Commodus. Including his own family. His sister, Lucilla, together with Quadratus, his cousin, got Marcia involved in a plot to kill Commodus just two years after I arrived, but his spies foiled it. Lucilla and Quadratus were topped but somehow Marcia escaped. At the same time Commodus's wife, Bruttia, had conveniently committed adultery, got herself exiled then murdered. And Commodus, believe it or not, chose Marcia as his favourite concubine."

"Lucky Marcia!"

"Not according to Aurelia. But some good came of it. Because of Petrus. Aurelia persuaded Marcia to convert to Christianity, and it took the pressure off. You see, Petrus was already ordained as a priest, although he still worked in the cattle market."

"And you were in a relationship?"

"For hundreds of years, priests, even popes, could

marry. But let's not get side-tracked. Because of Marcia, Commodus was tolerant of Christians. There was less persecution, though petty officials still had a go at us. Marcia tried her best, too. Got commended for restoration of the baths in Anagnia where Commodus spent his summer holidays."

"Get to the point, Craig! This isn't a history exam."

"Commodus got worse and worse. He thought of himself as Hercules, ensuring he beat his opponents in the arena by having them poisoned or knifed before a fight. The final straw was renaming Rome 'Commodiana', insisting every Roman citizen bore the name Commodianus and, the craziest thing of all, he decided to rename the twelve months of the years after his twelve f------ names. Twelve!"

"Language, brother."

"But he was stupid, like most evil men. I got myself trained to awesome fitness level. Then, in a kinda homage to Dylan, renamed myself 'Narcissus'."

"Why Dylan? Isn't a narcissus a flower?"

"Also the son of a Greek water god, and nymph, who fell in love with his own reflection. Dylan loved looking at himself in the mirror. Anyway, Marcia recommended me to the emperor as a wrestling trainer. After..."

Craig paused. He played with a tuft of grass as he struggled to find the right words. His sister looked at him. She could guess what was coming.

"After something bad happened?"

Craig nodded without looking at her.

"Petrus?"

"They said it was an accident. Trampled by a bull. But Aurelia was convinced it was her uncle. Hired a thug to push him under the animal. Until then, no way would I have come back to the twenty-first century."

"Forwards!"

"Commodus was delighted when he saw me fight. I even tried to persuade him to stop poisoning his opponents and fight fairly. Didn't cut much ice, though, but he accepted me into the palace. And I became their back-up plan."

"Back-up plan?"

"Marcia was furious when Commodus said he would parade before the people as a gladiator and not dressed up in his imperial robe. This made Commodus fizz with rage. He told his prefect and his servant, who also tried to dissuade him, so all three were added to the list of people to be executed the following morning. Happened all the time, mind you. Anyway, the pressure was on. They asked me to be around in case the poison didn't work. I warned them it might make the bastard puke. Plan A, that is. Poisoning him in the bath. Which is precisely what happened. So, Marcia came running to find me. I was Plan B."

"Plan B?"

Craig stared into the distance.

"I checked on Mum's iPad first thing after I got back this morning."

"And?"

The Melrose lad with the physique of a weightlifter turned to face his sister.

"Commodus was strangled by his wrestling coach, Narcissus, in AD 192. It said so."

Hannah appeared upset.

"You must understand why," her brother explained in his defense. "He was the head of an empire covering most of Europe and North Africa, and as mad as a pig in trainers."

"Why what?" Hannah asked.

Craig said nothing. Hannah stared at him for a while before suddenly opening her arms wide for a hug. Craig wept in her arms, but at the same time said how happy he was for her and Breth.

"Look!" Hannah exclaimed peering over Craig's broad shoulder before disengaging herself from the embrace. "Two people coming up the hill. A man and a little girl. They look Indian. Or maybe Pakistani."

Craig wiped his eyes before he and Hannah stood to welcome the two strangers. The man, presumably the child's father, was holding a sports bag.

"Hello!" the girl said, as they approached. "I'm Celandine. This is my dad. He's a very clever doctor and his professor asked him to sort out that skull they found with a bullet in it down there somewhere."

She had a refined Edinburgh accent and the composure of a young woman three times her age as she waved her hand at the River Tweed valley below to indicate where the skull had been discovered.

"Did he sort it out then?" Hannah asked, throwing Craig an anxious sideways glance.

"Very much so," answered Ranjit Desai with that little head wobble.

"We only know what we saw on the news," Hannah said, "but there were rumours about it being linked with the disappearances."

"One of several possible truths."

"Surely there can only be one truth?" asked Hannah.

Before her father could answer, Celandine asked whether Craig and his sister would like to see her rabbit.

"He's called Jimmy and he was made by magic," she informed them. "And that's the truth!"

"Magic, ay? My brother, Craig, and I would love to meet Jimmy. I'm Hannah, by the way."

"And my Daddy's called Ranjit. But I prefer to call him Daddy. In Hindi that's *'pitaji'* but I don't really speak Hindi because we only speak English at home."

"So where is Jimmy, Celandine?"

"In Daddy's sports bag."

The girl looked meaningfully up at her father who carefully placed the bag on the triangulation pillar, unzipped it and extracted Jimmy.

"I think I'd better hold him, sweetheart. Can't have him running away."

“Magical rabbits don’t run away, Daddy. You should know that. You’re a scientist!”

“Whatever. I’ll hold Jimmy whilst you tell him about your new friends here.”

And so, Celandine formally introduced the rabbit to the brother and sister, each secretly wondering whether the animal truly had been created by magic.

On their way back down the hill, Craig came out with it.

“The ‘what’ of my ‘why?’. I’m going to join a seminary to become a priest.” His sister took his hand, swung his arm forwards and backwards a few times, then answered:

“I know.”

Back home, whilst her brother searched the internet to find out what was required to make this come true, Hannah took out her laptop. She opened ‘Word’, deleted the file of her ridiculous, unfinished novel, opened a fresh document and typed, centre page...

THE FIRE HILLS

VERITAS

In AD 43, the Roman army invaded Britain, or 'Britannia', spreading northwards and reaching what we now call 'Scotland' by AD 79 when Julius Agricola was emperor. An important fort was established beside the River Tweed at the foot of the northernmost of the three Eildon Hills, aptly named 'Trimontium'. The Celts, a tribal people, spread across much of Northern Europe in Pre-Roman times, already occupied the Scottish Borders; the Selgovae in the hill country, including the Eildons, to the west, and the Votadini on the coastal plain to the east and to the north. A significant Celtic iron age settlement on the summit of the Northern Eildon had been in existence for long before the Roman invasion.

Whether or not the two communities lived in harmony or conflict is questionable. Perhaps a mixture of both, depending on circumstances and individual personalities. Although what happened between the Romans and the native Celts between AD 79 and around AD 180 is open to conjecture, there is archaeological evidence that, for periods, the fort of Trimontium was, for various possible reasons, deserted only to be re-occupied. However, shortly after AD 180, the Roman army left the fort for good, although whether the local civilians moved in we do not know.

On the Capitoline Hill in Rome stands a unique and magnificent equestrian Roman bronze statue; that of Emperor Marcus Aurelius, who died in AD 180. He was a Stoic philosopher whose thoughts on how he should conduct himself are embodied in his *'Meditations'*. Although sometimes 'sloganistic', his writing shows him to be a learned man who thought widely and deeply about human relationships and the behaviour of those in power, like himself. The historian, Herodian, wrote:

"Alone of all the emperors, he (Marcus Aurelius) gave proof of his learning not by mere words or knowledge of philosophical doctrines but by his blameless character and temperate way of life."

Commodus, the son of Marcus Aurelius, became co-emperor with his father at the age of fifteen. Few would disagree that the two men could not have been more different. Why the son's ascent to the imperial throne was allowed to happen when the father was clearly disappointed with the youth is a mystery, though this may have had something to do with the political climate of the period. Despite wars, epidemics and unrest, Marcus Aurelius held the uneasy empire together. Choosing someone other than Commodus to succeed him might have triggered civil war.

Commodus was evil. Much of what is described in this book relating to what happened after his father's death in AD 180 is well documented, including the failed attempted poisoning of the imperial monster, in AD 192, by his mistress Marcia, necessitating the implementation of Plan B by those trying to rid Rome of her megalomaniac leader: strangulation by the young emperor's wrestling partner, Narcissus.

Unrest in Rome under Commodus was reflected in Britannia. The Romans' iron grip was weakening. Trimontium was finally abandoned around AD 184 although Emperor Septimius Severus, who succeeded Pertinax, murdered only months after the death of Commodus, tried to regain Scotland. From his base in York he advanced northwards into Caledonia in AD 209, reusing Trimontium as a temporary camp. Outwitted by the guerilla tactics of natives, and following his death in York in AD 211, further attempts by Rome to quell the Caledonians were abandoned.

As for the Celtic Irish deer goddess Flidais, well...

Suggested reading:

The Trimontium Story published by The Trimontium Trust. *www.trimontium.co.uk*

Roman Britain, BBC publications.

A History of Scotland, Neil Oliver, 2009, Weidenfeld & Nicolson
A Roman Frontier Post and its People, James Curle, 1911 http://www.curlesnewstead.org.uk/
Scotland, A History from Earliest Times, Alistair Moffat, 2015, Birlinn Ltd
The Borders, Alistair Moffat, 2002, Deerpark Press.

The Author

Oliver Eade, born a Londoner, now an adopted Scot, retired from a career in hospital medicine thinking 'feet up and watch the TV', but this wasn't to be. After waking up one night with a ghost story in his head, he took to writing adult short stories. Over fifty have been published, several winning prizes, and many appear in a collection, ***Walls of Words***. A collection of young readers' stories, ***Stories for Children Ages 7 to 77***, illustrated by his nine-year-old Swiss granddaughter, Olivia, was published in 2017.

His first young readers' novel, ***Moon Rabbit***, a magical journey to Mythological China (Oliver's wife is Chinese), was published in 2009. It was a winner of the *Writers' and Artists' 2007 New Novel Competition* and longlisted for the *Waterstones Children's Book Prize, 2008*. The sequel, ***Monkey King's Revenge***, came out in 2011 and was a children's genre finalist for the *2012 People's Book Prize*. ***Northwards***, a young readers' dark eco-fantasy based in Texas and the Arctic, was published in 2010. ***The Rainbow Animal***, a fun spoof on war, is also set in North America where Oliver's two eldest granddaughters live. ***The Zookeeper's Daughter***, 2020, dedicated to Sir David Attenborough, concerns a brave little girl determined to save animals from extinction, because of what we humans are doing to our planet, after experiencing the lives of several endangered species.

His debut adult novel, ***A Single Petal***, which won the *Local Legend 2012 Spiritual Writing Competition*, is set in Tang Dynasty China and is a tribute to his wife and her Chinese family. ***Voices***, an adult novel of family love, intrigue and deceit, is set in London whilst the ***Parth Path*** is set in a post-apocalyptic Scotland run by women for women. ***The Terminus***, Oliver's debut young adult novel, returns to the city in which he was brought up: a city changed beyond recognition from the drab post-World War II era of the author's childhood, and which, in a post-apocalyptic world, gives humankind a second chance. The ***From Beast to God*** trilogy, ***The Golden Jaguar of the Sun***, ***The Merging*** and ***Revelation***, follows a Texan boy and Mexican girl on a life-journey involving drug gangsters, ancient Aztec, Mayan and Native Mythology, blending European and Native American spiritual beliefs. ***The Kelpie's Eyes*** was inspired by a visit, with the writer's two American granddaughters, to a famous Scottish waterfall, the Grey Mare's Tail, and weaves Scottish mythology into a tale of sisterly love. It won the *2018 Georgina Hawtrey-Woore Young Adult Novel Award*. ***Number Twenty-four*** takes a Scottish Borders teenager and his pretty Chinese classmate on a perilous journey to a land where the roles of humans and dogs are reversed.

In his fiction-fact story of the history of medicine over seven thousand years, ***In the Blink of an Eye,*** a 2021 Page Turner Book Award finalist, the author revisits his life as a doctor with stories of advances in medicine over seven millennia.

Oliver has also written several plays, one of which, ***The Gap***, inspired by being caught up in the Great Sichuan Earthquake of 2008 and shortlisted for the *Rowan Tree One Act Play Competition*, went on tour in Scotland in 2012. Another, ***The Other Cat***, a darkly humorous take on Schrödinger's famous feline, won the *2018 Segora International One Act Play Competition* and toured the

Scottish Borders with two more of his plays in 2019.

Although not confined to any specific genre, Oliver feels most comfortable in that magical space between reality and fantasy; the space into and out of which children slip so easily in their play; the place of dreams and of myths and legends deeply ingrained in cultures across the globe.

Websites:
www.olivereadebooks.org
www.olivereade.co.uk
www.oddproductionstheatre.weebly.com
www.olivereadephotography.org

Contact: *olivereade'at'googlemail.com*

For other Silver Quill Publishing books for adults, teenagers and young readers by authors from across the world, please visit: *www.silverquillpublishing.com.*

Printed in Great Britain
by Amazon

10320060R00140